The Pelican of Fernandina

cara

David Tuttle /Cara Curtin
The Pelican of Fernandina

www.caracurtin.com

Library of Congress Control Number: 2011933001
ISBN13: 978-0-9831094-1-9

Published by WordWorks Publishing
1417 Sadler Road #134
Fernandina Beach, FL 32034

Printed in the United States

Text Editing by Emily W. Carmain - www.noteworthyediting.com
Cover Art by Theresa Daily - www.theresadaily.com
Text Layout and Cover Design by Caroline Blochlinger - www.cbAdvertising.com

Other books by this Author(s):

- Murder in Fernandina
- The Leopard of Fernandina
- Fernandina's Lost Island
- Fernandina's Finest Easter
- City Sidebar: The Book

To order or more information go to www.caracurtin.com

DAVID THOMAS TUTTLE, SENIOR
February 17, 1941 – August 22, 2008

FROM THE DESK OF DAVID TUTTLE

TO MY WIFE

Barbara is not my life partner; she *is* my life. I met her in the eleventh grade and fell in love with her immediately. Our courtship years were wonderful, and our marriage has been one of many blessings. She has given us two wonderful sons, and the four of us traveled all over the United States. We enjoyed our travels and each other. Forty-six years later, it's still a romance. This book is for you, Barbara.

ACKNOWLEDGMENTS

Many people deserve recognition for their contributions to this book, and the first thank-you goes to you, the people who have followed the Wilson Mystery Series from its inception. I thank you for your loyalty.

Cara Curtin and I have shared not only a love of writing, but a rich military background as well. That common background has lent itself to a shared work ethic that has allowed us to produce a consistently well-told story.

Emily Carmain has been the editor for all of the Wilson books. She has such an easygoing way of helping me tell the story that it is pure joy to work with her.

Captain Jim Coe of the Fernandina Beach Police Department joined the team during the early days of the Wilson Mystery Series. Over the years, he has become a friend as well as a technical advisor.

I would also like to thank Lubana for her Arabic translations, as well as Kenneth A. Mertz, Jr., DDS, and Foy Maloy for their advice and friendship.

FROM THE DESK OF CARA CURTIN

This is David's book and the story he wanted to tell you. I have made only minor revisions to it. My job in writing with David was always to add tidbits of history throughout the story, and so I have added the subplots and their characters to deliver the history we all enjoy so much.

Like David, I extend my heartfelt thank-you to Emily Carmain for both her editing skills and her kindness in delivering those editorial comments.

Caroline Blochlinger has once again designed a killer cover for this book, and I thank her for it.

The pelican who glares at you so fiercely from the cover was painted by Theresa Daily of the Blue Door Artists on Centre Street.

Fernandina Beach Police Captain Jim Coe, now retired, has graciously provided technical advice and expertise for each book in the Wilson Mystery Series. Thank you, Jim, for saving us from several serious procedural gaffes.

I also wish to thank and acknowledge the Amelia Island Museum of History and its staff for helping me do the research for *Pelican*.

Annette Myers graciously invited me into her home and allowed me to ask her a thousand questions about Martha's Hideaway and the woman who had it built.

Mike and Jennifer Harrison shared with me their research on Old Town and made me feel welcome as I joined the group planning Bicentennial Day on April 2, 2011.

Cindy Glenn has been a friend and trusted Fernandina history fact-checker; thank you, Cindy, for catching several inconsistencies as I put the finishing touches on David's story.

I have saved the best for last and now thank my husband, Andrew, for his technical advice, moral support, and infinite patience as I worked to make David's book come alive.

TUTTLE FAMILY NAMES

Barbara and I had such fun with this. Every story has incidental characters who move the plot along. Assigning names to them makes the story more friendly, more real. Barbara and I decided to use Tuttle family names for these incidental characters and had great fun devising them. We hope you will enjoy this twist as you read the story they tell.

Character in Pelican   *Tuttle Family Member*

Elizabeth Cameron........Cameron Elizabeth Tuttle

Linda David................Linda Graham, David Thomas Tuttle, Sr.

Debbie Edwards............Debbie Mann, Joseph Edward Graham

Joseph Edwards............Joseph Edward Graham

Edward Graham.............Joseph Edward Graham

Sean Halter...............Sean David Tuttle, Barbara Halter Tuttle

Thomas Henry..............Thomas Henry Tuttle

David Hillary.............David Thomas Tuttle, Jr, Jon Hillary Tuttle

Barbara Joseph............Barbara Halter Tuttle, Edward Joseph Graham

Graham Lee................Linda Graham and Andrea Lee Toohey

Charlotte Mann............Debbie Mann and Charlotte Marie Tuttle

Jon Stewart...............Jon Hillary Tuttle

Ian Thomas................Ian Tuttle, Thomas Henry Tuttle

Lee Marie Toohey..........Andrea Lee Toohey, Charlotte Marie Tuttle

The Pelican of Fernandina

PROLOGUE

The sleek Learjet announced its intentions and headed almost due east over Carlton Dunes. Fortunately, the plane was still much too high to wake the residents of the high-rises the locals had dubbed "The Seven Sisters."

Now the pilot headed north to make his final turn to land on Runway 22 at Fernandina Beach Municipal Airport.

The ground crew at DuganAir listened to the pilot's slightly accented English as he made his final descent. Shorty Livingstone, by now a seasoned ground handler, slid off of his stool. "I got this one, guys."

Once outside, he grabbed a handy pair of the wands used to direct aircraft once they were on the ground. He hit the On switch so the wands would be more visible to the pilot of the Learjet in the early morning haze.

The aircraft stopped exactly on the spot Shorty indicated. He saw only one pilot, and knew that the man was busy with his after-landing procedures. He waited patiently until the door opened and the pilot began to descend.

"Welcome ta Paradise!" Shorty said. "Top ya off? What's the weather like where ya came from? Ya stayin' with us long, or are we just a quickie?"

The swarthy man ignored Shorty's impertinent barrage. "I have a rental car. Where is it?"

Shorty stopped halfway through his next question. "Yessir, I'll bring it to ya right away. What's the name?"

The pilot's look spoke volumes: How many people are picking up cars in this burg at the crack of dawn?

Shorty scuttled away and soon returned with a sparkling burgundy rental car, one that he'd washed himself. He stopped a convenient distance from the open cabin door and proceeded to open all four car doors and the trunk. "Help ya with yer luggage?"

The pilot merely held out his hand.

"Yessir, here's yer keys an' yer welcome." Shorty held on to them an instant too long while he shot the pilot a look of disgust over his poor manners.

Shorty and his fellow line rats had a lively discussion about how rude some people are. "An' chintzy, too," Shorty added. He grew quiet as Suzie and the others continued to bad-mouth their first visitor of the day. Something about this plane and its inhabitants made him a little uneasy.

He'd just taken his small notebook out when he noticed that the passenger was finally deplaning. Shorty could only get a glimpse of an unremarkable man dressed in unremarkable clothes. "You'd never notice him inna crowd," Shorty mumbled to himself as he wrote the plane's side number in his notebook.

"November two zero six four X-ray, got it." He stored the notebook in his pocket and the side number in the back of his brain.

"Welcome, my brother." Hakim Khalidi embraced his visitor. "How was your flight?" He led the way through the front door of one of Fernandina's fine old homes.

Once they were comfortably seated, Khalidi said, "When Jamal called to tell us you were coming, he was a little vague on what you might need during your stay. Is there anything that I can do or get for you to make your visit more pleasant?"

"Excuse me, sir, but your bags have been placed in your room," a shy, slight man interrupted. He disappeared when Khalidi thanked him.

"That was Bobby, our cook. You will eat well during your stay."

"Bobby?"

"It's a long story, one Jamal is quite aware of. Now, is there anything—"

Ali ibn Farouk found the other man's gentle probing an irritation and decided to end it. "No, nothing, except your famous Southern hospitality." He stood and said, "I'll unpack and check in with New London, if you will have someone show me to my room."

"I'll show you myself. Dinner will be at six-thirty, so you will have plenty of time."

Once Farouk had been settled, Khalidi went directly to his first-floor study to call national headquarters. "Our visitor has arrived," he reported to Jamal ibn Said in New London, Connecticut. They chatted for several minutes more, and Said never mentioned that he had already talked with Farouk.

Chapter 1

"Now, Charlie, I've asked you nicely three times, and all I'm gettin' is attitude from you. So I'm telling you one more time to have your man do this one small thing for me—quick, 'cause I need him now—and then both of y'all will be square with me."

God, I hate being called Charlie. Fernandina Beach Police Chief Charles Evans growled his agreement to the caller's proposition and severed the connection without bothering to say goodbye. He rummaged in his desk for an antacid and popped the chalky tablet in his mouth.

And he really hated it when some young pup talked folksy to him. It implied that he was just another hick redneck cop. *Well, cupcake, this ain't Sparta, Mississippi, and I ain't Sheriff Bill Gillespie.*

He placed another antacid on his tongue and grunted. *Raspberry. I always hated raspberry.* But what he really, really hated was when some smartass FeeBee tried to bully him. *Never mind, payback is a bitch.*

He had a small but evil smile on his face as he hit the intercom button. "Rose, find Captain Wilson and ask him to come to my office forthwith."

Wilson leaned back in his overstuffed desk chair and smiled. He'd been plagued with squeaky chairs since he'd moved to town some ten years ago. His troops had bought him this model when he'd made captain, and Jon Stewart had assured him that this one would not make a sound. Wilson took a moment to enjoy the silence that Jon had promised him.

He swiveled to look at the ego wall he'd amassed over the last decade, and then turned back to look at the newest photo on his desk. The harsh lines on his face softened as he looked at each person there: Dianne, his wife, his second chance at happiness. She was flanked by his daughters from his first marriage: Michelle, a too-mature seventeen, and Lisa, thirteen and blooming.

He grinned when his eye fell on Brian, his and Dianne's son. They'd had to bribe him to sit on his mother's lap for the photo shoot; he'd insisted that four was too old to sit there like some baby.

His grin disappeared when he saw the file folder sitting in front of the family photo. He'd made a promise to himself right after his promotion that he would find the time to investigate the few unsolved murders that the department still had on its books. The Haldad homicide was the third such case he'd looked into. While the first two had been resolved, the death of Petty Officer Benjamin Franklin Haldad remained a mystery.

The desk phone rang just as he opened the folder. It was Rose Isabel, the Chief's secretary. Wilson's eyebrows rose at the "forthwith," but he graciously thanked her for the invitation and told her he was on his way. *No need to kill the messenger.*

Chapter 2

They sat in unhappy silence.

"Dang," Captain Wilson finally said, "I am too old to babysit."

"I agree." Chief Evans had just explained why a police captain was going to spend the next few hours babysitting an FBI confidential informant.

"But I can't see a way out of this one."

"Me, neither," Evans agreed. The senior agent in charge at the Jacksonville Field Office had asked for their help. In reality, what the SAC wanted was for Wilson and Chief Evans to bail him out.

The informant was already at a Fernandina safe house, awaiting the arrival of a still-absent U.S. marshal. The SAC had explained the marshal's no-show by the emergency appendectomy of the original man; his replacement had telephoned the SAC at six this morning to announce that he was embroiled in the premature birth of his son.

The reward offered in return for Wilson's babysitting assignment was far too tempting to resist: if the chief rearranged Wilson's morning to do this small thing for him, the SAC would erase all of the favors they both owed him.

"If we do what he wants, we'll wipe the slate clean and get him off of our backs."

Wilson only snorted in reply. The ten years of their friendship had earned him certain small liberties. They had formed an almost instant bond when Charles Evans had inherited a police department in chaos after the arrest of his predecessor. John Cabe was still in Raiford for double homicide.

The murders of Robert LaFontaine and Cajun Jack had been Wilson's first assignment upon his arrival in town. It turned out that his second assignment had been to help Chief Evans put the department back together.

"Do you honestly think," he now asked, "that the FBI would ever let us off the hook?"

"No, but it will allow me the great pleasure of telling the FBI to pound sand the next time they call us to do their dirty work for them."

They shared a cynical grin and the tension dissolved.

"OK, tell me again what the Jax field office wants. And yes," he added before Evans could speak, "I will take the afternoon off as my reward for completely screwing up my morning—and thank you for offering!"

Evans watched glumly several minutes later as Wilson moved his marker to the Out column on the department's status board. *Wait until he finds out who the SAC is. He's gonna kill me.*

Wilson parked his car in the lot at the Miramar Beach Townhomes on South Fletcher and walked to the end unit. His knock was quickly answered and Wilson flashed his badge. He looked the man up and down before he asked, "You Walid?"

"Yes, I am Ahmahl Walid." He stepped aside to invite Wilson into the living room and closed and locked the door behind them. Wilson shot him a look. The man was not what he had expected. Walid was almost six feet tall, with blue eyes and sandy hair.

Walid ignored Wilson's scrutiny and returned to his writing. Wilson grunted to himself before taking a tour of the townhome's ground floor. Some high-priced decorator had gotten his hands on it. The décor had a nautical flair, with the predominant colors of sand and sea-foam green. Splashes of coral relieved the monotony.

The rooms were spacious, and the living room furniture was arranged to complement the sliding glass door that occupied most of the front wall. Two sand-colored loveseats sat across from each other and at right angles to the door, with a low table of dark wood between them.

Wilson quickly glanced around the galley-type kitchen, opened the sand-colored refrigerator, and extracted a bottle of very cold and very expensive spring water. He came out of the kitchen and looked over at Walid. The man was still scribbling on his legal pad. He had chosen to use the low table between the loveseats as his work station.

Wilson walked behind him on his way to the sliding glass door. His glance at Walid's writing told him very little. *Squiggles*, he muttered to himself before his brain kicked in. *Damn, it's Arabic. Haven't seen that since Desert Storm.* Wilson once again regretted not learning how to read or write the language. *With a name like Walid, I shouldn't be surprised at the Arabic. But he sure doesn't look like a Walid!*

Wilson continued to prowl the townhouse while he sipped water. He gave himself a tour of the second story.

The decorator had been consistent; the same bland tones graced each room up here.

He dropped his empty water bottle in the bathroom waste basket and quickly made his way downstairs. He glanced over Walid's shoulder again as he returned to the sliding door. The man was now drawing some sort of diagram. Wilson tried not to be too intrigued; after all, Walid was the FeeBee's problem, not his. He was looking at the restaurant down the street when Walid finally initiated a conversation.

"How 'bout some chow? You boys promised to feed me while I wait."

First I hafta babysit the FBI's brat, and now I hafta feed him. Good luck getting reimbursed. He had learned years ago to make lemonade out of lemons, so he decided to at least get a decent meal out of the deal. "How about something from Sliders, just down the way? They don't usually deliver, but I know a guy who works there."

Walid's order was simple. "A burger's fine, with a large Coke, fries and a side of fried pickles." He'd been massaging his writing hand while he placed the order, but now he returned to his work.

"Fried pickles? You mean someone actually eats those things?"

Walid's face went flat at the jibe. "Yeah, so?"

"Figures," Wilson said and pulled out his cell phone. He quickly placed the lunch order and said, "Is Jaybo working today? Good; have him run our food over when it's ready."

The delivery would give Wilson an opportunity to check up on that young man. He smiled as he pocketed his phone and reflected on how intertwined everything was in a small town.

Jaybo was a Shanks, a family famous in the area for

its various felonies and misdemeanors. Jaybo had been scared straight when his Uncle Cletus brought the entire clan down by murdering his wife and trying to kill his sister, Alice. Alice was now the wife of Jon Stewart, Wilson's good friend and co-worker. Wilson had helped the Stewarts in their attempts to rehabilitate Jaybo.

Wilson took another swig of water. He'd told Jon and Alice about the vacancy at Sliders that Jaybo now filled, a vacancy that Wilson had created by arresting the incumbent for dealing drugs.

Shorty's cell phone woke him up. He reached for it blindly on the nightstand and rolled over on his back. The light draft kicked up by the air conditioner felt a little cool on his naked skin. He brought the instrument to his ear without opening his eyes. "'Lo," he croaked.

His eyes flew open when he heard the voice at the other end. He quickly patted the other side of the bed. Thank God he was alone. He closed his eyes again to concentrate on what the caller had to say and could only grunt in acknowledgement before the connection was broken. He flipped the phone closed and laid it on his chest. He rested both hands on top of it and sighed. *Oh, hell. Another one's startin' up.*

He dragged himself up and sat on the side of the bed to get his heart started. *Damn, fellah, this job's gonna be the death of ya yet.* He groaned and headed for the kitchen and the coffee that was waiting. He looked around the living room on his way through to make sure there were no bodies lying there. It was empty, and a sour smirk crossed his face. *So begins another day in the life of Shorty Livingstone. Big whoop.*

The linoleum was cool on his bare feet, and he flinched when naked skin contacted cool cabinet surfaces. He poured his first mug of coffee. His eyes and brain began to focus more clearly with each sip, and soon he had a plan for the day.

First, a shower. He sipped on his second mug as he padded to the bathroom. He set the mug on the counter and regarded himself in the mirror over the lavatory. He rubbed a hand over stubble and grunted. It had only been a couple of days since he'd taken a razor to his face.

The air conditioner kicked on again and a swirl of air stirred up the stale smell of last night. A cautious sniff confirmed that he smelled like booze and cigarettes. He sniffed again and thought he detected a woman's cheap perfume. He grinned into the mirror. "Dang, that woman could dance!"

No need to shave, he decided, *and greasy hair is just part a' my charm.* He winked at the mirror.

An hour later, Shorty belched and used a toothpick to excavate the remains of a Huddle House breakfast out of his teeth. Bad teeth seemed to be another benefit of this job; if he didn't see a dentist soon his teeth would be beyond repair. He sat in his old beater in the restaurant's parking lot and let the sun warm him as he made a call. His mood had deteriorated badly by the time he finished his conversation. His next call only made things worse.

Damn them all. They know what's happenin' and they just don't care. He started the car and slowly eased out on to Eighth Street. *Or maybe they're doin' it on purpose.*

Wilson opened the sliding glass door at the townhouse to savor the light fall breeze. Summer's heat had softened into a gentle preamble of winter. He took a deep breath and detected the slight bite of salt air. *Paradise*, he thought.

He turned to check on Walid, but the man was still bent over his work. The breeze coming through the door had disturbed neither his papers nor his thoughts.

Wilson turned back to his contemplation of South Fletcher. Traffic was light, now that summer's visitors had retreated to where they belonged. He idly watched a food vendor unload his cargo down at Sliders. Movement in an upstairs window reminded him of his assignment, and he quickly retreated indoors. *That's all I need, to be picked off by a sniper while I'm babysitting for the Feebs. I'd be so embarrassed that I'd have 'em bury me in an unmarked grave.* He closed and locked the door.

He gave the street one last glance and saw Jaybo jaywalking through what little traffic there was. He was carrying two plastic bags that Wilson hoped contained their lunch.

He was waiting at the door when Jaybo arrived. "How ya doin', my man?"

Jaybo grinned and Wilson could see that his missing teeth had yet to be replaced. "Fine as frog hair, Mr. Wilson."

Wilson grinned back at him and handed over exact change for the meal. He waited for the youngster to pocket the money before he said, "Here, this is for you." Wilson held out a five-dollar bill.

Jaybo's grin grew wider. "Why, thanks, Mr. Wilson! I know exactly what I'm gonna do with this!" He turned and loped back to the restaurant.

Wilson shook his head as he closed the door. Why anyone would trust Jaybo with money was beyond him. He turned to extract their lunch from the bags, only to discover that Walid had moved them to the kitchen counter. A small sound from the living room made him look that way; Walid had found his lunch and was now eating out of the Styrofoam container in front of him on the low coffee table. He suddenly got up and passed Wilson on his way to the refrigerator. He bent slightly to get a bottle of water from it, and Wilson could see that he was chewing on a gigantic wad of food.

He shrugged at the man's eating habits and began to hunt through cabinet doors and drawers until he had a plate and silverware for his own lunch. He was ready to leave the kitchen before he thought to ask if Walid needed any silverware. The question died as he watched Walid use his fingers to cram even more food into his mouth.

He reluctantly joined Walid at the table. When the younger man saw that he was holding a paper towel to use as a napkin, he jumped up to get his own.

"Bring me a water, will ya?" Wilson asked to his back.

He glanced at Walid's place setting. He had plunked the food container on top of his work, making it impossible for Wilson to snoop. He couldn't read the squiggles, but he could see part of a diagram at the top of one page. *Wonder what that's all about*. Walid's cell phone lay beside the legal pad, and Wilson burned to check out its directory and call history. *Not a chance*. He suppressed a sigh of frustration.

Walid returned and plunked Wilson's water next to his plate. Wilson's mouth was full of fried oysters, so his "thank you" was garbled. Walid did not acknowledge it, and stuffed his mouth again with cheeseburger and French fries. He drank most of his Coke in a single slurp.

As Walid's table manners were almost nonexistent, Wilson tried to keep his eyes averted. He was aiming his fork at his next oyster when the first wave of nausea hit him.

He looked over at Walid as a second wave hit and discovered that the man across from him had stopped chewing, even though food still distended his cheek. He had a puzzled look on his face and was desperately trying to find Wilson through watery eyes.

The captain said, "Don't eat—"

Farouk answered his cell phone on the first ring. "Thank you," he said, and stood. "Time to go."
Bobby Slidell hurried to bring the car around. He had already put Farouk's bags in the trunk.

They were almost at the address that Farouk had given him, when the big man said, "Pull in here." Bobby quickly parked.

"Wait," Farouk said, and Bobby turned off the engine.

He returned less than ten minutes later. "Airport."

Bobby was becoming irritated at the man's abruptness and furtively glared at him in the rearview mirror.

Chapter 3

The pain woke him up. He struggled to focus his eyes and discovered a highly-polished man's dress shoe pinning his right hand to the floor. Someone wrenched a weapon from that hand. Wilson started to use his free hand to remove the shoe, but it retreated before he touched it.

"Gotcha!"

Wilson rolled onto his back once again and tried to identify the speaker through his still-bleary eyes.

"Man, your ass is grass. You're never gonna see daylight again!"

Wilson's vision cleared enough for him to see who was taunting him. "You!" He tried to jump up to confront the man face to face.

George Khee used his well-shod foot to push Wilson flat again, something he would have never been able to accomplish if Wilson had been in full control of his faculties.

"You son of a bitch! Get off me! Now!" Pure fury seared away the last cobwebs.

As he started up again, Khee used his foot to push back until he realized that Wilson was going to twist that foot and flip him aside. He took a step back and Wilson stood quickly.

"What in the bloody hell do you think you're doing?" Wilson rubbed his wrist. His eyes fell on the weapon that the FBI agent still held. "Is that mine? Gimme it!"

Khee said nothing while Wilson ranted, but his sneer spoke volumes. That sneer made Wilson even angrier, and Khee was enjoying the show. The ever-impeccably groomed Wilson was disheveled and bleary-eyed. He looked like he'd been on a three-day bender. What little hair he had left stood on end, and his black shirt with the FBPD logo on it had come untucked. A smear stained his once spotless khakis, no doubt from the contents of the plate he'd been lying on when Khee had found him passed out on the floor.

"Calm down or I'll cuff you right now," Khee said. His eyes did not leave Wilson when his fellow agent returned from checking out the second floor.

"Walid's dead. Master bedroom upstairs."

"How?"

"Gunshot. Took out one side of his head."

"Had to be something heavy."

Durwood Cratch gestured at the Glock that Khee still held. "That'd do it."

Khee held it up and sniffed. "Been fired recently." Both men looked at Wilson.

"Now look here—"

Khee made a small gesture with the gun, and in a flash Cratch was cuffing Wilson. "No, no, in front," Khee said. "Professional courtesy, Cratch. We don't want to treat our brother in law enforcement like a common criminal, now do we?" Cratch snickered as he wrenched Wilson's arms from behind his back to his front.

"Now wait just a damn minute, here! I—"

"Captain Wilson, you are under arrest for the murder of Ahmahl Walid, who was under the protection of the Federal Bureau of Investigation," Khee said loudly.

Cratch read him his rights as he marched him to the black Ford Escort that federal agencies seemed to favor. They put him in the back seat and cuffed him to the bar installed for that purpose. Cratch climbed into the driver's seat and Khee assumed shotgun. The FBI forensics team came to a halt beside them just as Cratch started the engine.

"Is that Forensics? Give me a GSR test before we leave."

"Shut up," Khee said as he exited the vehicle. Cratch kept the engine running and adjusted the rear view mirror so he could watch Wilson.

The door beside Wilson opened and a forensics technician silently administered the test for gunshot residue on Wilson's hands, arms, and shirt. He finished quickly and turned to leave.

"I want to see the results, you hear?"

The tech ignored him and slammed the door shut. Cratch snickered and Wilson glared at him in the rearview mirror. *Oh yeah, Khee is bringing you up right. You're gonna be a snot just like him when you grow up*, Wilson fumed.

Khee spent several minutes with the forensics team before he returned and opened Cratch's door. "Get out. I want you to stay with the body until the medical examiner claims it. You can get a ride back with Doc Hershey." Cratch left without a word, and only waved in acknowledgement when Khee shouted after him to watch and ask questions.

Wilson took a last look at the Miramar Beach Townhomes. It was going to be a long ride to Jacksonville.

The unfriendly Learjet was back on the ramp when Shorty arrived at the airport. He eyed it sourly on his way in the building. "Those guys back again, huh? Anything?"

His fellow line rats only snorted and Suzie grumbled, "Friendly as the last time."

"He was thirsty, though," Todd offered. "I put eleven hundred gallons in him."

Shorty said nothing, but did some rough calculations. That much fuel meant the jet could have flown about two and a half hours. *Wonder what's two and a half hours from here? Hell, that'll get ya well north a' DC.*

They listened to the conversation as Suzie buzzed the rental car through the security gate. She shrugged at the cryptic exchange. Four of them watched as the driver headed for the Lear. He opened the back door and his passenger climbed the few steps into the plane and out of sight. The chauffeur put the luggage in the baggage compartment, and then drove the car to the drop-off spot before he came in to return the keys.

"Thank you, sir!" Suzie chirped. The guys recognized the tone she used on customers who irritated her. "Was everything to your satisfaction?"

"Fine, thanks." The man scribbled his name on the contract and turned to leave without saying anything further.

"Have a nice day!" Todd said, but the man did not respond as he pushed through the door.

Shorty picked up the rental agreement, but the man's scribble was undecipherable. He pulled the fuel ticket and glanced at it with the same result.

The telephone rang on Suzie's desk, and the spell was broken. Todd and another lineman went out back to have a smoke, and Shorty headed outside himself. *Time to make another phone call.* He found a private spot under the wing of O'Leary's partially restored World War II torpedo bomber.

The phone rang as he was taking it out of his pocket. He listened for only a few seconds before he ran for his truck. He blew through the roundabout on the Parkway and raced up Fourteenth Street. He pulled into a parking lot across the street from the Miramar Townhomes just as Cratch and Wilson came from one of the units. He watched as the agent stuffed Wilson into the back of the SUV.

Shorty realized he was still holding his phone, so he used it to call in his eye witness report. This time, he had the chance to report the second visit of the Learjet. As he talked, he watched the van pull away with George Khee at the wheel. He ended the call after he reported that Cratch had gone back inside.

Durwood Cratch thought he was following his boss's orders, but he was merely making a pest of himself. He fired questions at the forensics techs until the team leader complained that he was interfering with their work.

"Hey, I'm the agent here; you guys are just lab rats. You work for me."

The techs erected a wall of silence around them until Cratch became frustrated and bored. "Jerks," he muttered as he went downstairs. He helped himself to bottled water from the refrigerator and plopped down in a living room chair.

"You should have asked me if this area had been cleared," one of the techs complained.

"Whatever." Cratch shrugged and slouched lower in the chair.

The drive up from Jacksonville this early autumn afternoon had been refreshingly cool, and John Hershey was smiling as he entered the townhouse. "The body's upstairs, I presume?"

Cratch looked over at the portly man in his early sixties. "You the ME?"

"I am."

"Special Agent in Charge Khee sez I'm to ride back to Jax with you."

Hershey's smile disappeared. He was no fan of SAC Khee, and he was rapidly consigning this young man to the same trash bin his boss occupied. "Not until I find the body."

"Upstairs."

Hershey grunted and headed that way.

"Do you have to play that trash so loud?"

"Yes!" John Hershey yelled and resumed his off-key whistling. He had turned up Del Shannon's "Runaway" to a thunderous level on the van's CD player. He had found this to be a very pleasant way to deal with unpleasant people.

"It hurts my ears!"

"My van. My rules," Doc Hershey grinned. "Or do you want to ride in back?"

Cratch shot him a venomous look and ignored him for the rest of the trip. They arrived at the field office with "Great Balls of Fire" blaring. Instead of whistling, the doc was beating tempo on the steering wheel. Cratch had the seat belt undone and the door open before the van's wheels came to a stop.

"You're welcome! Any time!" Doc Hershey yelled when Cratch slammed the door behind him. He goosed the van away from the curb, music still blaring. He waited until he was sure Cratch was out of earshot before he silenced Jerry Lee Lewis. His cheeks were tired from forty-five minutes of whistling, and his hands tingled from pounding on the steering wheel, but his slight discomfort was well worth it.

Cratch went directly to his boss's office, which was the third or fourth mistake he had made today. He already had a headache from the loud rock and roll, and the chewing out from his boss for failing to pump any information from Doc Hershey only added to his physical discomfort.

Dianne Wilson checked her watch as she climbed into her car. The afternoon had flown by. She had this Monday off and had used it to do housework in the morning and run errands in the afternoon. She cranked up her car and headed down Sadler. *Iced tea sounds good.*

I also need to talk to my husband. She glanced at her watch again and realized she hadn't heard from him all day, which was odd.

She dialed Wilson's number once she had put her purchases away. She took a large slurp of tea as the telephone rang and rang. It was Al Newman who finally answered.

"Hey, Al. I was calling Wilson but I'm glad you answered. I've been meaning to call Cassandra to see how she's doing."

"Hey back atcha, pretty lady! We're doing just fine, but the house is driving us nuts." The Newmans were the latest owners of the Sharpe House in Old Town.

Captain William Sharpe, one of its early owners, had been a harbor pilot during the latter part of the nineteenth century. Cassandra, a budding historian, had found his name on an 1893 membership list of the Cumberland Sound Pilot Association, but little else.

The Newmans had bought the house from a family with four boys, and they were about halfway through the long process of renovation and repair.

They shared a chuckle, and then Dianne said, "I'm looking for my husband. Have you seen him?"

"Not lately. Chief sent him on some babysitting detail, but that was hours ago."

"What's up with that? Isn't he a little senior to pull that kind of duty?"

Dianne had been a police officer long enough to know that junior personnel were routinely sent on the more mundane assignments.

"I dunno, lady—I just work here."

They laughed again and Dianne said, "Well, have him call me when he shows up."

"OK, but have you tried his cell?"

"Straight to voicemail. Oh—I almost forgot to ask how Cassandra's coming with her research on the house."

"Fine. She regaled me with the story of the difficulties they'd had when the owners decided to add a kitchen to the back of the house a hundred years ago."

They shared a laugh before Al warned her. "Watch out, though. She's chairman of the steering committee that's organizing the celebration for Old Town's two-hundredth anniversary in April. If you're not careful, you'll be right in the middle of it!"

"Thanks for the warning. At least she's not sitting around complaining about being bored. Have her call me when she has a spare moment. And have Wilson call me, too!"

Where on earth is my husband? We just might have to declare Girls Night around here if he doesn't show up.

In Jacksonville, Durwood Cratch was diligently downloading the files and photos in Wilson's cell phone. He grinned at the four messages that Dianne had left. He knew that she was Wilson's wife from his boss's detailed briefing. He also knew why Khee and Wilson hated each other.

Down the hall from Cratch's cramped office, Khee had spent the afternoon ignoring repeated telephone calls from Chief Evans. He grinned maliciously when his secretary handed him a collection of message slips, all from Charles Evans. He pulled out his cell and turned it back on. He'd killed it so he wouldn't be annoyed by its constant ringing. He listened to Evans say, "Khee, you sonofabitch!" in five messages before he deleted them. He reached for his desk telephone and smiled. *This is gonna be fun.*

"Khee, you sonofabitch! What have you done with my captain?"

"Me?" Khee put as much outraged innocence in his voice as he could. "How could you even think that—"

"Cut the crap. He was last seen under your so-called supervision."

Khee waited an extra beat before he answered. "I have your man. He is in federal custody." He grinned as he imagined Charles Evans bolting out of his chair.

THE PELICAN OF FERNANDINA | 25

"This better be damn good."

"Oh, it is, I can assure you. Seems your dear captain killed the man you—we—sent him to protect."

"No."

"And to think, I was trying to do you two a favor by letting this rookie assignment clear the favors you owe me."

"Are you out of your mind?"

"We have the weapon—Wilson's very own Glock. And it's been fired recently." He neglected to tell the chief that Wilson's GSR test had been negative. "I'm sure my forensics guys will match up the slug."

"I'm coming down there."

"No need. Your boy is tucked in for the night."

"Be there, or I'll come to your house and drag you down there." He heard Khee laughing when he hung up.

"HENRY!" The building went silent when Chief Evans yelled for his driver. Patrolman Thomas Henry came on a dead run.

"Mount up." The two men left, each dialing his cell phone, each telling his wife not to wait dinner.

Henry silently piloted the chief's vehicle through the late afternoon traffic.

"Remember that FBI agent, George Khee?"

"Yessir, I certainly do."

"Thought you might—you worked on the Leopard case, didn't you?"

"That I did. I was still a little green then, but I learned two very important lessons out of that experience."

"What were they?"

"I'd rather be a lowly patrol officer than a suit with an FBI badge."

Charles Evans' bark of laughter filled the big car. "What's the second lesson?"

"Stay away from George Khee."

Henry drove them in silence for several minutes before he checked the chief in the rear view mirror. "Uh, Chief?"

Their eyes met in the mirror. "Does Captain Wilson know that Khee is the SAC at Jax?"

"He does now."

Chapter 4

Evans took it as a bad sign when he received no professional courtesies at the field office. He had expected to surrender his weapon, of course, but no one offered to forego the security screenings. No one was waiting in the lobby to escort him to the SAC's office, either, and he cooled his heels for several minutes before a young and peeved agent appeared.

"The SAC's very busy this afternoon. Since you didn't make an appointment, you'll have to wait until his secretary can squeeze you in."

Evans had no response to this; he had learned long ago not to skirmish with underlings. His escort led him into the upper reaches of the building and eventually indicated the correct door. He kept on walking as Evans stepped through the door and presented himself to Khee's secretary. "He's expecting me."

She barely interrupted her typing to indicate a row of uncomfortable seats along the room's perimeter. He chose a chair, leaned his head against the wall, and closed his eyes.

He was refreshed and focused when he was finally ushered into Khee's corner office. The chair he sat in tipped him forward and off balance. *Little bastard's shaved a quarter inch off the front legs.*

He kept his expression bland as he glanced at Khee. He had to look up slightly to do so, and realized that the SAC's desk sat on a low platform that put him higher than the visitors who faced him. *Let the games begin.*

He shook his head and put a tired smile on his face. "Nice try with the chair and the desk, but most of the people who'll be sitting where I am will just be amused by it." He saw Khee's face tighten in annoyance. "Because they will have tried it themselves, back when they were as green at the game as you are."

Now Khee was angry, while the chief remained calm. And Evans knew that angry men make mistakes. He sat back and pretended to be comfortable.

Khee looked down his nose. "I may be *green*, as you say, but I have your man. You should be making nice."

"Bring him in here. I want to see him."

"Later, maybe. We have business to conduct first." Khee carefully laid out the case he had against Wilson. At its conclusion, he listed the charges he was contemplating.

"You haven't formally charged him yet."

Khee sneered and propped a foot up on the edge of his massive desk. He delayed his answer by running his eyes over the office walls he'd filled with his awards and commendations. "I'll sleep on it. Come back tomorrow."

"Bloody hell!" Evans erupted from his chair. "You son-of-a-bitch! Either charge him or let him go."

"I have seventy-two hours before I have to charge him, but as a professional courtesy, I will make the decision tomorrow."

"Now, see here, you—"

"Do you want to see Wilson before you leave or not?"

"Yes."

"Then be nice."

The chief resumed his seat and each man stared at the other for a few moments before Khee punched a button on his intercom. "Come in here."

Cratch arrived and listened to Khee's orders. He turned to Evans and raised an eyebrow. "You coming or not?"

They rode the elevator in silence. Evans followed Cratch to a door with a grated observation window. Cratch used the keypad to open the door, and Evans entered a small, windowless room that contained a table, two chairs, and Wilson. Wilson was the only thing not bolted to the floor.

"Ten minutes," Cratch said. The door locked automatically behind him.

"You OK?"

"Peachy. And how was your day, Mrs. Lincoln?"

Both knew that the room was wired for sight and sound, so they talked quietly.

"That bastard's making up his so-called evidence against me as he goes along. And, *and*, he's either ignoring the real facts of the case or he's too stupid to recognize hard evidence when he sees it!"

"Calm down. You've got more important things to worry about right now."

"No, no. You see, Walid was writing something, drawing something. On a legal pad."

"Wilson—"

"It's important, damn important. I couldn't read the Arabic, but whatever he was drawing looked familiar. Damn familiar, only I can't place it. Driving me nuts! I need to get my hands on that legal pad."

Evans knew that was never going to happen. He explained to Wilson that he would be detained overnight and watched as the other man's anger ratcheted even higher.

"Be cool."

"Ranger Rick never sweats."

The chief's mood brightened somewhat. Wilson's reference to his days as an Army Ranger meant that he was using those skills to cope with the current situation.

Evans arose from his chair and Wilson followed his lead. Their farewell handshake lasted a long time.

"What'll I tell Dianne?"

"Something came up and I had to go to Jax. Be back tomorrow. Have a nice night."

"She'll kill both of us when she finds out the truth." Evans cleared his throat and squeezed Wilson's hand even tighter. "This is it, buddy; I'm leaving."

At Wilson's nod, they broke the handshake and Evans loudly said, "So that's it then. We are agreed that Special Agent in Charge Khee is a real son of a bitch."

"We are agreed that Special Agent in Charge Khee is, indeed, a real son of a bitch."

Chief Evans moved in a little closer and softly asked, "What did you think about the 'Special Agent in Charge' bit?"

"Trash floats."

George Khee sat behind his big oak desk until Security informed him that Chief Evans had left the building. He finished reviewing the report in front of him before he placed the first of two calls to Washington. The first call was to the J. Edgar Hoover Building, while the other was to a nondescript structure elsewhere in the city.

His talk with FBI Assistant Deputy Director Frederick Page was short and unpleasant. He quickly reported the afternoon's debacle and then ADDIR Page began to talk. He talked for a long time. His words were strong and his orders were clear, leaving no room for interpretation. Khee said, "Yes, sir," again and again.

One last "Yes, sir," and the ADDIR hung up. Khee took a shaky breath as he returned the handset to its base. He rested his hand on the telephone and closed his eyes to regain some composure before he placed his second call.

Christine Mahmood was much more understanding than Page had been. Khee ended that call ten minutes later with his confidence restored. With Mahmood's help, he had several ideas about how to salvage this potentially disastrous situation. *And my good buddy, Captain Wilson, is gonna help me.*

He confirmed that his good buddy had been fed and was bedded down for the night before he left the building. He started to whistle the song that had been playing in his head all day long as he made his way to his car. Whistling made him think of Cratch's ride with the ME and he laughed out loud.

"Sorry I kept you so late."

"That's OK, Chief. Glad to help. See you in the morning." Henry walked away, pulling his cell phone out to call his wife.

Charles Evans used the landline in his office to call his own wife, Jacqueline. "I have one more thing to do, and then I'll be home." He expressed his appreciation when she promised him hot meatloaf and cold beer. He sat in his quickly darkening office for several long minutes before he picked up the telephone again.

He made himself sound upbeat as he explained to Dianne that he'd sent her husband on a simple errand that had turned into a can of worms. It was going to take most of the night to untangle the mess.

He was relieved when she bought his story. "I was beginning to wonder where he was. I swear I cannot keep track of him these days! I've been trying to get him, but his cell goes to voicemail every time."

"Uh, I think he left it in one of the cruisers down in Jax," he said and dug his hole a little deeper.

"Oh, well. I guess we Wilson women will just have to declare Girls Night!"

"What about Brian?"

"He's only four. We can still bully him."

The call ended and he felt a tug at his heart. The captain and his wife were two of his favorite people. *Let her enjoy a happy evening.*

Dianne ordered hot 'n' spicy wings from the Publix delicatessen, and then jumped in her car to pick them up. She had just put the last plastic bag in the back seat when she heard, "Hey there, Miss Dianne!"

She turned and Shorty Livingstone stood at her bumper, grinning from ear to ear. "You lookin' mighty fine this evenin'!" He made a show of looking around. "Where's that no-count man a' yours?"

"He up and left me to spend the night in Jax. How 'bout them apples?"

"Purty sour."

"Yeah, well." Dianne drooped a little. "We're all busy makin' apple juice!"

"I thought we did that with lemons."

Dianne laughed and backed out of her parking space. Shorty waved her goodbye and then pulled out his cell phone. "We have to talk."

"You on your cell?"

"Yeah."

"Call me when you're not."

Brian's palate had not yet developed an appreciation for hot and spicy, so he was very happy with his hot dog and potato salad.

The Wilson women had no such reservations and quickly filled their plates. "Where's Daddy?" Michelle asked.

"Down in Jax, straightening out some mess."

They spent the rest of the meal discussing the first issue of *The Pirate Press*. Michelle was a senior at Fernandina Beach High School and was the new editor of the school paper. She was excited about the first issue that would bear her name on the masthead. "I can't wait to show it to Daddy. I hope he's not off saving the world again when it comes out."

"Oh, hush; you know that he's rarely gone overnight." She turned to her younger stepdaughter. "You've been mighty quiet tonight. What's up with you?"

Lisa grumbled about not being able to get a word in, but soon she was chatting away about her visit with Elizabeth Cameron. A recent field trip to see "Post Mortem" at Amelia Community Theatre had caught her interest, and Dianne had arranged an after-school interview with the set decorator. Dianne had been mystified that a young girl wanted to work backstage instead of dreaming about becoming a famous actress, but Ms. Cameron had been thrilled.

Lisa and two classmates had met with her after school, and Dianne listened patiently as she relived the afternoon. Soon their plates were clean and all of the deli cartons were empty. "Let's do bath time, and then we'll try that nail polish I bought the other day."

The Wilson house went dark early that night. Dianne and the girls repaired to their respective beds sporting mauve nails with a hint of glitter, while Brian slept peacefully with his nails unpainted.

Wilson's nails were also free of polish as he stared into darkness and plotted revenge.

Chapter 5

"We leave in five." Someone banged on his door.

Wilson was startled awake, amazed that he'd slept at all. He rubbed his hands over his face and finger-combed his hair. There wouldn't be a shower or shave. *No breakfast, either*, he grumbled. He was starving after last night's skimpy dinner.

A clean and well-groomed Durwood Cratch was waiting with the Escort's engine running by the time Wilson had been outprocessed. He was a free man, with the cuffs removed and his personal effects in a large manila envelope.

He tried to open the front passenger door, but it was locked. When he knocked on the window, Cratch jabbed a thumb at the back seat. Wilson threw the envelope on the seat and climbed in after it. He buckled up before he retrieved his watch, wallet, and cell phone.

The van lurched and jerked its way to the interstate, and Wilson smiled sweetly into the rear view mirror. *Little bastard's whippin' this thing around on purpose. He's only four years old, I swear.*

"So, *Captain* Wilson, how did you enjoy our FBI hospitality?" Cratch was still smarting from the dressing down he'd taken yesterday for not chatting up the ME. Damned if he was going to get chewed out again. He looked in the rear view mirror to see how his conversation starter had worked.

"It met or exceeded all of my expectations. Uh, what did you say your name is?"

Who would do that to a baby? Wilson wondered after Cratch had supplied his name. "I hope he was a very rich uncle who left you a pile of money."

"Huh?"

Wilson waved it off and enjoyed the scenery. He became amused at Cratch's clumsy attempts to extract information from him. "Since I know for a fact that it wasn't me," he said in response to Cratch's wondering who killed Walid, "I'll leave it up to your oh-so-very Special Agent Khee and his crack team of G-men to figure it out."

He counted the money in his wallet before he returned it to his hip pocket. *Dianne's gonna have to boil these clothes before I wear them again— if I wear them again.* 'Since your guys are probably screwing up the forensics even as we speak, I doubt that anyone will ever know who done it."

Cratch flicked him a glare as he maneuvered north on I-95. "We have the finest forensics in the country. People from all over the world come to us for training."

Wilson had almost decided that Cratch's lurching trip out of the parking lot had not been designed to irritate him, but was simply the man's driving style. Cratch tapped the brakes and Wilson's eyes flew to the road. There was nothing to warrant the tap. *Oh, good; gratuitous braking.*

Wilson thought he would do a little fishing of his own. "If they're so great, why didn't they know anything about Walid's legal pad?"

"Of course they know about it! I watched them bag it myself!"

"Did you look at it? What did it say?"

Cratch opened his mouth to answer, but stopped. He glared at Wilson through the mirror again.

Wilson assumed his most innocent look. "I'm just sayin'! Hey, have you seen it since yesterday? Is it the same tablet? Maybe somebody switched it. Can you read Arabic? Does it say the same thing it did when you saw them bag it?"

"Shut up!" Cratch said and swerved the vehicle around slower traffic.

"Oh, nice. Is that how Georgie Boy's teaching you to behave?"

Cratch had no response, so Wilson clipped his badge on his belt and flipped his cell phone open to call Dianne. He closed it again without dialing. *It'd be just like Khee to bug it*, he thought. He didn't want Cratch to listen to him talk to his wife, anyway.

"Hey, where's my Glock?"

"Forensics—you know that."

"When will I get it back?"

"You know that, too. When we finish with it."

"Yeah, well, tell your boss I'm holding him personally responsible for that Glock. He's the one who confiscated it, and he's the one I expect to return it."

Cratch lurched to a halt in the curved driveway at the Lime Street station. Wilson thought that it had never looked so good. He had the door open before the Escort came to a full stop.

"Y'all come back an' see us again, ya heah?" Wilson slammed the door shut and walked into the station.

It felt odd when people greeted him as if it were any other Tuesday morning. Wilson returned their smiles, grateful to be back in his own world. He wanted to see the chief, but first he stopped at his desk and called Dianne.

"There's my man! Did you get everyone straightened out? I was beginning to think you were going to stay down there forever!"

"I haven't pulled an all-nighter in a long time. I'm going to clean up here, and then follow up on some loose ends." *Yeah, like who was this Walid character, and who killed him? And used my weapon to do it. And what in the hell was he writing?*

He left his questionable cell phone in a desk drawer and started towards the chief's office, but he turned back and added the watch to the phone. *I'm either smart or paranoid.*

Rose Isabel was on the phone when Wilson approached her desk, but the chief's secretary waved him on in. Chief Evans was also on the telephone, but he terminated the call as he motioned Wilson to take a chair.

Rose came bustling in with coffee in an FBPD mug. "Chief said you'd be in dire need of a good cup when you got back." Wilson's addiction to gourmet coffee was well known.

He thanked her and took a healthy swig. She smiled and left, only to return with a carafe. She placed it so both men could reach it and closed the door behind her.

The chief freshened his cup. "Give me a complete data dump."

Wilson talked steadily for twenty minutes. He provided facts and observations only. The conjectures and regrets would come later. "It's hosed," was Wilson's final observation.

"Yeah, it's hosed. Let's just make sure they don't use that hose to hang you."

"First thing I'm going to do is to talk to Jaybo."

"You think the food was doctored?"

"Damn straight."

"Doesn't sound like him."

"Hell, no. He's not bright enough to think of it on his own, and I think we've scared him too straight to do it for someone else."

Chief Evans said nothing, but leaned back and closed his eyes. Wilson gave him the minute to think. "Here's what we're gonna do," the chief said as he sat up. "Everything is going to be strictly by the book on this one."

Wilson started to protest that he always operated that way, but Evans held up a big hand to forestall him. "George Khee, for whatever reason, likes you for the Walid job. You two have been adversaries since that damned Leopard case. Wish we'd never agreed to that particular joint op." They paused for a moment to remember Wilson's almost fatal trip over David Levy Yulee's train trestle, as well as the people who had been injured and died during that exercise.

"You betcha! Especially when you stop to think that's when we first ran in to George Khee."

"Yeah," the chief agreed, "and you two hit it off just like a cat and a mouse. He'd give you life for jaywalking, if he could." He paused for a beat. "Your rear end is not quite in a sling on this one, but it will be if he can figure out how to put it there."

"Probably get another commendation out of it."

"So here's what we're going to do." Evans took a deep breath before he dropped the bomb. "We're going to put you on paid—paid, mind you—administrative leave."

"But—"

"No, that's what I have to do to protect you, to keep you out of Khee's line of fire." He waited patiently as Wilson ranted that administrative leave would pull him off the case and would therefore deny him a chance to clear his name.

It was only when his rant deteriorated into a harangue against George Khee that the chief grew impatient. He stretched his arm across his desk, palm up. "Badge and weapon. Now."

Wilson looked at his boss for several long moments before he stood to remove his badge. "The damn FBI still has my damn weapon," he said, and began to rant about the FBI in general and Special Agent Khee in particular.

"Enough!" Evans slammed his hand on the desk. "This is the way it's gonna be! I suggest, *Captain*, that you watch your temper and your mouth!"

Wilson was so angry that he could only glare at his boss.

"Go home. Clean up. Have breakfast. Then come back here for the meeting you're gonna set up with Lieutenant Newman on your way out the door."

"And just why am I going to have this meeting?"

"Because you're on admin leave and you're gonna turn your work over to him."

"And just how long is this leave gonna last?"

"As long as it takes."

Wilson stopped by Al Newman's desk to set up a two o'clock meeting. He deflected the man's questions before he retrieved his watch and phone from the drawer. He headed for the IT division to have them checked for bugs.

Sean Halter was Geek of the Day, doing intake in IT. Members of that division had been offended at first by that title, but stopped complaining when a wit pointed out that its acronym was GOD. Halter promised a quick turnaround time.

Wilson walked to his car, grateful for whoever had moved it from the townhome's lot to this one. He was behind the wheel before he saw the colorful piece of paper stuck under a windshield wiper. "Damn pizza places," he grumbled, forgetting that this was a secure lot.

He opened the folded neon yellow paper and read:

> *Words are easy, like the wind;*
> *Faithful friends are hard to find.*
> *—Richard Barnfield (1574-1627)*
> *The Pelican*

What in the hell does that mean? He glanced at the paper again and wondered at the signature. *Curiouser and curiouser.*

He started the car and headed for home. *I don't really need any of this pelican shit on my plate right now.* He smiled for the first time that day at that mental picture.

"I would have called you, but I think my cell phone might be bugged. No, no," Wilson cautioned as Dianne moved to hug and kiss him hello. "I smell like road kill. Let me clean up, and then you can give me all of the sugar you like."

Dianne laughed, glad to have her man back. "I'll fix lunch while you do that."

He checked his watch to see how much time he had before his two o'clock meeting, only to discover bare skin. He'd left his father's watch back at the station. He swore under his breath and headed for the master bathroom.

Wilson recounted his last twenty-four hours while he ate the hefty lunch Dianne had fixed. "So that's it. Walid, whoever in the hell he is, is dead, I'm screwed, and Khee is laughing his ass off."

"I can tell you're really upset because of your potty mouth. Am I going to have to get out the Cussin' Jar?" She smiled to take the sting out, but it didn't work. Wilson's response was earthy and to the point.

Dianne rolled her eyes and gathered up his dishes. "You owe the jar two bucks."

On his way back to the station, Wilson realized that he'd forgotten to tell Dianne about the note on his windshield. *Oh, well. It's probably just some do-gooder group spreading peace and love.* He buzzed himself into the parking lot and finally wondered how the do-gooders had gotten inside. *And who in the hell is the Pelican?*

The Learjet landed in New London just about the same time that George Khee and Charles Evans were arguing about Wilson's immediate future.

Ali ibn Farouk stuck his head in the cockpit to thank the pilot for his service. He grabbed his bags from the compartment and headed for his shiny new Mustang.

"I'm back," he reported into the cell phone on the way to his apartment. "It went well, praise be to Allah."

"Come see me tomorrow." Jamal ibn Said broke the connection and turned to the other men in the room. "The traitor is dead. We proceed as planned."

Chapter 6

Wilson returned to the station a much cleaner and calmer man. He had forked over the two dollars to Dianne and then held her tightly for a long time. "I'm sorry I scared you, sweetheart. This is nothing more than another one of Khee's little games. It'll be over soon."

He arrived at Al Newman's office with his arms full of files. Even though the grapevine had broadcast Wilson's latest dust-up with the FBI, Newman had rejected the gossip about his suspension.

"So it's true, huh?"

"Yeah. Khee's pulled another one."

"How long's the suspension?"

"Chief says as long as it takes, which is why I'm bringing you all of this."

The first folder contained the details of Wilson's speaking engagement at Florida Atlantic University in Fort Lauderdale. Al was dismayed. "Man, you know I'd rather have a root canal than give a speech."

"Sorry. You can delegate everything but the speech." Wilson forestalled Newman's next move when he said, "And don't try to bump it up to the chief; he's the one who gave it to me."

Newman held his head in his hands as Wilson explained that he would be addressing around one hundred students at the university's School of Criminology and Criminal Justice.

"Don't worry, everything's in automatic. The school has a speakers' program, so every other week, someone in law enforcement talks to the senior class so they can get an idea of what's out there. No big deal." Wilson pointed out the sheet of paper with the contact information for the woman who ran the speakers' program. "And here's a map of the campus I downloaded from the website." He closed the file and Newman grunted and pushed it aside.

The two men paused over each file and debated which of the detectives in the division would be best suited for that case. Newman would spread the work evenly among his team, but Sergeant Jon Stewart and Detective Karen Millen would inherit the more challenging assignments. Wilson made a mental note to plumb the extent of the FBI connections she had made during her first two years with the force. She had been loaned to the Bureau twice and had later spent time with FLETC, the Federal Law Enforcement Training Center in Brunswick, Georgia. He might need to use all of her connections before this was all over.

"But," Newman added as an afterthought, "I gave Millen the Quattlebaum case earlier today."

"As in J. Phillip?"

"Oh, yeah. Someone broke into Mr. Mayor's plumbing place and trashed it thoroughly." J. Phillip hadn't been mayor for several years, but he was still accorded the title.

"And we're putting one of our crack detectives on it because ..."

"Because no one has had the courtesy to commit a

major crime in the last twenty-four hours, and—"

"And Mr. Mayor threw his weight around with the chief."

Al Newman's large fake smile told him he was right. Wilson refused to let the never-ending drama of the Quattlebaums distract him from the thick file that he had saved for last.

"You know I said I would review cold cases when I made captain."

"Yeah. You already cleared up the Edward Graham and the Linda David cases."

"This is the third one, then. Benjamin Franklin Haldad. Caucasian male, twenty years old. Blue eyes, sandy hair. A sailor at Kings Bay, a sonar technician, I think. Found with his throat slit and his right hand cut off."

Newman winced. Fernandina had very few murders, and even fewer gory ones. "Who had the case originally?"

"Wilbur. It really killed him when he couldn't close it before he retired."

"What'd the Navy have to say?"

"It's all in there." Wilson finally handed the file over. "But I want this one back when my exile's over."

"I'll probably solve it while you're gone."

Wilson stood and pushed the chair in. "Good luck with that." He turned to leave, but stopped to say, "I'm sorry about the speech in Lauderdale. Maybe you can take Cassandra and make a mini-vacation out of it."

Newman was shaking his head before Wilson had finished. "Not with both of us gone. That'd leave Stewart at bat."

"So? Maybe it's time to give him a little more responsibility. He's not going to be a sergeant forever, is he?"

"I'll think about it."

When he left the building around three, Wilson realized that his almost sleepless night, as well as the tension and turmoil of the last two days, had finally sucked up the last of his energy. He headed for Seacrest.

He was glad no one was at home. He walked through the silent house and dropped his keys in the communal tray. He started toward the gun cabinet and winced when he realized he didn't have anything to put in it. The girls were in school and Brian was at daycare. He left his clothes in a heap on a chair and fell into bed. His last thought was to wonder finally where his wife was.

Dianne shook him awake. "You've got about a half an hour before dinner."

He emerged from the bedroom dressed in faded sweats. "Want a drink?" he asked Dianne on his way to the small bar. She declined, but he fixed a gin and tonic for himself. The first gulp was delicious.

They tried to have a normal dinner, but it was obvious to everyone but Brian that Wilson was distracted. The four-year-old kept everyone entertained about his first foray into preschool while his dad brooded at the head of the table. Lisa and Michelle tried to fill in the blank spots. Lisa talked about her involvement with Amelia Community Theater and Michelle worried out loud about her role as the editor of *The Pirate Press*. Dianne said nothing when Wilson poured himself a third glass of wine.

The girls cleaned the kitchen while Dianne and Wilson wandered into the den. "Want anything?" Wilson hoisted the wine glass he'd brought from the table.

She declined and hid behind a magazine, only to

peek over the top to watch her husband brooding and drinking. *Not good.*

Michelle and Lisa brought them a freshly bathed Brian to say good night. Wilson smelled the soap and shampoo they'd used when his son hugged him. He envied the boy's innocence.

Dianne watched her husband after the children had left the room. He stared off into space and sipped wine until the glass was empty. He seemed to rouse himself and blinked several times before he noticed that his wife was studying him. He crooked an eyebrow at her and announced they'd have a family meeting when the girls finished their homework.

They put on light sweaters as they gathered on the deck. Everyone but Wilson had a mug of hot tea, and Dianne monitored her husband as he talked and sipped yet another glass of wine.

Wilson gave them a slightly sanitized version of Walid's death and his subsequent detention by the FBI, but did not hesitate in regaling them with his theories and opinions about the last couple of days.

"George Khee. I want you all to remember that name. If he or anyone else from the FBI tries to talk to you, or tries to make you go to FBI headquarters, I want you to yell like a banshee and run like hell! And don't forget to use any of the defensive moves you learned at the *dojo.*"

"Why is Mr. Khee being so mean, Daddy?"

"George Khee is a real sonofabitch who's decided to ruin my life." Wilson's large gulp emptied his wine glass and he reached for the bottle he had brought with him.

"That's not fair!"

Wilson took a large sip of wine before he answered. "I know, but I want you—and you, too, Michelle—to realize that things and people don't always turn out the way you want them to." He burped gently. "And you'll also have to realize that garbage floats and that's why people like that asshole Khee is now in charge at the damn Eff Bee Eye."

The girls had never seen their father like this and they turned to Dianne for help.

"Language, Wilson, language."

"My language is not the point! The point is that someone—someone, hell! Someone named George Khee is screwing with my life. He's a fu—"

Dianne jumped up. "OK, that's it, ladies. Bedtime for Bozo!" She hoped that their family joke would lighten the mood. Michelle and Lisa were quick to deliver a hasty good night.

The girls rinsed out the tea things and put them in the dishwasher. Lisa said, "What's wrong with Daddy?"

"He's being a jerk because he's so mad at this Khee guy."

"I've never heard him talk like that."

"Mom will have his head for it, you'll see," Michelle said. "We'll get an apology in the morning." She looked at her watch. "I want to look at some stuff about the paper. See ya." She grabbed an apple on the way out.

Lisa stood in the middle of the kitchen. She heard her sister's bedroom door shut. She did not understand what was happening and that was scary. She sighed and helped herself to a handful of pretzels. She would share them with Miss Blossom. Miss Blossom's raspy purr always made things better.

"Blossom! Blossom! Miss Blossom! Here, kitty." Even though she called for her repeatedly both in the house and outside, Lisa's cat did not appear.

The Wilson family's self-appointed guardian angel

had watched it all. He swore under his breath when the family scattered at Wilson's foul-mouthed tirade. He watched Dianne speak to her husband after the girls had left, and he watched her stride stiff-backed into the house when he'd responded to her by taking yet another swig of wine.

Chapter 7

I don't think I've been this beat since I moved here. Karen Millen unlocked her Honda and began to drive out of the lot. *No rest for the weary,* she sighed. She had errands to run before she could go home and work to do once she was there.

It had been a brutal day, and she grunted with weariness twenty minutes later as she placed her dinner from Gourmet Gourmet on the back seat. Captain Wilson's predicament had shaken everyone, and then to add to it, the lieutenant had redistributed the captain's workload.

Her plate had already been full. The Edwards case, the prosecutor had assured her, was a slam dunk. An hour on the stand, max, and she'd be outta there, he'd said. But Joseph Edwards had a crack defense lawyer who was complicating the process. *I better memorize my field notes before I climb up on that stand.* And then the lieutenant had given her the Quattlebaum case a couple of days ago. She rolled her eyes in the privacy of her car. J. Phillip's melodrama was prolonging the process of finding out who trashed Quattlebaum & Sons.

She giggled suddenly, remembering her amazement at how anyone could go into hysterics over the smashed commode lying in pieces on the floor. *Nobody should pay that much for a pee pot*, she snorted, *and who'd want to own a lavender one, anyway?*

Thankfully, the lieutenant had given the Haldad case to Jon, as well as the order to give the Bureau any support it might need on the captain's case. Both men had automatically glanced her way and she had graciously offered to provide any assistance Jon might need. *Idiot, that's just more work*, she sighed and turned onto Lewis Street. *It's magic. Every time I drive into American Beach, I begin to calm right down.*

She took a quick left at Ervin and then crossed Julia Street. No matter how tired she was, she always felt the history of the place wash over her. No wonder; its rich legacy had earned American Beach the right to be the first site listed on the Black Heritage Trail in Florida back in 1992.

Nearly six decades earlier, Abraham Lincoln Lewis had been a vice president of the Afro-American Life Insurance Company when he bought just over two hundred acres of island beachfront. In 1935, his vision was to create a seaside resort for company executives, and he'd named its streets after himself and other company officers—Gregg, Waldron, and Price—as well as entrepreneurs and business owners.

Karen smiled when she remembered the faded photo she'd seen of Julia Brown Lewis. A.L. had immortalized his mother by naming one of the community's major thoroughfares after her. Karen's own house was on a street named after Louis Ervin, who'd owned and operated a popular gathering place called Ervin's Rest for decades.

She pulled into her driveway and hit the remote for the garage door. She always felt a little pang of regret whenever she drove in. Martha Hippard, the original owner of the property, had been a fun-loving woman. An inveterate gambler, she had built this structure, near the main home, as a party house for her famous get-togethers. Over the decades, the little house had been reduced to its mundane role of garage. *There's a lesson there, but I'm too tired to figure it out.*

Wilson looked at his bedside clock. *God, my head hurts. Just how much wine did I drink last night?* He started to throw the covers off, but stopped. *Why get up? I have no job. I might not even have a future if Khee has his way.*

Dianne lay beside her husband with tears in her eyes. She had felt him start to get up and then stop. She rolled over and they held each other tightly until her alarm announced the start of her day.

She silenced it and turned back to her husband. "I love you. Don't shut me and the children out. We are all on your side."

"I know, I know, but I'm fighting for my life here."

"We know that, and we will do anything we can to help you, even if it's only a good dinner and clean skivvies." Dianne was relieved when he smiled at her lighthearted promise.

He kept out of everyone's way while they got ready for school and work. He watched as Dianne finally backed out of the driveway. Now he knew how dogs felt when everyone left them home alone.

He sighed and shuffled back to the kitchen. He had told Dianne that he would clean up the breakfast dishes, but now he pushed the cereal bowls aside and poured himself another cup of coffee. He brooded through a second cup before Miss Blossom interrupted his pity party by complaining that her water bowl was dry.

He cleaned up the kitchen, and then wandered into the master bedroom. He automatically made the bed and then gathered up towels from both bathrooms to start a load of laundry. He was measuring the detergent when it struck him that he was in danger of becoming a househusband.

"To hell with that," he announced to the load of towels. "I'm a detective—and a damn good one!"

He returned to the spotless kitchen and brewed another pot of coffee. He found a yellow legal pad and a couple of pens and then sat down to detect. He had spent so much time obsessing about Walid over the past two days that he did not need time to think. He began making a list of all of the questions he wanted to ask. About six questions down, he ripped the sheet off and started over.

He turned the tablet sideways and made a matrix of sorts. Down the left side he wrote his original six questions and added to them until his list was several pages long. He returned to the first page and to the right of each question he listed who he could talk to, where he could go, and everything else he could think of that would help him find out just exactly what was going on.

First thing he was going to do was to talk to Jaybo. He smiled to himself and added one last question: Who the hell is the Pelican?

Jamal ibn Said watched the others as they filed in. This was his fifth year as the East Coast coordinator of the Muslim Military Jihad in America. He considered the assignment both an honor and a test of his faith. He greeted each man warmly and invited him to the tea and small cakes that had been set out along a side table.

He began the meeting only after the last man had arrived and had helped himself to the refreshments. "My brothers, let us begin." The chatter died and Jamal said, "Ali ibn Farouk has returned from a successful trip to Florida, praise be to Allah."

The others murmured their praise and Jamal nodded to Farouk to begin his report. "Our mission in Fernandina was more successful than we envisioned. The traitor is dead, and the two men investigating his death hate each other. Instead of looking for Ahmahl's killer, they will try to destroy each other."

"Thank you, Ali. God has been very good to us; it is clear that He approves of our plan in that town," Jamal said. "And that plan remains unchanged, despite the loss of Ahmahl."

"*Because* of the loss of Ahmahl," Farouk amended.

Jamal nodded in agreement and said, "Hossein will replace Ahmahl, as we agreed earlier. He will leave tomorrow. He will make several stops on his drive down and will get to Amelia Island next week in time to celebrate the Sabbath with his new brothers."

The others congratulated Hossein Mousavi on his promotion to cell leader, and he shook each man's hand.

Jamal once again assured the assembly about the Fernandina cell. "Before all of this unpleasantness, I spoke with Ahmahl about his plan. I told him then that it was a good plan, and it still is. And now Hossein will make sure that it is a successful one."

Mousavi began to speak quietly. "They—" He stopped himself and began again. "*We* are almost through the planning stage. I will review the situation quickly, and then we can start staging men and materiel."

The meeting broke up soon after Mousavi's remarks. On their way out, each man congratulated him again and wished him success in his new assignment.

Chapter 8

Wilson lost track of time as he filled in the matrix he had designed. An empty stomach and full bladder finally pulled him back in to reality. He fixed himself a lonely lunch and put the plate on top of his morning's work. He ran his hand over his chin as he took his last sip of milk. He needed to clean up. *And then what?*

He began to move swiftly after he had decided to go to the station for a few minutes. He'd just pop in and out quickly to retrieve the telephone numbers he needed, and then he'd be on his way.

The car was hot from sitting in the driveway all morning, and Wilson concentrated on cranking up the air conditioner. He was fastening his seat belt when he finally noticed a yellow flyer tucked under the left windshield wiper. "Damn garage sales," he muttered and unbuckled.

He stood perfectly still beside the car when he realized that the paper was not a flyer, but a second note from the so-called Pelican. He scanned it quickly and checked the street. Nothing was out of place, so he climbed in and buckled up again.

The air conditioner was finally throwing out icy air, and he reread the note in its blast.

*If you know the enemy and you know
yourself, you need not fear the result
of a hundred battles.*
—*Sun Tzu (544 B.C – 496 B.C.)*
The Pelican

"What in the hell is that supposed to mean?" he asked out loud. He balled up the note and threw it over his shoulder. It landed beside the earlier note. "Am I gonna get these things every day?"

After a few seconds of thought, he got out to retrieve both notes from the floor behind the driver's seat. *These things might be important.* He read both notes again before he stuffed them into one of the files lying on the passenger seat. *One thing's for sure; this Pelican guy knows a lot about what's going on in my life.*

"Attaboy," the Pelican muttered from his perch.

Wilson pointed the car out of Seacrest and realized that his suspension had one bright spot. He was finally going to contact an old Army buddy he'd been meaning to call for a long time.

He parked the car in the station lot and automatically checked for his weapon and badge. He winced at their absence. It had been decades since he'd been without them and he felt naked as he walked across the lot.

Of course, Chief Evans was the first person he saw. "What are you doing here?"

"I work here, remember?"

"Can the attitude."

"Can the suspension."

They glared at each other until the chief relented. "Hell, man, I am on your side, you know that. But what on earth are you doing here, anyway?"

"I forgot a couple of things yesterday, so I came to pick them up."

The chief grunted and went on his way, making a mental note to watch his favorite captain closely over the next few weeks. Wilson had avoided eye contact, and that was a bad sign. Then again, there was no need for direct eye contact to detect his hurt and anger.

Al Newman watched the exchange from a distance. He couldn't hear what was said, but he could read their body language quite well. *Whooee*, he thought and picked up the telephone to postpone his staff meeting. He watched Wilson walk to his desk. It was painful to see how awkward people were with him.

Wilson grew unhappier with each false smile and wary greeting. He was almost bleeding by the time he reached his desk. He had no idea that this brief visit would make people so uncomfortable. *Treatin' me like I'm contagious.* He shook his head to clear it and realized that someone had already been through his desk. His stapler was missing, as were a couple of gel pens out of the FLETC mug he used as a pencil cup. He opened a file drawer, and it took him a couple of seconds to realize that he'd given the missing files to Newman. He sighed and turned on his computer. *Wonder what they've helped themselves to in here?*

He wrote down the information he needed and backed out of the program. He was turning off the machine when he was suddenly desperate to leave the station. He scooted back his chair and nodded politely to the few people brave enough to speak to him on his way out.

He sat in his car and smacked the steering wheel. *Dammit! I'm gonna get to the bottom of this if it kills me!* He let that thought reverberate in his head as he headed for home.

What the hell, he thought as he turned a corner. He drove past the entrance to Seacrest and turned on to South Fletcher. Five minutes later he was on The Surf's deck with a cold beer in front of him. He checked his watch. *Three-fifteen. Huh. Let them suckers work all afternoon. I might as well enjoy this little vacation.*

Al Newman watched Wilson leave. He had never seen him with that lost look before. And he'd kept patting the empty spot where he usually wore his badge. Newman winced at the memory. He shook himself out of his reverie and called his two best sergeants to their belated meeting.

"The captain has delegated his work load to us. Some of it's front burner, and some of it can be pushed to the back. So let's get started. Karen, what have you got going besides the Edwards case?"

Karen quickly explained that her testimony at the trial of Joseph Edwards for the murder of his wife, Debbie, would probably be early the next week. "I've already been prepped."

"How about the Quattlebaum thing?"

She rolled her eyes. "Mr. Quattlebaum is quite upset that the—I kid you not—lavender commode that he'd special-ordered for a customer had been destroyed in the attack."

"Lavender?"

Karen rolled her eyes at Jon's question and continued her report. "And he was distraught to think that anyone in this town could have the 'unkind audacity,' as he put it, to throw a brick through his expensive window."

Newman couldn't stop his grin. "Don't tell me there was a note tied around it. That'd just be too trite."

"OK, I won't, but I will read it to you." She pulled a clear plastic evidence bag out of the folder and read, 'People who get in over their heads usually end up drowning. Stay out of the water on this one.'"

"What on earth is that supposed to mean?" Jon Stewart asked.

Millen shrugged and said, "J. Phillip thinks it's because someone has the mistaken idea that he's mixed up in all the rumors about developing the downtown waterfront."

Newman finally relaxed. "Oh, those rumors go around every ten years or so. This thing'll die down about the time J. Phillip gets his window fixed. What else you got?"

She hesitated a moment and then said, "I hate to bring it up with everything that's going on, but I have to meet with Graham at four-thirty today. And I'll probably have to meet with him several more times over the next week or so."

"Damn, that's bad timing." Newman took a deep breath and smiled. "But we can work around it. We knew this renovation project was going to eat up some of your time. How's it going, anyway?" Al had recommended Graham Lee Renovators to her because the firm had done such a fine job on the Newmans' home in Old Town.

Karen Millen had moved to Fernandina three years ago when she inherited an old family home on American Beach. Now she quickly explained that they were reaching what would be one of many critical points in the process.

"Yeah, I know he's a stickler for doing it right. I'll give you all of the leeway I can on time off, but if there's a crunch, you'll just have to reschedule."

THE PELICAN OF FERNANDINA

"Understood. Thanks."

Al looked at his watch. Millen's appointment wasn't for several hours, so there was no need to rush the meeting. He shifted his attention to Jon Stewart.

Jon reminded his boss that he'd closed one case this morning. They quickly reviewed two more of his active cases.

"I'll hand these over to the other guys so you can concentrate on the captain's work." Newman shoved a thick, well-worn file folder across the table. "This is a cold case that Wilson had just started on." When the sergeant seemed puzzled at the assignment, Newman added, "I think you'll find it interesting."

Jon flipped through several pages of the Haldad case to give him time to choose his words carefully. "This case has some relevance to our captain's current, uh, situation?"

"Read and decide."

"I'll get right on it, but—"

Al sighed. Everyone had a "but" this afternoon. "What?"

"Alice and I have that appointment I told you about. It's with the obstetrician at nine tomorrow morning."

"Oh, boy," Al grinned and cracked a joke about first-time fathers. Jon blushed at all of the right moments, and for a few minutes there was laughter in the Investigations Division.

Wilson returned to Seacrest with two beers in him and several more bright ideas. He also had a question for the chief, and he fought off the beer-induced drowsiness to make the call.

"I'm already late for a meeting, so this better be good."

"One question: Why did Khee ask for me to be the one to babysit Walid—and just who was this guy, anyway?"

"I'm telling you, Wilson, drop this right now. Trust me, you do not want to investigate this case on your own. You have no badge, no back-up. And when you get in the way, and you will get in the way, I will damn well arrest you—as a civilian—for interfering in a police matter!"

Charles Evans had started speaking calmly, but by the time he reached the end he was shouting into the receiver. He slammed the phone down without saying goodbye. *Great. Now I have to go make nice to Cassandra Newman and her bicentennial steering committee.*

Wilson looked at the dead receiver. *Guess I'm not gonna learn anything about Walid's phone log or what he was scribbling on that legal pad, either.*

At least he was stone cold sober. The chief had blasted the last of the beer haze from his brain. Soon he was at his desk with a mug of freshly-brewed coffee.

He rearranged the papers on his desk while he weighed his options. He could either work on his tan and do all of Dianne's honey-dos, or he could do what he did best. *Hell, I'm a cop, a detective. So, I'll detect! Besides, they can only kill me once.*

He punched in George Khee's number. He would ask him those same two questions, but with a twist. When this was all over, he'd know whether Khee had set him up or not. If he had, he'd have Khee's badge on a plaque over his mantle.

The SAC was unavailable, and his secretary became quite snappish when Wilson demanded to know his whereabouts. He backpedaled and thanked her as politely as he could, but Ms. Toohey did not soften.

He hung up and checked his watch. He had time to work off the day's frustrations at the *dojo* before everyone with a real life came home.

The technician at Baptist Medical Center Nassau squeezed a liberal dollop of gel in her palm and rubbed her hands together until they were slimy. She wiggled her fingers at the Stewarts. "Ready?"

Alice grinned and put her hands on her belly. Jon held her a little closer. He could see the pulse beating in her throat. "Yes," they said in unison and Annie Howard quickly rubbed the gel onto Alice's stomach.

"Let me put on clean gloves and we'll be ready for the next step," Annie said.

Alice and Jon had been married two years. They had had a small ceremony shortly after the bride had recovered from her brother's brutal attack.

Cletus Shanks would be in Raiford for a long time. He had been convicted not only of the attempted murder of his sister, but also for beating his wife to death. Laurel Shanks had lingered for months, but she had finally died during Cletus's trial for his assault on Alice. When that trial ended with a guilty verdict, he had pled guilty in Laurel's death, too.

Alice had no thoughts of the difficult past as Annie bustled over with the sonogram machine. The technician kept up a steady stream of chatter as she pushed buttons and flipped switches. Finally, she was ready. She held the wand aloft and grinned again.

"Ready to meet someone new?"

She didn't wait for the Stewarts' answer, but began to drag the wand slowly back and forth across Alice's stomach. The three of them watched the small display screen intently. Jon thought that Annie was the only one who understood what they were looking at, but he still couldn't turn away.

After several minutes of concentration, she smiled at the nervous parents-to-be. At their nod of approval, she traced the fuzzy image on the CRT and said, "Sergeant and Mrs. Stewart, meet your new daughter."

Alice gasped and laid her hands on her sticky belly. Jon lowered his head and kissed his wife's shoulder.

"Would you like a picture of her to take home?" At Alice's tearful yes, she pushed yet another button and printed a hard copy of the image.

While the strip of paper slowly emerged, Annie cleaned Alice up and gave them both tissues to mop eyes and noses.

Jon barely remembered the rest of the day. He returned to work, had two meetings, and went to a farewell luncheon for a city official. When he finally drove home, he tried to remember what he had agreed to during the second meeting and could not.

He opened the front door and called, "I'm home!" Alice yelled hello from the kitchen and Sara Jane came hurrying from her bedroom to join them.

"Ummm, that smells good. What is it?"

"Stir fry shrimp," Alice said, "if you don't eat all of the vegetables first." She slapped his hand and he dropped a piece of raw cauliflower.

Mary Martha and Amelia paced back and forth across the kitchen floor. They had been his first family. He had adopted the two flamepoint Siamese cats a couple of years ago when he had investigated a series of break-ins at Cats Angels. He liked to say that Alice and Sara Jane were his second choice.

Now he bent down to talk to the cats. "What do you two want?"

"*Meowww!*" they said in unison. They were more interested in the freshly-peeled shrimp than they were in vegetables.

Alice added the vegetables to the skillet before she checked on the rice. "Dinner's in about a half an hour, so you have time to do your thing."

Jon kissed a cheek warm from cooking and began his nightly ritual. He padded down the long hallway to the shower. The washing machine was chugging away when they sat down to dinner several minutes later. Alice had finally given each cat a shrimp, so they were happily occupied.

Grace had been said and Jon's wine had been poured when he nodded to Alice. She pulled the sonogram image out of a pocket and handed it to Sara Jane.

Sara Jane had a mouthful of stir fry when her mother handed her the funny looking piece of paper. She was still trying to decipher it when her mother asked, "See anyone you're related to?"

Sara Jane jumped up and ran circles around the table. "OMG! OMG! This is the baby! I can see its head!" She kissed Alice and then ran to kiss Jon.

Mary Martha, the bolder of the two Siamese, came to see what all of the excitement was about. Sara Jane scooped her up and said, "We're gonna have a ... We're gonna have a ..." Sara Jane stopped beside her mother and asked, "What are we gonna have?" Mary Martha took this opportunity to escape, but no one noticed.

Alice held out her hand for the print-out and pulled her first daughter in close. "See here?" she said, and began to trace the image with her free hand. "You, my dear, are going to have a sister."

Sara Jane went perfectly still. "A sister," she whispered. "I'm going to have a baby sister." She did a little jig.

When she settled back down at the table again, Jon turned the conversation to selecting a name for the baby. It quickly became a comedy routine. "I know, let's name her Spot!" When Sara Jane shrieked, he added, "Or Ludmilla! Gumby! Summerfallwinterspring!"

Sara Jane spent the rest of the meal peppering them with questions and considering where in her library of "word" books she could search for odd and antiquated terms for the situation.

By bedtime, she had chosen *preggers* for her mother's condition and *soeur* for the sister who would soon join them. Her parents merely smiled. They knew that these were only the first two of a long list of words Sara Jane would compile over the next several months.

After the dishes were done and Sara Jane was safely in her room with homework, Jon spoke more seriously about their new daughter's name. "I'd like to name her Ruby Dell."

"After your sister."

"Yeah."

"You don't talk about her much. Are you ever going to tell me about her?"

"Soon." He kissed the top of Alice's head.

"How old was she when she died? How old were you?"

"Four. She was very small, even for four." He paused. "I was six, the big brother. I was supposed to take care of her."

"What happened?" Alice whispered.

Jon squeezed her fiercely for a heartbeat before he said, "I'll tell you all about it, love, but not right now. This is supposed to be a house of joy tonight."

Chapter 9

Hossein Mousavi pulled his SUV into the driveway of his new home on Ash Street, late on a Thursday evening. He was glad to be here. He had been on the road for a week, and he was very tired. He had left New London last Monday and had stopped to visit several cells along the way. In Norfolk, he had spent two nights delivering documents too sensitive to trust to the mail. The cell at the Naval Operating Base in Norfolk and the one at Little Creek Amphibious Base in Virginia Beach were both on track with their plans. The new cell at Dam Neck was barely operational, but its members were bright and eager.

He'd spent another two nights in Charleston, again delivering and gathering information. His next two days had been spent in the Savannah area, touching base with the cells located at Fort Stewart and Hunter Air Force Base. He'd slept in this morning and had treated himself to beignets on River Street before a late start to Fernandina.

He had exited I-95 about a half an hour ago. His first impression on A1A had been of a corridor typically lined with car dealerships and fast food emporiums. *Of course*, he'd sneered as he drove by Target and Super Wal-Mart, *every burg has to have its big box discount stores.*

He had driven up Eighth Street and taken a left at the light onto Centre. He was not particularly charmed with the brick crosswalks and the lighted trees. He had no idea of the history that surrounded him that afternoon, and in the days to come, he would show his disinterest in learning about it. He would never know that the house he was about to enter, a block south of Centre Street, had contributed greatly to the community's rich history and folklore.

He was stretching the kinks out when the front door of the former Addison House Bed and Breakfast Inn opened. The backlight silhouetted a tall, lean man.

"*Salaam*." He moved to the edge of the porch. "You must be Hossein."

"And you must be Hakim."

"I am. Welcome to your new home. There is tea." Hakim Khalidi opened a front door that had once graced the nineteenth-century Egmont Hotel. "The others are anxious to meet you."

Mousavi nodded tiredly on his way up the porch steps. "That's good. Perhaps it shows that they are still committed, in spite of recent events down here."

"I think," Khalidi stopped to explain, "that we are eager to show you that our loyalty and dedication remain unchanged."

"We never doubted it," Mousavi lied to his second in command and followed him inside.

There were several men around the dining room table, with the vacant chair at its head waiting for their new leader. Mousavi took his seat and glanced around while the youngest of the group brought him tea and cakes.

Khalidi remained standing to make the introductions. "Our leader, Hossein Mousavi, comes here from the New London cell," he said. "While directing our operations, he will also be working at the Civilian Personnel Office at Kings Bay, as a GS-12."

He turned to Mousavi and smiled. "You know that I am your second, so let's start with the third most important man in the unit, the cook." Everyone laughed and the baby-faced man who had served Mousavi his tea blushed at the attention. "This is Culinary Specialist Third Class Bobby Slidell. He is a cook at the enlisted galley on the submarine base."

Slidell murmured his greeting and Khalidi added, "He also feeds us quite well." Mousavi noted the man's Western name, but said nothing for the moment.

"Next is Azziz Eid, also stationed at Kings Bay, a personnelman at the submarine group there." Mousavi was pleased. Eid would be able to track ships' movement for them.

"And Malik Gamil is at TRF—the Trident Refit Facility—so he knows which boat is scheduled to come in for work." A tall, slim man down at the end of the table lifted a hand in greeting. His rimless glasses reflected the light so Mousavi could not see his eyes.

Mousavi did not stand when he told his new team how glad he was to be there and how impressed he was with the assembled talent and dedication. When he began his conclusion, Khalidi signaled to Slidell and the young man quietly left the room.

"Thank you for your kind remarks," Khalidi spoke from down the table. "We are proud to welcome you to your new home. Your room is ready. Why don't we help you bring your things in while Bobby puts the finishing touches on dinner?"

It was quickly done. He owned very little, and he assured them that he could unpack later.

Hossein Mousavi was Persian-American, while everyone else at the table had a distinctly Anglo-Saxon origin. His parents had fled their homeland during the Iranian Revolution in 1979 and had joined friends in Ohio shortly before their oldest son's birth. Mousavi's swarthy Mid-Eastern looks soon set him apart first from his classmates in Dayton's public schools and then later at Ohio State University. By the time he joined the civil service, he had grown proud of this distinction and sought out other Muslims as he moved about the country from one job to another.

Mousavi took his place at the head of the table again and was surprised when Slidell presented a meal that could have come straight from the kitchens of Cairo or Tehran. "What is this?" He waved at the serving dishes. "I was expecting hamburgers or beef barbecue, but this is a wonderful meal!"

"When he joined the group, Bobby vowed to learn how to prepare the *halal* or clean foods," Khalidi explained.

Slidell blushed again, and Mousavi could see pink skin glowing through his thin crew cut. He turned even pinker when Mousavi added his own compliments about the meal.

Khalidi looked at his watch. "It's almost time for study before evening prayers. You know the drill."

Every man except Slidell carried his dirty dishes to the kitchen. Eid stacked Mousavi's dishes on top of his own before he disappeared. Slidell pushed his chair back and nodded to them before he disappeared upstairs.

"Slidell does not clean up. The rest of the men do that while the leader—you, now—and I talk before study, prayers and lights out."

"We will talk about the external operation tomorrow, when we have more time. First tell me why Slidell has not yet taken his true name."

Khalidi hesitated before answering. He did not want the man to get off to a bad start with the new boss. "He is younger than his years. He has just turned twenty."

"You tired of babysitting?"

"Not yet. Slidell is dedicated with the fervor that only the very young can muster. He wants to choose his true name very carefully. He says that it will be the name he will have to live up to for the rest of his life."

"Touching," Mousavi said, and Khalidi checked to see if the other man was being sarcastic. He wasn't and Khalidi relaxed a little as his new boss added, "It is very touching. And you're right about the fervor of the young."

Khalidi took a sip of tea before he began to brief Mousavi about the team. "Before I tell you any more about Slidell, let me say that there's bound to be some friction now and then in any group."

Mousavi nodded, so he continued. "Well, first there's me, who everyone says is anal. I just think that an organized life is the best way to live. And to fight."

"There's a fine line between organization and obsession."

"I agree. Have no fear; the others tell me when I stray too close to that line."

"Oh, for the good old days of blind obedience," Mousavi said, and they both chuckled.

"Next, I want to talk about Malik Gamil, our training officer. He is almost as bright as he thinks he is, so he gets impatient with the rest of us when we can't keep up."

"Shades of Imam Majid, right?"

"Except Gamil doesn't ask Allah to strike us dead for our stupidity! He was born Nathan Broadstreet in Connecticut. I mention his home state only because his disdain for Southerners sometimes causes friction."

"Any real problems?"

Khalidi shook his head. "Nothing serious. Gamil won't win any popularity contests, especially with the locals, but he's OK.

"He's been here about a year, a yeoman at the Trident Refit Facility at Kings Bay. He tells us when the big Trident submarines come and go up there. He's our yeoman, too; provides the team with any admin support we might need. He also runs our religious studies program, using the syllabus from New London."

"Busy man."

"That's OK. He has more energy than he knows what to do with." Khalidi took his last sip of tea. "Our only two problems, if you want to call them that, rest in Azziz Eid and Bobby Slidell. In different ways, of course.

"Slidell is, as you have seen, very young for his age. He doesn't always think before he does or says something stupid. This tries the patience of the other guys. They give him a hard time, call him 'Baby,' which enrages him. That makes them laugh even harder."

Khalidi chuckled and went on, "Two or three months ago, Eid started calling him 'Kermit' because he's so green. When he'd walk in a room, he'd be greeted by a few bars of 'It's Not Easy Being Green.'" Khalidi shook his head. "Had to put a stop to that.

"I've had to step in a couple of other times, mostly after Bobby's tried to 'prove' himself. Bottom line is, he is sincere in his faith and is definitely genuine in his enthusiasm."

"And he's a damn fine cook."

"Ah, yes, there is that. If it's true that an army travels on its stomach, we are going first class all the way."

"You've saved Eid for last. Any particular reason?"

Khalidi had spent the last few minutes sizing up his new boss. Judging him quickly, he decided that he would trust Mousavi with his life—and with the lives of the other men.

"Azziz Eid," he began, "is a very angry man. He is hard to control, and he needs to be watched. He's Personnelman Second Class Jared Cummings, stationed at Submarine Group TEN at Kings Bay. He's our weaponsmaster."

"How's that coming?"

"He'll give you a full briefing later, but it's right on track."

They were interrupted by Gamil, who came in from the kitchen, wiping his hands on a dishtowel. "Clean-up's almost done. I'll go set up the room."

"Since we have so much space in this big old house, we turned the back parlor into a training room," Khalidi said.

"How old is this place, anyway? Some of the light fixtures look like they belong in a museum."

"Built in the 1870s for a local merchant named Simmons. Frank, I think."

"Huh. What's the training on?" Mousavi was uninterested in the local history.

Khalidi grinned. "Remember those TV ads you always see for that video language course? We're using one to learn Arabic." He looked at his watch. It was time to join the others. "We have an hour of Arabic and an hour of the Holy Book before prayers, then bed."

"Every night?"

Khalidi shook his head. "Three nights a week. And

we observe the Sabbath. Ours is the Muslim week—
Friday is Sunday and Saturday is our Monday."

"Does Gamil teach *The Book* as well as the language?"

"Yes, he uses the guide issued out of New London.
Would you like to sit in?"

Mousavi smiled. "Thank you for your kind offer,
but I wrote most of that guide."

"You did an excellent job, then."

"I will unpack while the rest of you train. Have
someone knock on my door and I will join you for
prayers."

Chapter 10

Wilson waited patiently while everyone with somewhere to go got ready to go there. When the quiet house was his, he raced through his new morning routine of beds, dishes, and laundry.

He took a mug of coffee into his study and sat at his desk. He grunted in satisfaction. He had spent most of last night organizing it to be his command post at home. He pulled the telephone closer to him and checked the list of people he wanted to call. When he'd been a rookie, a crusty old sergeant had taught him that when you swallowed a live toad first thing in the morning, the rest of the day was a piece of cake. *Might as well swallow the biggest toad first.*

Lee Marie Toohey's response to his request to speak to her boss was delivered in clipped monosyllables.

"To be frank, I don't remember much about the other day, except I have an idea I might have been a little abrupt with you," Wilson said. He waited for her to thaw.

It was a long time coming. "I know that you and Agent Khee don't get along, but he really is a good man."

Wilson let that one slide. He'd heard Lee Marie's explanation before: the higher Khee climbed up the FBI ladder, the more good he could do.

"Do you have any idea when he'll be back?"

Lee Marie hesitated before she whispered, "He really is out of the building, but I guess you should know that he's told me not to put your calls through to him, even when he's here."

"Thank you. I know it was hard for you to tell me that. Don't worry about it. You have a nice day, now." *How did a nice girl like her end up working for such a jerk?*

Wilson's mood brightened when he saw the next name on his list. He hadn't talked to Ray Forbes in several years. They were old Army buddies who had been in and out of touch several times since Desert Storm.

He was smiling as he punched in all eleven digits. He knew from the 202 area code that it was a DC number, but he held the receiver at arm's length in disbelief when the woman on the other end of the line identified it as FBI headquarters.

"Hello? Hello?"

"Uh, is Ray there? Ray Forbes?"

"Who's calling, please?"

Wilson identified himself as an old friend who just wanted to say hello.

"I'm sorry, but Mr. Forbes is in a meeting upstairs that I expect will last most of the day. Can I take a message for you?"

"I just wanted to say hello. It's been a while." He gave her his contact information and hung up. *Two down. Now what?*

Al Newman was rushed and wary. Somehow, Wilson knew this call was not going to go well. "It's me, just checking in with you. Who'd you give the Haldad case to? It's a screwy one, all right."

"I gave it to Jon, but I don't think he's had—"

"That's OK. Who's workin' my case? I hope they're

havin' more luck than I am—"

"Say, Captain, sorry to cut you short, but I gotta run. Good hearing from you though. Hang in there. Catch ya later!"

Wilson glared at the receiver as if it were to blame for the frustrating responses coming out of it. *Jeez Louise. Three strikes an' yer out! Khee, Forbes, and now Newman.* He headed for the shower. An early lunch at Sliders tiki bar sounded good. He needed to put gas in the car, too.

He put his wallet and change in his pockets and headed for the door. His hand was on the doorknob when he remembered one last detail he should attend to. Miss Blossom came running at the sound of kibble hitting her dish, but stopped at the kitchen door when she saw Wilson. "Yeah, I love you, too, cat."

He knew that you're supposed to take care of your horses before you take care of yourself, but he was suddenly very hungry. And thirsty. He pulled into a parking slot at Sliders. He'd feed the car later.

"Is Jaybo here? I'd like to talk to him."

The waitress returned with his beer and the news that Jaybo's shift started at four. *Figures*, Wilson groused and took his first sip.

His mood had improved somewhat after another beer and one of Sliders' signature burgers. He left a generous tip and headed up Sadler to finally see to the car's needs. He'd catch up with Jaybo another day.

He was pocketing his change at the Shell station on the corner of Sadler and Eighth streets when Shorty walked in.

"Hey, Hoss, how's it hangin'?" Shorty grinned at him.

Wilson finished stuffing his wallet into its pocket and held out his hand. "Well, well, well! If it ain't my fav-o-rite vertically challenged person!"

"Hell, I'm the only one you know!" Shorty shook his friend's hand and pulled him down to his level. "Scoop is you're in deep doo-doo," he said quietly. "Wanna talk about it?"

"Not here. Let me run the car through the wash and I'll meet you somewhere."

"How 'bout the coffee shop over there?" Shorty jerked his head back toward Sadler's intersection with Fourteenth Street.

Shorty was halfway through a gooey chocolate gut-bomb and a fancy latte by the time Wilson joined him. Wilson shook his head. He'd never figured out how a little guy with such bad eating habits managed to stay so trim.

With only minimal prompting, Wilson let his black coffee grow cold and told Shorty his sad tale, complete with his suspicions, frustrations, and editorial comments about the *dramatis personae*. George Khee did not fare well, and even Chief Evans took a few hits. Shorty's eyebrows shot up more than once.

When he finally ran down, Shorty sat quietly for a few seconds before he discarded their trash and returned with freshly filled mugs. "Have you told Khee or Evans how ya feel about all of this?"

"Khee has instructed his secretary not to put me through, and Evans already knows that I'm terminally pissed at him."

Shorty looked down and took a slow sip of his coffee. "Ya know that Evans may be yer very best friend right now."

"Huh. Damn sure don't act like it. He could be a little more cooperative, you know."

Shorty pierced him with a look. "You have no idea what, exactly, he's doing for ya, even as we speak." Wilson blinked at Shorty's sharp tone. "So I don't think ya should irritate him any more than ya already have."

"You're giving *me* advice on how to handle authority? Shorty merely glowered at him. "You, the thigh-bite king? The guy who has a 'Question Authority' tattoo?"

"Now ain't that a crock a' beans? Me tellin' you how to bee-have, an' all?"

Running into Dianne later that afternoon downtown was pure coincidence, but Shorty was quick to take advantage of the unexpected meeting. He knew it was the end of the day, but he thought she looked whipped.

"Hey, Miss Dianne, how's it goin'?"

A tired smile lit her face. "End of my shift, and I have to go back to the station for a meeting. How about you?"

"Fine as frog hair. Uh, I heard about the ruckus with the captain."

"Yeah, well. What can I say?"

"Ran into yer guy earlier and we had a cup of coffee." He watched her grow even more tense.

"Coffee?"

"Yep, an' we talked for a long time. Or, he talked and I listened."

Now her face was completely closed. "And just exactly what did he have to say in all of this talking?"

He knew that Dianne would want it straight. "He's purty angry. Ever'one's a sonofabitch, especially that Khee fellow." Shorty paused a beat before he added, "Can't say I blame him."

"Oh, he's mad, all right. Even the cat's giving him a wide berth these days.

He knew she was wondering about it, so he added,

"And he's a little ticked at you 'cause yer not bein' all Nancy Nurse-like with him."

"Uh-huh. And what was his language like?"

"That boy has got hisself a terminal case a' potty mouth!"

They both chuckled over that, and Shorty left her with a reminder that he would always be there if they needed him. "Don't fergit—words is easy, but faithful friends is hard ta find."

Wilson was excruciatingly polite to Lee Marie Toohey, and was rewarded by being allowed to talk to George Khee.

"Thanks for taking my call, Special Agent in Charge Khee. I didn't know you'd been promoted until I had my little sleepover at your house. I suppose I should congratulate you."

Khee was suspicious. "Thanks. What do you want?"

"Who'd you screw over to get it? Heard you got all sorts of goodies out of that botched Leopard job. You parlay that up to the top floor?"

"What do you want?"

"I want to know who that Walid character was. I want to know why you had the bright idea for me to babysit him. And I bloody well want to know why you tried to arrest me for murder!"

"Get off my back! Even if I could tell you anything, I wouldn't. It's a federal case; stay out of it."

"What do you mean, 'even if you could'?"

"I do not need this grief from you! Stay out of this, and stay off of my phone!" Khee slammed the telephone down so hard that it bounced off of his desk.

He put it back where it belonged with yet another bang.

When Khee had calmed himself, he dialed Charles Evans. He was surprised that the telephone still worked.

Evans, on the other hand, made a point to be gentle with the telephone when he ended their conversation.

But his exchange with Wilson was not nearly as gentle. "Get your ass in here. Forthwith."

"Don't bother to sit down," the chief said to Wilson several minutes later. "When I finish with you, you're not going to have anything to sit on, anyway." Wilson stood a little straighter and braced himself for whatever was coming.

"I just got off the phone with George Khee. He reminded me that he is the SAC down there, and that he—not you—is in charge of the Walid investigation." Wilson said nothing and stared past the chief's shoulder.

"One more telephone call from Khee, or anybody else for that matter, and I will dump a whole pile of it on your head."

Wilson still had nothing to say and his boss glowered at him. "Got it?"

"Yes, sir."

"Git."

Wilson executed a sharp about-face and marched out of the chief's office. No one was brave enough to speak to him on the way out.

"You wanted to see me, Chief?"

Charles Evans had spent the last twenty minutes calming himself down after his conversations with Khee and Wilson. Now he pasted a sincere but tired smile on his face and greeted Wilson's wife. He was glad that this day was almost over.

He gently explained to Dianne that he was putting her on desk duty until the situation with Wilson was resolved.

Dianne was stunned. "Boy, I didn't see that one coming. Am I being punished because you're mad at my husband?"

"Shame on you—you know me better than that. I'm not mad at him, and you're not being punished. It's just that traffic duty can be dangerous, and you need to be in top form every day you go out there."

Her only response was a glare, but he continued, "You have to be distracted by all of this. If your husband goes home and acts like he does around here, I hate to think what your nights are like."

Dianne's shoulders slumped and he knew he'd gotten through to her. "You and Wilson are two of my most valuable employees. You are good at what you do, and you're enthusiastic about doing it. Besides that, you two have been good friends to me and Jacqueline. Wilson's going through a rough spot now, but he'll come out of it. We all will.

"And I'd hate for anything to happen to you or the children." She shot him a questioning look, and he said carefully, "We don't know who this Walid guy was or who wanted him dead."

"You think Wilson could be in the same cross-hairs."

The chief nodded and said, "And you. If something happened to you or to the kids, God forbid, it would destroy him. You have to know that the bad guys have figured that out. Hell, they'd probably decide to kill you and the kids and not him; it'd be too kind to kill him, too."

"I get it, now. I just thought he was so angry because he's getting shafted. And he doesn't know who or why.

And he doesn't seem to be able to find out anything about it."

"Well, yeah, there is that element to it."

"And because of all of this, I have to push papers."

"Only until it blows over."

"Huh. Thanks, Chief, for everything. Now I'll go home and thank my dear husband for the desk duty."

Evans spent the next few moments visualizing what kind of evening the Wilson family was going to have. "Rose," he said as he picked up his car keys, "it's been a long day, and I'm going home."

Rose Isabel said nothing as he walked out, but looked at the small clock on her desk. It was only four.

Wilson stormed out of the station and gunned his car out of the parking lot. He knew that he was too agitated to drive, so he tried to concentrate on the road. But his mind wandered, and so did the car.

He cut another driver off at the Fourteenth Street light and headed for home. "I can't believe George Khee made SAC," he said out loud. "S-A-C, huh. In his case, that stands for Sack A' Crap." Amused by his wit, he did not notice the car pulling on to Fourteenth until it was almost too late for him to swerve out of its way.

Knocking over the full trash can at the end of his driveway was the last straw. "Who the bloody hell put the bloody trash can in the bloody driveway?"

Dianne and Michelle came running from the kitchen. Michelle skidded to a halt a safe distance away, but Dianne was not so cautious.

"Who in their right mind puts—"

"STOP!" Dianne held her hand up like the traffic

cop she was. "I am responsible for the trash can. We were trying to help you by doing this chore for you."

"I didn't—"

"We were going to say 'you're welcome' when you thanked us, but I don't think we will."

"Now just a minute! I—"

Dianne pointed to his study. "In there! Now!"

Wilson blinked in surprise. *Sounds like my old sergeant at Basic.*

She closed the door behind them. "What on earth is wrong with you, coming into the house screaming like that?"

"What's wrong? I'll tell you what's wrong! This whole bloody thing is what's wrong! And George Khee is what's wrong! I cannot, *cannot* believe that he made SAC. Well, I'll tell you something, he did it on all those dead bodies in that Leopard case. Almost got me killed, too." Wilson paced up and down the room, arms waving. Dianne had subsided into a chair to watch her husband disintegrate.

"SAC, for God's sake! I decided on the way home that stands for 'Sack A' Crap.' Witty, doncha think?"

She said nothing but watched him as he continued to prowl around the room. He would stop and pick up a knickknack, then put it down and move on.

"And I'll tell you another thing, Grace, I'm fed up to here," he patted the underside of his chin, "with this whole mess. I'm half a mind to tell 'em all to stuff it and go fishing, or whatever. Move to the Keys. Run a T-shirt shop."

"You called me Grace." Dianne fought tears.

"Did not."

"Did, too."

Wilson stood in the middle of the room with his

hands on his hips and looked at her before he sank into a nearby chair. He put his face in his hands. "God," he said through the mask of fingers, "I am so very sorry. I must be out of my mind."

"It hurt."

"I know, sweetheart. I was upset. I'm sorry." He realized his uncontrolled anger was what hurt her more than his accidentally using the name of his late wife. He had grieved with his two small daughters when cancer removed Grace from their lives, but that loss belonged to the past. He and Dianne had built their own warm, tightly knit family during their years together.

Dianne let his apology hang in the air before she finally began to talk. She spoke quietly and calmly for several minutes before she summed up her remarks by saying, "I love you dearly. The girls adore you, and Brian thinks that you're God.

"But you are scaring us. We have never seen anyone as out of control as you are. You are doing a great deal of damage, both to yourself and to the people who love you." She looked over at him, but he was staring down at the floor. "And I have a horrible feeling that you're doing the same thing in your professional life as you are in your personal one."

They listened to the clock tick while Dianne composed her final shot. "You need to get a grip or everything you love—your life, your work, your friends and family—it's all going to run through your fingers."

He had not changed his mind about the situation, but he realized that he was going to have to watch himself if he wanted to get his life back. He forced a smile on his face and stood. He held out his hand, and Dianne took her time in placing hers in it. He pulled her close and murmured, "I love you. I love all of you. And

I need every one of you to make it through every day."

"We love you, too. Now go make nice to your daughters while I finish fixing dinner."

She heard him knock on Michelle's door and then their murmurs as they began to visit. Several minutes later, she heard him knock on Lisa's door.

She nodded in grim satisfaction and realized that she was also very glad she had not told him about her unwilling reassignment to desk duty. Conversation around the dinner table was stilted and Wilson knew he was to blame. His family was waiting for the next blow-up. He turned to ask Michelle about school.

He wandered out to the deck with a drink in his hand after dinner. The evening was cooler than he had anticipated, and he didn't plan to stay long. He took a sip of the twelve-year-old single malt he'd just poured and refused to count how many other drinks he had poured that night.

Chapter 11

Friday, the Sabbath. Hossein Mousavi awoke quietly and looked around his room. It was on the first floor, at the back of the house, and faced a private courtyard with a fountain. He could hear it burbling in the early morning stillness.

He spread his rug on the cool bricks of the courtyard and began his morning devotions. He always spent a longer time in prayer on the Sabbath, and this Friday was no exception.

The others had just started breakfast when he walked into the dining room. "What time do we leave for the center this afternoon?" he asked the table in general.

"Right after work," Khalidi replied. The Islamic Studies Center was on the other side of Jacksonville. If they left around six, they would have plenty of time for the commute and for visiting several of the center's Islamic scholars before the service.

"And our visit with Imam Sharif?"

"It is all arranged," Gamil spoke up. "He is looking forward to seeing you again."

"Yes, it's been too long." Mousavi looked at his

watch. "This departure time gives us the chance to review our plan if we all come straight back here after work." He looked around the table and everyone nodded in agreement.

Sara Jane searched for her best friend. She barely spoke to the other kids as they milled around before the first class at Fernandina Beach Middle School.

"Lisa! Lisa! Over here!"

"You're mighty excited this morning," Lisa Wilson grumbled.

"I'm gonna have a baby sister! A *bambina*, a *niña*!" Sara Jane was hopping with excitement and failed to notice that Lisa was not hopping along with her.

"Isn't that great? A baby sister I can play with—" Lisa's lack of enthusiasm finally registered. "What's wrong with you? Are you sick or something?"

"Dunno," Lisa shrugged. There was no way she was going to tell anyone that her dad had come home screaming last night and then proceeded to drink too much. "Guess I got a bug, or something. It's great about your sister, though. When will she get here?"

Sara Jane looked more closely at her friend. If she didn't know better, she'd say Lisa had the same look that she herself had had when her dad and Uncle Cletus had kept her scared all of the time. "Let's walk up to the Doo-Wop Diner after school and talk."

"Maybe. Meet me here right after our last class." Maybe Sara Jane would be interested to hear about Ms. Cameron and how she was letting her help decorate the set for the next play. *At least Sara Jane's eyes will be focused and she won't slur her words.* Suddenly the day seemed a little brighter.

"Ray, you old hound dog! I been chasin' you for days!"

"Wilson, my man! It's good to hear your voice. And you know DC, one meeting after another." Ray Forbes looked at his watch. "I have a little time before I have to go brief this fellow about one of my projects. Whatcha got?"

"First, I need a name. It's been driving me crazy for weeks. Do you remember Popeye?"

"That boy loved fried chicken more than sex."

"Hell, where we were most of the time, there *was* no sex!" They both had a good laugh and then Wilson said, "I was thinkin' about him the other day, and suddenly I can't think of his name."

"Uh, give me a minute. Keep talking, it'll come to me."

"Well, I'm also a little fuzzy about what happened to him."

"Oh, I know that one. You're gonna love it. He went back to Michigan, Lansing, I think, and bought a franchise for—"

"No!"

"You got it. Popeyes Chicken."

"Does he still have it?"

"No, man, some dude tried to rob his place and he thought he was still Ranger Rick."

"Dang! What happened?"

"He died in the ER, but the dude was DRT—Dead Right There—smack dab in front of the fryer." Forbes paused and said, "The obit listed a wife and two little girls." His brain pulled up the image of the newspaper clipping, and he snapped his fingers. "Got it. Hillary. David Hillary, that was his name."

"Yeah, that's it, all right. Sorry to hear about poor ol' Popeye. Listen, I know you're busy, but I wanted to ask you a couple of things on the professional side."

"Shoot."

"You know anything about George Khee, the SAC in Jax?"

Forbes was suddenly wary. "I may have heard the name. What about him?" He pulled a tablet close and took notes as Wilson talked. He grew more alarmed with each sentence.

"Whew! That's quite a story! You OK?" Forbes worked hard to maintain the folksy, friendly tone of their conversation.

"Oh, hell, I'm fine, but I do have a couple of questions about this whole thing. Thought I'd ask you to help me track them down." No need to tell him about being banned from the case or suspended from the job.

Forbes's bells and whistles were getting louder and louder. "Uh, what are they?"

"No one at the local office, namely Khee, seems to know or care who this Walid character was. And let me tell you, he didn't look like any Walid I've ever met. He was as American as apple pie—sandy hair, blue eyes, corn fed, and choir practice on Wednesday. Probably had freckles when he was a kid in Iowa, or somewhere."

Forbes could hardly hear him over the alarm bells going off in his head.

"Of course, Khee won't share evidence. This Walid character was writing and drawing something, but I can't get my hands on his legal pad," Wilson said. "And please tell me how in the hell did a screw-up like Khee get a plum assignment like Jacksonville?"

"Sounds like you got your hands full down there, ol' buddy. I'm afraid I don't have any answers right off the top of my head. Let me check around and get back to you."

From the silence that followed, Forbes could tell that Wilson was trying to keep from muttering "yeah, right." Nevertheless, he gave Forbes his email address and cell phone number, and his voice now had returned to the low-key tone of earlier in the call.

"Or maybe I'll just come up there and buy you a drink while you fill me in about the Walid/Khee thing," Wilson said.

"Sounds like a plan. I'll call you in a couple of days or so." They ended the conversation and Forbes took a moment to gather his thoughts.

"Cindy, is he available? I need two minutes."

Cindy Gordon put him through. He had worked for Assistant Deputy Director Frederick Page for a decade as they both climbed the federal ladder. He gave his boss a synopsis of Wilson's story and they agreed to meet after Forbes had delivered his briefing.

It was Page's turn to contemplate the receiver before he finally decided to place his call.

"Hello, Frederick."

Christine Mahmood was the only person who called him by his full name. He rather liked it. "Isn't Caller ID wonderful? You can decide whether or not to talk to the person on the other end," he said.

"I will always take your calls. What is on your mind today?"

Her slight Afghan accent made even the most mundane statement sound interesting. "There's something going on down in Florida I want to make sure you are aware of."

She had a good idea of what was coming next, but she grabbed her note pad anyway. She jotted several notes as Page told her things about Walid's death that Khee had failed to mention during his earlier telephone calls.

There was no need for her to lock her notes away every night along with the other sensitive papers on her desk. Her bad handwriting, combined with a personal shorthand peppered with Pashto slang, made anything she wrote a cryptographer's nightmare.

"Ah, yes, Ahmahl Walid, better known as Ronnie Hightower."

"You know him?" Page jotted the man's Western name down.

"Of him and the organization he belongs to, the Muslim Military Jihad. Have you heard of it?"

Page scribbled that name below Hightower's. "Muslim extremists do not fall in my area of expertise. Keep talking."

"The MMJ had its roots in the Iranian Revolution in 1979, with the leadership eventually coming from all over the Middle East—Saudi, Yemen, Iraq, you name it. The general membership is mostly Westerners who've converted to Islam and have embraced its more extreme attitudes," Christine said.

"Young American military men who are disenchanted with their lives are recruited into a local cell. At first, they are presented with the kinder teachings of Islam, but gradually they are introduced to the Jihadist mission of MMJ. Once they are converted and trained, they go about their military duties, but in such a way to harm or impede the smooth working of the command they're assigned to."

"You mean sabotage?"

"Sabotage is hard to define and prosecute, especially

in peacetime. But they do things like damage equipment, install parts backwards, and even make costly accounting or administrative errors," she said.

"A Navy yeoman out in San Diego sent the fitness reports—you'd call them annual performance reviews— of all of the lieutenants in his command to an MMJ buddy in Adak, Alaska. They were the last reports the board would see before it considered them for promotion to lieutenant commander. The guy in Adak sat on them until after the promotion board had met. Not one of those lieutenants made it."

"Yeowch!"

"Oh, it gets worse. Some cells are chosen for what they call an 'External Operation.' That's when they mount an attack on a military installation, like an Army post or a Navy ship. Did you hear about that accident at a US Marine Corps ammo magazine out in Twenty-Nine Palms last year?"

"As a matter of fact, I did; a friend's son was injured in that one."

"Well, it was no accident. One of the fatalities was a member of the local MMJ cell. Took us forever to figure that one out."

"So what about this Walid guy down in Florida? Or Hightower, or whatever you call him?"

"It took us a while to turn him. He was finally coming in, and he was bringing the plans for the external operation assigned to the Fernandina Beach cell."

"So who took him out?"

"We're not sure yet. The SAC in Jax and I have talked a couple of times, and he's coming up here for debriefing."

"George Khee."

"I am surprised you know the name."

"I don't. The guy who called Ray Forbes has a real hate-fest for Khee. He spent most of his nickel telling Ray what a low-life the Jax SAC is."

"He is very ambitious, and that does sometimes cloud his judgment. Just exactly was the purpose of this man's call to Ray? What was his name again?"

Page checked his notes. "Captain H.L. Wilson of the Fernandina Beach, Florida, Police Department." Page riffled through his notes again. "He wanted to know a couple of things about Walid and his death, but Ray stalled him. Told him he'd have to do some checking and then call him back in a day or two."

Christine thought a minute. "Tell Ray not to call him back, to wait for Wilson to call him again. That will give us a little more time to get our ducks in a row."

"He joked about coming up to get the info in person."

"That might not be a bad idea. When he calls back, Ray can invite him here, and we can put him up at one of the hotels we use. Then we can put the fear of God—"

"Or Allah."

"Or Allah in him so he will go back to flyover country and disappear. He sounds like a loose cannon who can very well wreck several years of hard work."

"Talk about sabotage."

"Pure *puduu!*"

Page had heard her favorite epithet before and smiled. The woman could read and write four languages and get by in a couple more. But she had adopted a curse word used by a podracer in Episode I of "Star Wars."

"You're right; it is *puduu*, indeed."

They ended the call with promises to keep in touch. It was getting late, and Page checked his watch before he dialed Forbes's number. Their conversation was short.

Each man was tired and ready to end his day. They quickly agreed that Wilson would be coming to DC; he just didn't know it yet.

"I am impressed," Mousavi said as he stood in the door of the training room.

Gamil smiled and quickly pointed out the supplies and equipment the cell had at its disposal. A table with a lectern on top faced a room full of long tables.

Khalidi saw Mousavi's eyes rake the back of the wall, but invited him to sit at a table before he explained. "Azziz, here, is our weaponsmaster, as you may recall." The young man sat a little straighter at the attention. "And he has done an excellent job of building our weapons stores."

"Were the inscriptions his idea?"

"And a very good one, too," Khalidi replied.

Eid quickly explained that inscribing the boxes with holy verses would be inspirational. "After the briefing, I'll show you our small arms locker, if you want."

Khalidi spoke again and Mousavi turned to face him. Khalidi stood at the lectern, and the screen behind him displayed a green background with "Muslim Military Jihad" inscribed in white Arabic letters.

"I have been serving as the cell leader and plan coordinator since Walid's departure. I am delighted to turn some of those duties over to you." Mousavi grinned and Khalidi continued, "With Azziz Eid as weaponsmaster, we now have our full complement of launchers and most of our small arms."

Eid nodded in agreement as Bobby Slidell came in with a cart loaded with a samovar and tea glasses. "Bobby, here, will rent an RV we'll use to stage the weapons when the time comes." Slidell's face went rosy on cue as he fixed a glass for himself.

"He's been camping at Fort Clinch off and on for a couple of months now, and the rangers all know him." Khalidi's casual reference gave no hint to the fort's rich history of almost two hundred years.

"It's easier to get a campsite since all the tourists left," Slidell explained, "so it's easier for me to chat 'em up. They don't hardly check my truck anymore." His face brightened and he said, "It's really a neat place. Named after a real guy, ya know. A general in the Seminole Wars way back in the 1800s. 'Cept he was a colonel when the war—"

"'Nuff a' that," Eid piped up from the back of the room. "We're makin' our own history, an' right now, not a couple a' hunnert years ago."

Mousavi picked up on the tension between the two men and hastened to defuse it. He was not familiar with Slidell's twang and asked where he was from. Everyone chuckled and Slidell grinned.

"Tennessee. Spent early days backwoodsin' with my kin, so this camping thang is just up my alley."

Mousavi smiled at the kid's enthusiasm, even if he wasn't interested in listening to his babbling about local history. Khalidi had said the guy was only twenty, but had the exuberance of a twelve-year-old. *Keeping this enthusiastic holy warrior is worth listening to a few unwanted history lessons*, Mousavi sighed inwardly.

"'Sides," Slidell grumbled, "one a' the rangers is from a coupla hollers over from us."

"Hollers?"

"It's a type of valley," Khalidi explained impatiently and once again took control of the conversation. "Slidell and Eid will move the weapons to the fort when the time comes.

The screen changed to show an aerial view of Fort Clinch, and Khalidi's laser pointer illustrated how they would use the fort to launch their attack against the submarine base in Georgia—just north of Cumberland Sound.

Mousavi nodded in satisfaction. It was an excellent plan. It was still on track despite Walid's defection, and the cell members remained committed to its success.

Chapter 12

Alice wandered into the living room, wiping her hands on a dish towel. "I know it's early, but we are beat. Ruby Dell and I are going to read ourselves to sleep."

Jon put down his own reading and gathered his wife to him. He kissed the top of her head. "That's OK. The two of you are working hard. Other than tired, how do you both feel?"

"We feel fine, but December seems so far away."

"It will fly by, you'll see." When she grumbled in protest, he reminded her, "Most of the time you're so busy you don't even realize that the week's over, remember?"

"Easy for you to say." She gave him one last hug and left to pour a cup of tea from the pot steeping under its cozy.

Jon poured his own tea before he returned to the sofa and the papers scattered there. He was about halfway through the last file Wilbur Jordan had assembled before he retired.

Benjamin Franklin Haldad, Jon read, had been a Navy petty officer stationed at Kings Bay. He'd lived here, though, and Jon recognized the address of an apartment complex within the city limits.

When Haldad had failed to show up for work, Base Security requested that FBPD do a wellness check. Patrolman Derek Frank had found him in bed with a missing hand and a slit throat. He'd called it in, and Wilbur had caught the case, his last, as it turned out.

Jon yawned. He was never going to get through this if he didn't wake up. He looked at his watch and groaned. It was only nine-thirty. His tea was long gone; maybe he'd wake up if he got a refill and rinsed out the pot.

He returned to his seat with a new cup of tea and a second wind. Before he could resume his work, Mary Martha jumped up and demanded attention. Her first owner had named both cats after women prominent in Fernandina history. Mary Martha, the bold one, was named after the wife of Governor Reid. Amelia was named after the wife of William B.C. Duryee, a prominent merchant whose building on Centre Street now housed the Marina Restaurant. Amelia was nowhere around, but Mary Martha settled down nicely beside him. He returned to the Haldad file.

"Whoa, what's this?" he muttered and scanned Wilbur's notes from a meeting with a Naval Criminal Investigative Service agent at Kings Bay. *Wonder why NCIS got in on it? The murder happened in town, away from the base.*

He read on to discover that Petty Officer Haldad had also been known as Tariq el Ramadan. The Wisconsin native had converted to Islam long before he arrived in Fernandina.

"Huh," he grunted when he saw the entry about a wife back in Wisconsin. *Wonder if anybody looked into her?* He pulled his pad over and added that question to a growing list.

He had just noticed a big red MMJ scribbled in the margin when Mary Martha jumped down and ran to the French doors in the kitchen. Amelia soon joined her. Both cats meowed loudly and Jon got up to see what the fuss was about.

"I'll be damned. I think it's that big black tomcat from The Bookworm." He and Poe had met when Jon was trying to keep someone from killing Sue Nell Borden, owner of the town's premier bookstore.

"Poe, is that you?" Jon opened the door and the cat strutted in like visiting royalty. Mary Martha and Amelia were certainly treating him as if he were a royal.

Jon watched in fascination as Poe gave himself a tour of the place, took a sip of water, and helped himself to a generous portion of kibble. A quick romp with the girls, and he was ready to go. Jon shook his head and closed the door behind him. *I swear, that cat acted like he was looking for something.* He left Mary Martha and Amelia with their noses pressed against a bottom pane of one door.

He went back to his reading, but soon began to nod. He awoke some time later with Amelia asleep in his lap and Mary Martha beside him. He petted Amelia awake and removed her from his lap.

He started to return his papers to their file and enjoyed the short tussle with Mary Martha when he tried to retrieve the papers she was sleeping on. Jon pressed the wrinkles out and teased her about getting kitty drool on official documents.

He tossed the messy file on the table, and then lunged to keep it from falling off. Neither he nor the cats noticed the photograph that fell under the table.

He padded off to bed, and saw the light under Sara Jane's door. He tapped on it as he went by as their nightly signal for lights out.

Sara Jane closed the latest book about words that her mom had bought her. Sue Nell had promised that it was filled with wonderful old words, and she had been right. She hadn't found anything related to her sister's eventual arrival, but she'd enjoyed the search. She fell asleep smiling at "Adam's ale," an ancient euphemism for water. Jon continued his journey to bed and was barely conscious when he spooned himself next to his sleeping wife.

Amelia awoke later in the night to use the litter box. She had a sip of water and a kibble or two before she wandered into the living room. She spotted the photograph underneath the coffee table immediately. After a quick sniff, she batted it and then chased it as it skittered away. Her attack eventually dislodged the sticky note that Wilbur had put on the back. Amelia sniffed the glue before she pierced the paper with her sharp kitty teeth. When she batted it again, it joined the photo out of sight under a heavy piece of furniture. Amelia rejoined her sister in bed, while the photo and note waited to be rediscovered.

Saturday morning chores found Sara Jane daydreaming as she vacuumed the living room. She thrust the wand under the large chest and it made a most gratifying *thwoop* sound. She shut the machine off and a slightly mangled photograph fell to the floor. Pin-sized holes told her that it had been cat-handled. When she bent to retrieve it, she discovered a yellow sticky note lying beside it.

Neither of the people in the photo was familiar, and the lady had what looked like a black tablecloth over her head. She knew what it was called, but could not dredge up the word. "Mom!" she called and started down the hall. "Look what I found!" The cats raced ahead of her. "Who are these people?"

Alice came out of the main bathroom that Sara Jane would be sharing with Josephus this weekend. She always said a little prayer of thanks whenever she thought of her nephew, now transformed from when he had been known as Jeeter. He and his twin, Skeeter, were the sons of her brother, Cletus. Skeeter had grown into a carbon copy of his father, and had left Fernandina more than a year ago.

Jeeter, on the other hand, had risen like a phoenix from the ashes of the Shanks clan. Shedding his nickname, Josephus had also shed the bad attitudes and criminal ambitions of his family. With Alice and Jon's support, he was almost finished with his welding course in St. Augustine. Job offers were beginning to come in.

Alice sank down on a dining room chair; Ruby Dell seemed to be sapping most of her energy this morning. She looked at the photo Sara Jane was holding and saw a young man, probably in his early thirties, with light brown hair and a scraggly beard of the same color. The woman's features were in the shadow created by her black cover.

"I don't know, honey; perhaps your dad can tell us when he gets home."

"Will this help?" Sara Jane stuck out an index finger with the yellow note attached.

"Huh. 'Birthday – Tariq and Jasmine.' Well, that explains the whatsis she's wearing."

Sara Jane snapped her fingers. "I remember now; it's a *burqua*. Middle Eastern women wear 'em."

"Smarty pants!" Alice tweaked her nose. "Did you learn that from one of your books?"

Sara Jane's only response was a giggle as she and the

cats raced back down the hall.

"Put those on your father's desk!" Alice called after the rapidly retreating trio.

Ah, he was safe. Evans held the department head meeting this time every week. He looked at his watch; by now, they were trying to impress each other as they sat around the conference table. Evans would be at its head, listening and watching.

Wilson casually walked to the evidence locker and greeted its long-time attendant. Charlotte Mann had been an up-and-coming patrol officer until a liquor store robbery left her with a permanent limp. Her second career as the department's evidence custodian had come as a welcome surprise to everyone.

She guarded her domain fiercely and treated each piece of evidence as if it were part of the national treasure. She was also an inveterate gossip and ran what she called the Information Bank.

She rarely left her cage, thereby offering a captive audience to anyone who stopped by her "bank." Her clientele included uniformed and plainclothes officers, civilian employees, county and state LEOs—law enforcement officers—even the building's custodial staff. Some of her visitors would make deposits, while others withdrew tidbits of information. She was judicious in her disbursements, which ranged from a recommendation for a hairdresser to a contact who might be crucial to an investigation.

"Charlotte, my dear friend. How are you this morning? Let me see your nails."

She was also famous for being vain about her hands. Her weekly appointment at Magna's was sacred. She chose a different color scheme each time she went, the more outrageous the better.

She greeted him warmly and held out ten lime green nails for inspection. She waited patiently for him to get to the real reason he stopped by. She had known about Wilson's suspension before he'd left the building that day. There was no legitimate reason for him to appear at her service window this morning. "Nice timing, Ace."

Wilson did his bad imitation of a shy young man, "Well, ya know, I don't hafta get up as early as the rest of you working stiffs. Couldn't get movin' any earlier."

"Uh, huh. And to what do I owe the pleasure of your stirrin' your lazy butt to come see me so late this mornin'?"

He loved it. "I need to make a withdrawal from your world-famous Information Bank." He paused to see that he had her attention. "You don't have any of the Walid evidence, do you?"

"Never saw it. I hear the feds went in and took everything. Damn near took the paint off the walls."

"I was afraid of that. Any words of wisdom?"

Charlotte lowered her voice. "Watch out for Khee, but I reckon you already figured that one out. He's gonna get somebody killed; make sure it ain't you, cupcake."

Wilson nodded, and she continued, "You should also watch out for his protégé, Durwood Cratch." She looked around to make sure they were still alone. "Now, there's a piece a' work. Know him?"

Before Wilson could answer, he heard Jon Stewart's voice. "Hey, I'm glad I ran into you; we need to talk."

Jon stopped himself to make a point of greeting Charlotte and inquiring about her health. He had barely survived an early gaffe that had taught him to treat her with the respect she thought she deserved.

"Can I buy you some lunch?" Jon said to Wilson. "I

need to pick your brain about—"

Chief Evans inserted himself between the two detectives. Jon was knocked off balance, and Charlotte reached through her window to steady him. They both watched in fascination as Evans and Wilson stood nose to nose.

"This is your very last warning. If you do not stop messing around in this case, I will damn well ban you from the entire building for the duration of your suspension. Got it?"

"Got it."

"You're sure? Because I can extend your suspension long after this Walid mess goes away."

"I'm sure." Wilson wisely kept his responses short and, for once, did not argue with authority.

Evans turned and glared at the two mesmerized witnesses. He jabbed a finger at each of them in a silent order to keep quiet about this exchange before he stomped off.

"Whew! Meeting must've broken up early," Charlotte observed.

"Yeah, I'd say. Tony's at noon tomorrow OK with you?"

When Jon nodded in agreement, it was Wilson's turn to stomp down the hall. He tried to calm down during the short drive to the Miramar Townhomes. He had chased its rental agent for weeks before he got this appointment, and he was not about to stand her up.

Jon and Charlotte looked at each other after Wilson left. "What did we just watch?" he asked.

"Now you know, if you didn't already, why you never, ever, want to cross Chief Evans," Charlotte dispensed this unnecessary bit of advice to the former street kid standing at her window.

Chapter 13

Wilson pulled into a spot in the Miramar Townhomes parking lot. He had left the station with a queasy feeling in his stomach. He hoped that this visit to the townhomes ended better than his last one.

He finally found the office and knew he was in trouble the moment he stepped inside. The striking young blonde who sat behind a cluttered desk was whining into her telephone.

"But, Harlan, you don't—oh, never mind!"

Wonder if that's Harlan Quattlebaum. Wilson had less than pleasant memories of the man as an erstwhile suitor of Sue Nell Borden, back before she married Doc Mueller.

Harlan's father, J. Phillip, had been Fernandina's mayor at the time. Hadn't he seen J. Phillip's name in the paper about some waterfront development scheme?

"No, I'll just do it myself!" She slammed the receiver down and a look of irritation crossed her face. Her "Can I help you?" sounded more like "What do you want?"

Wilson couldn't help himself. "Was that Harlan Quattlebaum you were talking to?" He hurried to explain when she hesitated in answering him. "I met him a couple of years ago, but I haven't run into him since our business was finished. How's he doing?"

The young woman stuck out her left hand to display one of the largest diamonds Wilson had ever seen. Always the cop, he wondered how Harlan had paid for a rock that size.

"He's my finance—oh, I mean fiancé," she giggled. "I have trouble keeping those two words straight."

I just bet you do. He made his smile gentle when he told her that he had an appointment with the rental agent.

She pulled a rental agreement out of a drawer. "We usually do this by email or letter, but I guess you can do it in person."

"No, I don't want to rent a unit; I have an appointment with a Mrs. Joseph." He watched as she struggled to process his words.

Suddenly her face cleared and she said, "She's not available right now. Can I take a message?" Her smile was blinding.

"No," he repeated patiently, "I want you to find her and ask her to come to this office." Wilson spoke pleasantly and slowly. "Is she on the property, uh, facility?"

"Director Joseph is in the Princess Amelia Suite talking to Karl."

"Does the director have her cell with her? Please call her and tell her I am here for our meeting."

She turned to punch in the numbers and Wilson finally noticed the name plate on her desk. He almost groaned aloud. He was attempting to communicate with someone named Muffy. Another glance told him that "Muffy" had been taped on top of her given name. He could only see the "Mar" at the beginning and the "ret" at the end. *Margaret? No, not Margaret; she's definitely a Muffy.* He tuned back in to Muffy's end of the conversation.

"Director Joseph, I'm sorry to bother you, but there's this guy here to see you. What? Oh, his name?"

"Wilson," he supplied.

"A Mr. Wilson, and he wants to see you."

"I have an appointment."

"And he says he has an appointment."

He settled in for a long wait when Muffy announced that the director would only be a few minutes. He picked up a brochure on the complex and began to flip through it. His attention was caught by an engraving of John Percival, the Earl of Egmont, the namesake of one of the suites in the complex. The good Earl had died before he could set foot on this island, but his wife and executors continued his work.

"Yes, ma'am, I'll tell him. No, ma'am, I won't." It was Muffy's tone of voice that caught his attention, rather than her words.

"Honestly!" she said as she hung up the phone. "Everyone treats me like I'm a baby! Of course I know to ask you to wait and apologize for the director's latiness!"

Latiness? Whatever polite remark Wilson's brain was forming evaporated at Muffy's choice of words. He smiled sweetly at the girl, and she bent her head to return to her work.

Bored again, Wilson went back to reading the brochure. Another suite was named after Princess Amelia, the daughter of George the Third of England, and a third was named after Stephan Egan, superintendent of Lord Egmont's indigo plantation. Egan and the Earl's slaves had built a large house on the north end of the island where the Egan family lived for several years. *Funny, I don't remember Dianne ever mentioning anything about that house or any artifacts from it. I'll have to ask.* And all he knew about Egan himself was that several places around the island were named after him.

Barbara Joseph bustled through the door ten minutes later. "I'm so sorry to keep you waiting. Let's go in here." Wilson started to lay the brochure aside, but thought better of it and tucked it in a pocket. Dianne and the girls would enjoy looking at it.

She led him into a small, neat office. "Muffy, dear, would you bring coffee in for me and Mr. Wilson?"

"I'm sorry, Director, it's all gone. I can turn the pot back on and make more?" She ended the offer with a question mark.

Wilson shook his head to decline the offer.

"No, just bring us a couple of bottles of water, please."

There was a slight pause and then a small, baby-doll voice said, "You said I could leave early today so I could stop at Wal-Mart to buy a couple of cases on my way to Momma's."

Barbara Joseph, Wilson noticed, was now using the same tone of voice with Muffy that he had. "That's fine. Don't worry about it." It was obvious that the director had long ago grown weary of Muffy and her various deficiencies.

She looked at her watch. "Tell you what, why don't you take off even a little earlier to run that errand?"

They waited impatiently while Muffy slammed drawers and doors and reloaded her purse with the personal detritus she had scattered about. A final bang of the office door, and she was gone.

They enjoyed a moment of silence before Wilson asked, "How long has she worked for you?"

"A thousand years."

"How long are you going to keep her?"

"She's the owner's niece."

"My condolences." He looked at his own watch. He'd been here thirty minutes and had yet to conduct any business.

"Now, Mr. Wilson, what can I do for you?"

"I'm sure you remember the shooting that occurred here a couple of weeks ago."

"In the Egmont Suite, yes. We had to replace all of the carpet upstairs. The owner was quite upset."

He still thought it rather pretentious to name a unit in this modest complex after the eighteenth-century British Earl but offered only an encouraging murmur.

"The police cut huge chunks out of the carpet in the master bedroom and its bathing suite. And they smeared this awful black powder everywhere."

"'Police,' you said. Do you mean the Fernandina Beach police?"

"Oh! I never stopped to think! I suppose so. I was up in St. Simons for my monthly meeting with the owner the day that poor man was killed, but I saw the damage when I got here the next morning." She stopped to think. "Who else could it have been?"

"Who, indeed. Let's see; can you tell me—these are rental units, right?" She nodded and he continued. "So who rents the Egmont Suite?"

"I'm afraid I'm not at liberty to say. Our clients expect a certain level of discretion and privacy."

Her face closed and he knew he'd lost the battle when she belatedly asked him what his interest in the murder was and why he wanted to know about the suite.

"Oh, I'm with the police." She said nothing, and he knew that she was waiting for him to flash the badge that was resting in his boss's desk drawer. "But I'm on vacation, so I thought I'd do a little sleuthing on my own." *How lame can I sound?*

"I see. Well," she stood to end the meeting, "if you have access to police files, you already know more than I do."

He didn't budge. "That may be true, but I do not know who rents the Egmont Suite."

"You know I can't tell you."

He was getting nowhere. He stood to leave and asked one more question. "Can you tell me who owns this townhome complex?"

"A very wealthy man who wishes to maintain his privacy. And he definitely does not want his name associated with this sordid business." She had herded him to the front door, and now she opened it for him to leave.

He stopped short of the threshold and asked one last question. "If you can't tell me who rents it, can you tell me the name of the man—it is a man, isn't it?" She nodded almost imperceptibly. "The man you deal with on a day-to-day basis?

"I'm sorry, but—"

"Does his name start with a K?"

Her reaction told him everything he wanted to know. He finally stepped through the door. "Thank you for your time. And good luck with Muffy."

She smiled and winked. "My youngest child just started his last year of college. He graduates, I'm outta here!"

Wilson checked his watch as he slid into a booth at Tony's. He was early. *Yeah, like I had trouble fitting this into my busy schedule.*

His hangover was almost gone. After his fruitless visit with Barbara Joseph, not to mention the mind-numbing Muffy, he had stopped for a session of liquid therapy before going home.

Dinner last night had not been pleasant. The kids ate and ran, and Dianne had clearly been irritated about something. He'd tried to sort it out with a drink on the deck, but it was too cold to stay out there for long. Dianne had already gone to bed when he'd come in. Her goodnight kiss had been perfunctory, and she'd only grunted when he said he'd be up for a while.

What a mess, he groused and looked around. *Why is the whole world dumping on my head?*

Jon Stewart's arrival brought a welcome halt to his introspection. Jon ordered a diet Coke and didn't seem to mind when Wilson ordered his first beer of the day. Since he had rejected having one for breakfast, Wilson now felt he deserved a reward for good behavior.

"Do you want to eat first and then work? Or the other way around?" Jon asked.

"Work now," Wilson said and told the waiter to delay lunch. "But keep an eye on my glass, hear? When it gets close to empty, I want to see you with a new one in your hand."

Wilson slowly sipped his beer as Jon talked and riffled through the Haldad file. "Sorry the photo is so mangled. One of my cats got to it."

Wilson grinned and held out his hand. "At our house, we would say that Mr. and Mrs. Haldad had been cat-scanned."

Jon grinned and began to review the case. He pulled out his list of questions. "What did the NCIS have to do with this case?" He flipped Paul Patterson's business card across the table.

"I was getting ready to see if Patterson is still at Kings Bay. NCIS would get involved to some extent, even when a sailor is killed out in town." He took a small sip of beer. "Oh, and have you had a chance to look at the evidence in our locker?"

"On my list."

"Charlotte may be able to give you some inside dope on the case. You know that she talks to everyone, and that they tell her the darnnedest things."

They grinned at her gossip-mongering before Jon asked the next question on his list. "What's with this all-American boy taking a name like Tariq el Ramadan? Isn't Ramadan a Muslim holy day?"

"More like a month, I think. Lots of fasting. You can check, but I don't think he changed it legally. It may be like a street name or even a gamer name."

"Know anything about this big red 'MMJ' scribbled here? Did you do that or did Wilbur?"

"Wilbur. I was going to ask Agent Patterson about it." This conversation was almost as frustrating as the one at the townhouse yesterday. Besides, he was almost out of beer. "Sorry I'm not more helpful. I'd only looked at the file a couple of times when, uh ..."

"That's OK." Jon saved him from having to finish the sentence. "You've given me good leads to track down. Ready for some of Tony's famous pizza?"

"Holy moly!" Jon's vocabulary had changed drastically since Alice and Sara Jane had joined him.

Too full of pizza to concentrate on paperwork, he had decided to Google MMJ. Now he stared at his computer screen in disbelief. Typing in that acronym had sent him directly to the FBI terrorism watch website. He grew even more alarmed as he scanned what it had to say about the MMJ.

He tracked down Karen Millen in the break room and she followed him back to his desk. She sat in his chair and read the screen. "The good ol' MMJ." She used her finger as a cursor. "Muslim Military Jihad."

She smiled at the shock on his face. "It's been around since the late Seventies, and I don't think it's ever going to go away. It was born during the Iranian Revolution in '79, and then migrated to Detroit." When Jon's eyebrows rose in surprise, she added, "Detroit's got the largest Muslim population in America."

She swung her seat around and asked why he had pulled up this information. Jon explained about the cold case and where it was leading him.

"Haldad's death may be telling us that MMJ has a cell here." She tapped her front teeth in thought. "Who have you talked to about this?"

"Just Wilson, so far. It's one of his cold cases. But I've got some leads I'm going to follow up. This MMJ thing was one of them. And I've got the name of an NCIS agent over at Kings Bay—"

"No, you need to talk to the FBI in Jax first. No, wait; you need to brief the chief so *he* can talk to the FBI."

"Uh, Khee's not exactly high on our list at the moment."

"That doesn't matter. That's who you need to talk to." She looked at her watch. "Gotta run. I have to argue about paint colors with my contractor at the Hideaway."

She was gone before Jon could thank her. *One day I'm gonna remember to ask her why she calls it the Hideaway.*

"Dammit!" Wilson had rummaged through every shelf of the refrigerator, but could not find a single can of beer. His lunch with Jon had put him in the mood for another brewski or two, but there was not a can to be had. He didn't want to start on the hard stuff this early in the day, and only wimps drank wine in the afternoon.

Maybe Dianne had let him run out of beer to reduce his intake. "Damn the woman!" he exclaimed, and Miss Blossom quickly exited the room. He was immediately ashamed at his thoughts. *Dianne wouldn't do that. Or would she?*

Wilson poured iced tea instead, and wandered to his recliner in the den. *Now what do I do with myself?* He picked up the copy of the *Pirate Press* lying on the coffee table and hit the recline button on his chair. He began to nod off before he finished the front page. He remembered that his daughter was this year's editor just as he fell over the edge of sleep.

Thirty minutes later he was awake with a fuzzy mouth and a slight headache. Mouthwash, aspirin, and coffee cleared away the cobwebs, and he sat down at his desk. Ray Forbes had never called him back; it was time to bug him.

"Buddy, I'm sorry I haven't gotten back to you. Things have been at their usual insane pitch around here and then, quite frankly, people haven't been too ready to talk about that Walid thing in Fernandina."

"Welcome to my world. Have you made any progress at all?" Wilson's headache was coming back.

"Well, you know me and my bright ideas—"

"More like cockamamie schemes that'd get us either arrested or maimed. I remember the time in Kuwait City—"

"God, she was *sooo* beautiful!"

"Yeah, and her four brothers were *sooo* homicidal!"

"OK, let's don't go there. Just listen to me for a minute. How about coming up to DC? We can play catch-up and have a long talk about our favorite part of the world."

When Wilson hesitated, Forbes sweetened the deal. "I'll even pull some strings and put you up at one of the hotels we use for visiting pooh-bahs."

"Oh, goody. I always wanted to stay at the Willard."

"Get real. Say, why not bring along the wife and kiddies? I'll see if I can't score you a suite."

"Hope you have to throw some sheikh out."

"Call me back with a couple of dates when you can come up. And plan to stay two or three days so we can have a good visit."

Wilson's mood—and headache—had improved greatly. He agreed to call back with possible dates and said goodbye. He couldn't wait until everyone came home.

Forbes called his boss immediately. "He bit. I'll let you know when he decides on the date."

Frederick Page had merely grunted and broken the connection so he could place a call of his own. Christine did her own grunting and agreed to get a dog-and-pony show ready for the loose cannon from flyover country.

Mousavi looked around the table at his team. The last few weeks had been busy. The plan for the Kings Bay external operation had been well on its way when he had arrived; equipment and munitions were either in place or arriving on schedule, and the men were doing their jobs. He had told Khalidi that he felt as if he were trying to merge on to a fast-moving interstate.

A sharp retort broke his reverie and he saw Eid and Slidell exchange glares. Those two were a growing problem. He made a mental note to talk to them soon.

He quickly dispensed with the administrative and housekeeping portion of the meeting and asked for weekly reports.

As Slidell was handing out the coming week's menu, he mentioned that he would be camping at Fort Clinch again this weekend. The reservations clerk now knew him well enough to make sure he got his favorite spot.

Khalidi was next. He reported that the quarterly disbursement from national headquarters had arrived, as had the first hand-guns. "Eid will give you the particulars; my point is that the bookkeeping and supply side is running as smoothly as one of Slidell's sauces." Everyone except Eid chuckled when the cook blushed.

Mousavi nodded to Gamil, the yeoman at Trident Refit Facility. "The new drydock schedule is due in a couple of days. I need to know if we're ready to target one of the boats on the schedule."

An electric shock went through the room. The plan was suddenly real, not some electronic war game. They looked at each other, and then turned to their leader.

Mousavi looked each man in the eye before he answered. "Yes, I think we are ready to target a sub. Bring me the list when you get it."

The meeting was soon over. Mousavi was making his way out of the training room when he heard Eid. "Fat little Cherie's takin' up her time tellin' you all those stories about the fort 'cause she's hot after yer bones, Slidell." Bobby said nothing as they continued down the hall, but Mousavi could see the back of his neck turn scarlet.

"Aww, lookathat! Baby's turned bright red, just like a cherry!" Eid slapped Slidell on the back. "Cherie, that's just about right, ain't it? Do ya get it, fellas? Cherie, as in Cherry?"

"Shut up, Eid," someone in the group growled before they all disappeared around a corner.

Mousavi shook his head. Khalidi had mentioned that Slidell's virginal state was of great concern to the man and a source of amusement to everyone else.

Wilson heard the garage door open. When Dianne deposited grocery bags on the counter, he wandered into the kitchen with a glass of Merlot in his hand. He saluted her with it and started to tell her his good news.

Dianne looked at the wine and her mouth tightened in annoyance. He decided to wait until a better time to bring up the trip to Washington.

"We're out of beer, so I had to settle for red."

"I have not had a very nice day, and I am not in the mood for your booze-induced shenanigans tonight."

His wine glass stopped halfway to his lips. "I have a handle on—"

"Can it." Dianne took a deep breath and leaned against the counter. "I know this is a very unhappy time for you, but I would really like to take a break tonight from your obsessing about this case." She began to put the groceries away and Miss Blossom darted by in a fast exit.

"She sure has been skittish lately," Wilson said.

Dianne shot him a look. "I wonder why."

Wilson said nothing, but watched his wife carefully. He took another sip of wine.

"I'm sure that all of us, including Miss Blossom, would dearly love it if you could refrain from drinking your way through the evening. Again."

Wilson began to help her with the groceries and silently stowed a chilled six-pack in its usual spot in the refrigerator. He straightened from the chore and said, "I'll be in my study." He left his empty glass on the counter.

Dinner began in silence. Wilson complimented Dianne on dinner and she accepted it as the olive branch it was. The girls ate rapidly and silently, but Brian gave his nightly report on his day at preschool at St. Michaels Academy.

Wilson bided his time and finally refilled his wife's wine glass before his own. "I have good news." Three faces turned to him in eager anticipation. Brian, having regaled them with his latest run-in with Sister Sue, began to shovel his dinner.

Wilson quickly recounted his conversation with Ray Forbes and delivered the invitation, along with its free lodging, to spend a few days in Washington.

Dianne fell back in her chair. "Wow. I mean, when? I'd have to have time to clear my work schedule, do something with the girls and Brian—"

He overrode all of her objections. Michelle had started to refuse to go, but then had second thoughts. "Could we go to Arlington, please? The National Cemetery, I mean. I want to find Flossie Borden's grave."

Her request stopped the discussion. "You mean the Flossie Borden who lived in the Villa Las Palmas? What's she doing buried there?" her father wanted to know.

"She and her husband, Nathaniel, had a son who joined the Navy when he grew up. When the son died, he was buried in Arlington, and when Flossie died—years after her son did—she was buried next to him."

"Huh. How about that," Wilson said. "I may not have time to go, but you and your mother certainly can." He turned to Dianne. "Are you up for that traffic in DC?"

Dianne started to nod yes, and then laughed. When Wilson asked her what was so funny, she recounted the tale about Mrs. Borden causing the first automobile accident on Amelia Island, back in the early 1900s. She ended her story with the punch line, "She backed her car right into the one owned by Dr. Waas!"

"As in the Waas House on Seventh Street?" Wilson wanted to know.

"Yes, and Waas Drug Store, don't forget."

Michelle ended that discussion with yet another idea. "And I could go to the Newseum! It's on the corner of Pennsylvania and Sixth. There's even a Metro station nearby, so I could even go by myself while you and Dad are doing your stuff."

"We'll see."

"You are not riding the Metro by yourself," Wilson added.

Michelle opened her mouth to protest, but Dianne forestalled her with a look. Then Lisa spoke up.

"I don't want to go if it's gonna interfere with my meeting with Miss Cameron," she said. "We're supposed to talk about what she's gonna let me do to help her decorate the set for 'Our Town.'"

"Maybe she could stay with Sara Jane," Michelle offered.

They soon disbanded to continue their nightly routine of dishes, homework, and getting Brian ready for tomorrow's battle with the young nun. Dianne fell asleep in front of a chick flick on television and Wilson once again retreated to his study with a glass of wine.

The Pelican had watched it all. He had noted the smiling faces and animated conversation around the dinner table. *Somethin's up.*

Chapter 14

Slidell pulled his Silverado up to the entry booth at Fort Clinch with his money in his hand. He knew the ranger on duty and they exchanged pleasantries.

"How long are you staying this time?" the man asked as he looked back at the truck's bed. "You look like you're movin' in, permanent-like." The bed was jammed with an odd assortment.

Slidell looked in his side mirror. "Oh, that. Most of it's junk I was too lazy to offload. See them long boxes?" Slidell had thrown in a couple of empty launcher boxes so the rangers would get used to seeing them. "Got three or four of the dang things. Picked 'em up at a surplus store. They're great for storin' all sortsa stuff." Slidell usually let his Tennessee twang roll out when he talked to this ranger.

The ranger was now bored and waved the truck through as he stepped back. "Yep, surplus is a good deal. Y'all have a good un."

Slidell smirked to himself. *Pretty slick for a baby*, he thought as he parked at the small building that housed the check-in desk. Cherie was next on his list and he remembered she always dotted the "i" in her name with a heart. Time to put away the good ol' boy and get out the shy young man.

"Hello, Miss Cherie-with-a-heart." He smiled bashfully and the pudgy young woman behind the counter almost squealed. The other ranger on duty rolled her eyes and moved as far away from them as she could.

"Here's all of your paperwork, Mr. Slidell—"

"Bobby."

"Yes, Bobby. I saw your name on the reservation list so I already gave you your favorite spot. All you have to do is sign your John Hancock right there."

He glanced at the hot pink heart she'd drawn next to the signature line. "Do you think it would be all right if I signed it 'Bobby Slidell' instead?"

Cherie did squeal at this second witticism, and the other ranger brushed past her, muttering something about fresh air.

Slidell picked up his permit and turned to go. He took a step toward the door and turned back to see that Cherie was watching. He grinned and winked at her and pulled the door open. He heard her squeal again the door closed behind him.

He groaned when he was safely in the truck. He'd forgotten to make reservations for when his "cousin" came with him over Thanksgiving. *Dang,* he chastised himself. *I guess I can do it when I check out. With any luck, Cherie won't be on duty then.*

He spent a pleasant afternoon chatting up the rangers on the grounds and walking one of the trails. A simple dinner and a good night's sleep brought him awake just before dawn. He found his favorite spot and quietly said his prayers as the sun came up.

Someone other than Cherie was on duty when he checked out, so he made his Thanksgiving reservations without benefit of her squeals and pink hearts.

Karen Millen had just poured a mug of coffee when Dianne walked into the break room. "Hey, girl, how're ya doin'?" Karen looked the other woman over and did not like what she saw. "Let's go sit outside and play catch up."

They chose a bench in the courtyard between the building's wings and cradled the mugs to warm their hands. The air was cool, but both women preferred it that way. It was not the only trait they shared. They had formed an instant bond upon Karen's arrival almost three years ago. Both were dedicated to law enforcement, and both were passionate about family.

Karen's discovery of her ties to the Delaney clan, plus her inheritance of Martha's Hideaway, had awakened an interest in her ancestry. Dianne had shown her how the town's history was entwined with that of the Delaneys and now the detective eagerly looked for more of those connections. The two women regularly exchanged new information about long-dead family members and the contributions they had made to Fernandina lore.

Now Dianne's family was in trouble.

"How's our favorite captain doin' these days?" Karen asked.

Dianne was too tired from last night's domestic drama to be cute. "Not worth a damn." She took a sip of coffee to hide a trembling lip.

"Which means, of course, that the rest of you are right down there with him." She looked around to make sure they were out of earshot. "Talk to me."

Dianne needed little encouragement. Her coffee was long gone before she finished her monologue about Walid, Khee, and even Evans. Wilson's tale about his encounter with Muffy provided a much-needed chuckle.

"But the thing that's making him crazy is that no one will talk to him. I mean, it's not like 'go away kid and don't bother me,' or even 'I'm not at liberty to discuss this.' Wilson says he asks a question and the other person either changes the subject or acts like he hadn't said anything at all. Stares at him with what Wilson calls the 'dead fish look.'"

"Flat affect."

Dianne threw her a look. "Well, Wilson's *affect* is anything but flat!"

Karen was glad to hear a little humor in the midst of all the worry. "Besides being inaudible, what else is bugging him?"

"No one seems to know, which is ridiculous, who this Walid character was. Or they won't tell him. Either way, Wilson still hasn't a clue. And why send a captain to babysit the guy? Did Khee set him up, and if he did, why?

"And another thing he keeps ranting about is the legal pad the guy was scribbling on. Wilson thinks it was in Arabic."

"Can he read Arabic?"

"No, but he can recognize it. And, right before they started eating, Walid was sketching something."

"Sketching? You mean like a person?"

"No, more like a building or maybe even a map. Wilson said it looked familiar, but he couldn't place it. It's driving him crazy. And he's driving us crazy!"

Dianne traced the rim of her mug with her finger. "And then there's the drinking." She whispered it, but Karen heard her.

"How much?"

"Too much." Dianne did not look up from her mug.

"He starts early and is still at it when I go to bed." She shrugged. "Of course, I go to bed very early these days."

"How are the kids handling it?"

"They're hurt, scared. Dinner is a nightmare. The girls eat and run."

"How about the four-year-old?"

Dianne smiled for the first time that day. "He's so wrapped up in his ongoing battle with Sister Sue that he isn't really aware of anything else."

"Hmmm, I wonder where he learned that?"

They had a laugh and parted on that cheerful note.

Karen watched her friend walk back to her desk. Diane hadn't mentioned it, but it had to be killing her to be riding a desk instead of a cruiser. She headed for her own desk and resolved to make a few calls.

Bobby Slidell was still smarting from Eid's latest attack. *I'll show them who's the baby,* he thought as he turned onto Inverness.

He had taken Walid's death hard. The former leader had been the only team member who had treated him right. Slidell remembered once, after a particularly disastrous day, Walid had taken him aside and explained Slidell's worth to him and the team. The older man had explained that he was their chance to educate and nurture a young mind so that he would grow into a true follower. Those few sentences had given him the confidence to cope with the two worlds he inhabited, as well as the bullies who lurked in each of them.

He let the truck roll to a stop in front of Captain Wilson's house. Finding the address had been relatively easy, thanks to the internet locator. He had targeted the captain because he was convinced Wilson was responsible for Walid's death. Slidell fought tears as the truck idled. He sorely missed his friend, still unaware that the man had planned to betray him and their holy mission.

He dabbed his eyes and saw a fat calico cat interrupt its trip across the Wilsons' front porch to stretch first one leg and then the other. He hated cats. His Aunt May had a dozen of the nasty things. Her house made his eyes water. His lip curled as he remembered her hysterics when she'd found one of them hanging from a tree in her backyard. *Huh. Nasty thing deserved to die. Got away with it, too.*

His eyes were dry as he pulled away from the curb. It wouldn't be smart to linger in front of a cop's house. He spent the rest of the drive back to the old Addison House picturing the fat calico swinging in the breeze.

Dianne pulled into the garage, but stayed in the car after she shut the engine off. It was the first time she had been alone all day. She leaned back on the headrest and closed her eyes. Her talk with Karen had been the only bright spot in her day.

The chief thought that work would distract her, so he had piled her desk high. And then, of course, everyone had to drop by to check on her and get an update on her husband. She was very tired of smiling and telling everyone that things were going well. She felt her eyes mist. *What I need is a good cry.*

The door to the kitchen opened. "I thought I heard you pull in. What are you doing sitting out there in the dark?"

She gathered her things and walked into the kitchen.

She automatically checked the stove top. She had called him mid-afternoon to ask him to put tonight's dinner ingredients there to thaw. The spot was empty. She turned to face him while he ranted about the frustrations of his day. He used the hand holding his beer to jab a point home. Beer slopped out of the can and landed on his hand and the floor. He did not seem to notice, but continued his tirade.

"That's it! I've had it!" Wilson stopped in mid-rant. "I am sick of hearing about these people! You are obsessed. This is all you talk about, think about. You are so wrapped up in your woes you can't even remember to take out the hamburger, like I asked you to!"

"Well, *excuuuse* me for—"

"Do you even know, much less care, that your daughter is the editor of this year's paper? Has it registered with you that she's been walking on cloud nine because of all the compliments she's been getting about the first issue? Have you even looked at it?"

"Yes, I have looked at it, and yes, I do know that she's the editor." Never mind he'd fallen asleep before he finished it.

"Or that she's going to be the coordinator for the student aides at this year's Amelia Island Book Festival?" There was a pause. "No, I thought not."

She had yelled herself out, so now she said quietly, "Lisa is knee-deep in set decorating at ACT. All she talks about is Miss Cameron this and Miss Cameron that. Do you recognize the name? Have you even heard Lisa mention it?"

Dianne saw only anger in her husband's eyes and she knew that she had failed to get his attention. "The bottom line is that you're not here anymore. You are in some dark world filled with evil FBI agents and Mid-

Eastern low-lifes. I don't like it, and I most definitely do not like what it's doing to you!"

Wilson slammed the now-empty can on the counter. It bounced to the floor. "Oh, yeah? Well, maybe you don't like me, either!"

They stared at each other in stunned silence. Michelle and Lisa, who had been eavesdropping in the hall, leaned into one another. Lisa wiped a tear from her cheek and Michelle patted her aching stomach.

Wilson put a conciliatory hand on her arm and Dianne forced herself not to flinch. "Call Arte Pizza," he said, "and I'll go pick it up."

She had changed clothes and Michelle was setting the table when he appeared with the car keys. "When I get back, we'll talk more about the DC trip." Neither of them responded, and he left the house feeling a little martyred.

The Pelican watched from his nightly perch. *Another night of Wilson family bliss. I'm gonna hafta do something about this soon.*

"Here's the idea I've been kicking around for the last couple of days," Wilson said as soon as everyone had a slice of pizza and a bowl of Greek salad.

"Let's leave for Washington next Tuesday. We'll take two days to drive it, stop in Florence, South Carolina, at that motel we like. We'll hit Washington before rush hour on Wednesday."

"Why so early in the week?" Dianne asked. "I was hoping we could stay over the weekend."

"We can. I'll have meetings Thursday, maybe Friday. We'll have Saturday and Sunday to play. We'll start back on Monday, get here on Tuesday." The table was silent as everyone considered his plan, so he pressed on. "That'd put everyone back to school and work no later than Wednesday." He looked over at Michelle. "You'd miss five days of fast Fernandina action, but that thing never leaves your side." Her iPhone sounded off right on cue.

"I already talked to Sara Jane. She said her mom's cool with whenever I come," Lisa offered.

That's more like it, the Pelican thought as he watched the excited family as everyone talked at the same time.

The girls retired to their rooms after the dishes were done, and Wilson knocked on Michelle's door shortly after it closed. He had some fence-mending to do.

He left her door open, and Lisa soon joined them to find out what all of the laughter was about. She found a spot on the end of the bed, and Wilson said, "Say, now that I have you two together, how would you little ladies like a bedtime story?"

Michelle and Lisa collapsed in laughter. "Oh, Daddy," Lisa said, "you *really* haven't been paying attention if you think we still need stories!"

He saw Michelle's eyes dart to her computer screen yet again and took the hint. "C'mon, punkin, let's leave your sister, the editor, alone."

Lisa climbed into her own bed and gave her dad a resounding kiss when he offered a cheek. She was half asleep but managed to mumble, "Can you bring Miss Blossom in? I forgot."

"OK, but a big favor like that will cost you!"

He awoke some time later with his notes scattered about him on the sofa. The nights had finally become too cool to sit on the deck, so he had chosen this cozy room for his work after everyone else had gone to bed. The house was quiet as he glanced at the framed photos on the bookshelves and the needlepoint pillows that his mother had made for her own home. He fervently hoped that he would be sitting in this same spot a year from now. He glanced at his wine glass, but the deep red liquid held no appeal for him. Perhaps he wasn't turning into the village sot, after all.

He stuffed his papers back in their various file folders before he returned them to his desk. He dumped his wine down the kitchen sink and began his nightly security check of doors and windows.

He opened the door to the deck and stuck his head out to check the temperature. He suddenly remembered Miss Blossom. "Here, kitty, kitty," he called softly. Miss Blossom liked her warm spot at the foot of Lisa's bed, so she couldn't be far.

He stepped out onto the deck and closed the door behind him. He called for her again. When she still didn't come, he left the deck and began to walk around the house, calling her name every few seconds.

"Hey, Wilson!" someone called softly. He crouched and reached for his absent weapon.

"Don't shoot! It's yer pal, Shorty!" He emerged from the shadows.

"What on earth are you doing here, man? It's the middle of the night!"

Shorty answered Wilson's question with a couple of his own. "What's up? Why are you walkin' around out here?"

Wilson quickly explained about Miss Blossom, and the two of them continued the circuit. They were standing on the front walk when Shorty said, "Oh, my God!" He began to run toward the front porch.

Wilson whirled to follow him. His eyes never left Miss Blossom. When he reached her, he saw that someone had used a clothesline to hang her. They had threaded it through a bracket for a hanging basket and left her to twist ever so slowly in the night breeze.

Wilson stood in stunned silence. Had he thought to look, he would have been equally taken aback at his friend's uncharacteristically fierce expression. He reached out to touch the cat. "She's still a little bit warm."

Shorty wordlessly produced a pocket knife. Wilson cut her down and Shorty cradled her in his arms. "Glad we found her before yer girls came flyin' outta here first thing in the mornin'."

Wilson ran his fingers through his hair. "Lordamighty, who would do this? Could it be a prank?"

"Dunno 'bout that, but I do know I'd like ta get muh hands on 'em."

"Can you hold her for another minute or two? I need to find something to put her in."

"I got just the thing. Let me take her, an' I'll get her back to ya by the time everybody's awake."

"Uh, sure." That didn't quite make sense to Wilson, but not much in his life was making sense lately. He turned his head to see if their search and discovery had awakened anyone. Shorty was already walking down the walk by the time he turned back. Wilson watched him disappear with a cell phone plastered to his ear.

Chapter 15

Jon was halfway to the car when he turned around to fetch a jacket. Florida's version of autumn had finally arrived. Alice grinned at the sink when he said "Brrrr," and continued to the hall closet.

His wardrobe still consisted of khaki slacks and polo shirts with the FBPD logo embroidered on the left breast. The blue windbreaker he pulled out of the closet carried the same logo. He stuck his tongue out at his wife when she giggled at him.

He left Amelia Park and stopped at the light at Fourteenth. He knew that Alice would opt for an extra layer this morning, too. He smiled to himself when he realized that the entire family, even the cats, preferred warm weather.

He parked the car at the station and hurried inside. He was grinning because he'd just figured out that he was surrounded by beautiful women: his wife, Alice, of course; and then there were Sara Jane and the two flamepoints, Amelia and Mary Martha. Ruby Dell would join this harem in a matter of months.

"Good mornin', Miss Charlotte, and how are you today?"

"My, my, my, ain't we chipper today?" Sensing a little gossip coming her way, Charlotte Mann eyed this young sergeant carefully. She had not been the only one to comment that he had mellowed since his marriage. Once quiet and all business, he had grown happier and more relaxed with Alice and Sara Jane in his life.

"Most people think of me as Jon, but you can call me Chipper if you like."

"Jokes, even. You must have had a great night," she fished.

"Ms. Mann, I am surrounded by beautiful women, yourself included; how could I possibly be anybody but 'Chipper'?"

"Uh, huh. And just how can I help Your Chipperness this morning?"

He filled out the form and in a few moments she put the Haldad evidence box on the counter. He signed it out and saw Wilson's signature on the line above his. The check out and return dates told him that Wilson had been looking at it just days before his suspension.

A glittery purple fingernail tapped the sign-out log. "Speakin' of our dear captain, how's he doin'?"

Jon knew his answer would be embellished and broadcast. "He's doing great. Had lunch with him the other day."

"I know that, darlin', that's why I'm askin'." One of her nephews was a waiter at Tony's and had recognized both men. He'd earned himself a ten-spot for being so observant.

Jon flashed his best shy boyish smile, but it didn't work.

"How many beers did he have?"

He was trapped. He knew better than to lie, so he tried evasion. "I didn't really count. He's on vacation, you know."

"Some vacation. Not that he's takin' any time off. I hear he's makin' a downright pest of himself, tryin' to investigate his botched babysittin' job."

She was baiting him and he knew it. He dropped the boyish grin and went for a more feral look. "I don't think whoever told you that he 'botched' it knew what he—or she—was talking about."

"I give you high marks for loyalty, darlin'." She lowered her voice. "I hear that our dear Sergeant Millen loves a good lunch at Brett's. A little food, a little champagne … That'd be some lunchtime conversation, let me tell you, what with all of her close friends and contacts at the alphabets. Whooee!"

Jon's smile was sincere this time. "You're a treasure, Charlotte. I knew I'd be glad I talked to you!" He winked at her and carried the box to his desk.

He had good intentions of going through it right then, but his telephone rang. He sat down to take notes and his eye fell on his sticky note with the reminder to call Paul Patterson up at the Kings Bay NCIS office. *Jeez, I'm going to have to start keeping a To Do list.*

"Is he in a good mood today?" Dianne asked Rose Isabel. She wanted to talk to Chief Evans about time off for the Washington trip, but not if he was on one of his famous rants.

Rose chuckled softly. "He's on the phone and he's not yelling at the person on the other end. That's a good sign, isn't it? You want to talk to him in person or on the phone?"

"In person, I think." Dianne knew that he would ask Rose why she wanted the interview, so she quickly explained about the trip. She billed it as a reunion of Army buddies, and neglected to mention any illicit information gathering.

"I'll call you when he's free." She paused a moment before she added, "And, Dianne, I know that people are driving you crazy asking about Wilson, so I'll just say that I'm lighting lots of candles for all of you."

Dianne laughed. "Between the two of us, St. Michaels is going to run out of the darn things!"

She was in the chief's office ten minutes later. His reaction to her request and the reason for it was typical. "Fine! That'll keep him outta my hair for a couple of days!"

She had just finished telling the high school the dates that Michelle would be absent, when Karen Millen dropped a sheaf of papers on her desk. "What's all this?" She skimmed the first few lines and her eyes flew back to Karen.

"Don't ask, don't tell."

"I can't believe this! It's the evidence inventory from the Walid case."

"Keep reading."

The last two pages were Khee's official report on the incident. Dianne had tears in her eyes when she looked up again. "Thank you from the bottom of our hearts. I hate to think what you had to do to get this."

Karen winked and said, "You don't wanna know, girl, but it involved a bottle of Dom and lots of whipped cream!" She continued on her way to the lieutenant's office. She needed a couple of days off herself.

"Dammit! Doesn't anybody do any work around here?" Al Newman laughed and leaned back in his chair.

"No, Loot; you're the only person in the entire division who earns his paycheck!"

"I suppose you want the time off for that house you inherited. Just how old is the Hideaway?"

"It's almost as old as American Beach itself. Martha Hippard had it built in 1938 by a local contractor, Johnson and Son. Frank and Frank Junior made the concrete blocks for it one by one out in the front yard, and then laid them when they were dry."

"I bet Graham Lee won't be making his own bricks."

"Those days are gone forever. And I think maybe women like Martha Hippard are gone, too."

"I've heard the name, but Jacqueline's the historian in the family, especially since we moved to Old Town. Refresh my memory."

Karen knew Jacqueline Newman quite well in her capacity as the chairman setting up the Old Town anniversary celebration. Since the Newmans had bought and renovated the Sharpe House on the corner of San Fernando and Estrada streets several years before, Jacqueline had been an invaluable source of information and advice. The two women regularly exchanged newly-discovered tidbits about the history of both their homes and their families.

She and Jacqueline had laughed over the colorful first owner of the Hideaway. Karen sat down on the chair beside Newman's desk and smiled as she started the story. "Ms. Hippard was the richest and most powerful black woman in Fernandina. She owned a restaurant and lounge, the Plum Garden, on North Third. She also had a home downtown, one that her daddy bought for her. And Lemuel, her first husband, had a bakery and grocery store downtown."

"I haven't heard the Delaney name yet. Where does that come in?"

"From my mother's side. She never talked much

about family, and certainly not anyone in Fernandina Beach. I never heard of this place until I went through Mother's papers after she died. Even then, I didn't think much about it. Then the letter from Finegan and Finegan arrived, so I dug out her papers again. And here I am. I—"

"Wait a minute, I know that name."

"Finegan's a prominent attorney—"

"No, that's not it." Al Newman thought a moment and snapped his fingers when things fell into place. "Got it! Joseph Finegan was a Confederate general. Built a huge mansion right where the School Board offices are on Atlantic."

"That's the one, all right," Karen agreed. "He led the Confederate troops—to victory, I might add—in the Battle of Olustee over near Lake City."

"I'll be darned. I hadn't put it together that he was *that* Finegan. Even more embarrassing, we've been to the reenactment several times." Newman paused while he tried to do the math. "And so this lawyer who contacted you, he's the general's—what?"

"Great-great-grandson. He has the papers to prove it, he said. The good general's picture is in the waiting room, glaring down at his poor secretary."

Newman grinned. "This town never ceases to amaze me. Now that we've determined the pedigree of your lawyer, how about your contractor? Is Graham related to anyone I should know?"

Karen laughed, "All I know about Mr. Lee is that he does what he promises to do and that he's good at what he does."

"OK, OK, so if he isn't going to make bricks in the front yard, what is he going to do?"

"Here's where the serendipity comes in. My brick

sidewalk and chimney need some work, so Graham's going to tackle that small chore before he starts on the really big jobs. The serendipity is that my Great-uncle Birdie Delaney did the original work. He and his part of the clan did a lot of the brick work around town."

"That doesn't sound like much of a job for a man of Graham's talents."

"Oh, we're just getting started! When he finishes the walk and chimney, we're going to clear out the furniture in the downstairs and refinish the floors. All of the floors in the house are heart pine, and somebody's already refinished the ones upstairs. Now I have to do the downstairs."

"I'm glad you're an overpaid officer of the law!"

"Oh, yes! You should see my villa on the Riviera!"

Dianne was queasy when she finished reading George Khee's report. She had waited until the chief had left the building before she pulled it from its hiding place. She had skimmed the evidence inventory first and had found the dead man's legal pad listed there. She'd have to get her hands on the forensics report to find out what it said. *Good luck with that*, she thought and turned to the report.

SAC Khee's account of the Walid incident jived with the version she had heard from Wilson. But the conclusions and recommendations were frightening. In the succinct language of all such reports, Khee had implied that Wilson's arrogance hindered his ability to perform his duties and endangered his coworkers.

He had ended by saying that he felt responsible, to some extent, for Walid's death. He had begun to have doubts about Wilson's competency several years before, during the Leopard job, and had heard rumors since then about his faults and failures in other assignments. Manipulating him into taking the babysitting assignment had been his attempt to find out if the captain should be removed from the field. Walid's death had been a sad proof of Khee's reservations about the captain's fitness for field work. Perhaps a psychological evaluation and a desk job before early retirement would be in the best interest of both the department and the Wilson family, not to mention the community at large.

Dianne closed her eyes and took deep breaths before she returned the report to its drawer. There was no way she was going to show this to her husband. He was already playing into Khee's hands with his obsession about the case, not to mention his alcohol-fueled rants. On the other hand, to keep it from him bordered on criminal negligence.

Her face must have registered her feelings, because Chaplain McGuinty stopped on his way by and said, "Are you all right?"

She made a snap decision. "Do you have a minute?"

Roger McGuinty read Khee's report through twice. His expression was as grim as hers when he finally looked up. "What are you going to do?"

"I don't know whether to show this to Wilson or not. He's already frustrated and angry. He will go critical mass if I show it to him."

"Oh, my goodness! You must show it to him. The man needs to know what he's up against."

Dianne was so ashamed that she almost whispered when she told him what life with Wilson was like these days. She had tears in her eyes when she asked him, "Can you check him out for me? I'm worried that he's losing it.

We're leaving for DC next Tuesday. Wilson's going to talk to an FBI buddy up there about this mess."

"He definitely needs to see the report before he talks to his friend. It will help him decide what questions to ask while he's up there."

"Now we're gettin' somewhere!" Wilson exclaimed and hung up after Dianne called to tell him that she and Michelle would be able to go with him to Washington. He glanced around to see if his voice had spooked Miss Blossom again. He winced when he remembered that Shorty had brought her back in a sealed wooden box. Lisa had conducted a touching ceremony, and the cat now rested peacefully under a pine tree in their back yard.

But the good news, he reminded himself, was that Dianne said that the DC trip was a "go." She and Michelle had cleared their schedules to leave Tuesday. Lisa was excited about staying with the Stewarts, and Brian would join the Newmans' twin granddaughters in Old Town. "What's one more?" Al had asked. "Besides, the kid is already used to being bossed around by girls."

Wilson's conversation with Ray Forbes was short, as usual. "We'll get in early afternoon on Wednesday. You and I can talk Thursday, Friday if we have to. I'll have a day or two of family time, and then we'll head back here to Paradise."

Forbes snorted at the island's description and forced himself to sound enthusiastic. "Can't wait to see you, buddy. I've got a couple of people I want you to meet. And don't worry about the hotel; I've got it covered."

Frederick Page merely grunted when Forbes provided him with the dates a few minutes later.

"Crikey! That soon?" Christine's time in Australia had added to her already colorful vocabulary. She would have to scramble to get ready for the rogue policeman. "The three of us need to talk before he gets here." She checked her PDA and said, "I'm booked solid until five this afternoon. Come about six, why don't you, and bring Forbes with you. I'll serve refreshments," she added as an incentive.

Chapter 16

"You did what?" Mousavi was deadly calm, but Slidell saw a muscle in his jaw working. For the first time, he began to have doubts about what he had done.

He had bided his time during today's meeting while everyone else made their reports. He wanted their undivided attention when he made his own so they could finally appreciate his contributions to the team.

Gamil's announcement that the *USS Indiana* would be arriving at the drydock during the first week in November had startled him as much as it had the others. They had spent the remainder of the meeting fine-tuning their timetable.

Finally, Mousavi had asked if anyone had a last input before he adjourned the meeting. Slidell said, "I have one more thing." He ignored Eid's groan and told them in great detail how he had hanged Captain Wilson's cat.

There was silence around the table when he finished instead of the congratulations and cheers he had expected. He looked from man to man, but no one would look at him except Eid, who said, "Man, you've really stepped in it now."

"The rest of you are dismissed. Slidell, you stay right where you are." Mousavi signaled his number two to join them. "Tell me everything," he ordered when had closed the door after the last man. "I even want to know how you got this cockamamie idea in the first place."

Slidell looked from one man to the other. He could not understand why they were not congratulating him for his bravery and incentive.

"NOW!" Khalidi's palm slapped the table and Slidell jumped and began to talk. He started by telling them about his aunt and ended with a slightly embellished account of his night's work at the Wilson household.

"Very well. You can go," was Mousavi's only reaction to his tale. Once Slidell was gone, Mousavi and Khalidi huddled together.

Khalidi shrugged and said, "It is in our best interests for him—and everyone else, for that matter—to believe that the cop is responsible for Walid's death. It would shake their faith in one another to know that they had harbored a viper in their midst."

"You have a good point, but do you think we should discipline Slidell? Does this thing with the cat endanger this cell and our mission?"

Khalidi played with his empty tea glass before he answered. "No, he is too well established at the fort to remove him. And perhaps this thing has given him the courage we need when we mount the attack next month."

They finally eased their chairs back and began to leave the room. "Besides," Khalidi whispered, "our mission is dangerous. Only Allah knows who will survive it."

Ray Forbes did not enjoy the ride from the Hoover Building to Christine Mahmood's office. He was tired and cranky and wanted to go home. He sneaked a peek at his watch. He should be in his recliner now, with a beer and a snack to tide him over until dinner. He looked around the back seat of the Escalade. Page's driver was supposed to put fresh bottles of cold water in the cup holders before every run. There had been only one bottle, and Page had snagged it. Forbes gave himself a mental shrug. *Get over it. His car, his driver. His water.*

He was startled out of his reverie when the driver made a sharp turn into an underground parking garage. He had driven past this sandstone building a thousand times but had never given a thought to its contents. The bland façade hid one of the country's most secret and successful intelligence gathering organizations.

Christine Mahmood's office was not bland. From its size and the view from its windows, Forbes belatedly realized that she was not the mere functionary he had assumed her to be.

The visitors' chairs that faced her desk sat on a rich Afghan rug and the tea she drew from the samovar was nothing like any tea he had ever tasted.

"Tell me about the cop," Christine said when the amenities were taken care of.

Page began the core dump she wanted. Forbes played his usual supporting role by providing dates and other minutiae.

Christine turned to him when his boss came to a stop. "Anything to add?"

He chose his words carefully. "Wilson and I took turns saving each other's butts during Desert Storm, on duty and off. He's the straightest arrow I know. Having his professionalism, and especially his personal integrity, questioned is driving him nuts."

"That's what we're afraid of," Page interjected. Forbes threw him a dirty look before he could stop himself.

"Nuts or not," Christine said, "here's the deal. This guy is in way over his pay grade and security clearance." She waited a moment for one of them to object before she continued. "If we don't get him under control, he's going to get people killed.

"Some of those dead people will be little guys like him. He'll probably be the first one to go. Then there are our contacts and confidential informants all over the Middle East who are working this problem, men like the late Mr. Walid." She checked them again, giving them another opportunity to contradict her argument. Page was nodding slowly, but she thought that Forbes looked a little pale.

"Now, on to more positive things." She refilled her cup at the samovar and invited her guests to do the same. Forbes helped himself to the honey and sesame seed cakes he had learned to love in the Middle East.

"I have blocked out two to four on Friday afternoon for the good captain. We are going to show him that he's putting himself and his family, along with many other people, in grave danger."

She walked to her window and gazed at the city scene for a beat or two before she turned back to them. "I have no doubt that this man is a relatively sophisticated law enforcement type. But this far exceeds the home invasions, burglaries, and even the homicides he's used to handling. He has no idea of the mayhem he is inviting into his life."

"You've convinced me; two o'clock it is," Page said, and looked over at Forbes. He still looked a little shaken so Page decided to continue ignoring him.

Christine saw Forbes's distress and offered him a brusque thank-you for recognizing the problem in plenty of time for it to be fixed.

"Do you think we can fix it?" he asked.

Both Christine and his boss assured him that Wilson and his family would survive, which made him feel better, at least for a few minutes.

Page nodded to him, and that was his cue to leave. He sat on a particularly uncomfortable chair in the waiting room while his boss and the mysterious Christine talked behind the closed door.

Wednesday morning dawned crisp and cool in Fernandina. The stores were ready for Halloween and were gearing up for Thanksgiving. *Tempest is fidgeting,* Jon Stewart smiled and thought of the slightly dotty lady he'd stolen the phrase from. Great-aunt Tootie had added welcome bouts of comic relief a few years ago as he had struggled to keep her great-niece from being murdered.

He was the last to arrive at the staff meeting and the first one to be called upon. He gave his boss his weekly report, and then began to talk about the cold case. "I've learned that our Petty Officer Haldad is known in some circles as Tariq el Ramadan. His particular circle seems to be the MMJ, the Muslim Military Jihad. Ever hear of it?"

Al Newman's eyebrows almost disappeared into his receding hairline. "Not me; Karen?"

Karen gave them a quick explanation of the MMJ and added that she thought its presence in the area was a recent development. Her coworkers listened carefully as she shared information gained during her close association with several federal agencies in the past few years.

"I wish I could agree with you, but Paul Patterson over at Kings Bay says they've been here for several years. Haldad/Ramadan, whatever you want to call him, was trying to establish a cell down here as long as four or five years ago."

Karen had a smile on her face as she explained that Middle Eastern cultures thought in terms of centuries, not years. "There's a wonderful story still floating about that the Shah of Iran claimed that his navy was twenty-five hundred years old." Everyone chuckled. "The MMJ itself is thirty, so Haldad's membership drive four years ago is, indeed, 'recent.'"

"Recent or not," Al Newman interjected, "It was successful, since we now think we have an active cell right here in Paradise."

"That's very true. And the chatter is that this cell has accepted an external operation that involves attacking Kings Bay." Her announcement was met with stunned silence. "And they think that the attack may very well be launched from our own Fort Clinch." She could see sweat pop out on a couple of foreheads.

Newman was outraged. "I just took the twins there last month, when the 1st New York Volunteer Engineers had their First Weekend Union Garrison!"

"I read a little bit about the fort. Wasn't it built in the 1800s?" Karen asked.

"Yeah," Newman said. "They started it then, but never had the chance to finish it. And it's still not finished, for that matter."

"Finished or not, these low-lifes plan to use it as a launch pad," Karen said.

"Holy moly!" Jon Stewart whispered. "Any ideas when this'll go down?"

Karen shook her head no. "That's what Walid

was going to tell Khee that day at the safe house." She couldn't tell them that she had gotten this information from her pirated copy of Khee's report, and they knew better than to ask.

"Is anybody uncomfortable about the FBI maintaining a safe house here? And that we didn't have a clue about it until this Walid thing blew up?" someone down the table asked.

"We'll talk about that little bit of business when we are sure our captain is safe," the lieutenant promised.

"I have another question," Jon said and did not notice everyone's impatience that the meeting was taking so long. "Do you think there's any connection between the Haldad and Walid murders?"

"My sources haven't finished analyzing all the intel they've got. But—" she looked around the table to make sure she had everyone's attention. "If the same person killed those two, they may very well decide to target Wilson to stop his snooping."

"If that's true, we're in way over our head. We need help," Jon said.

"I'll talk to the chief," the lieutenant promised and adjourned the meeting.

A quick call to Rose got Newman a nine o'clock with the chief tomorrow morning. He would take Stewart and Millen with him as backup.

Karen turned to Jon Stewart as they left the lieutenant to his telephone call. "Why don't we grab a quick lunch and visit this fort you and the Loot have been talking about? I've never had the chance to see it, and besides we can get a much better idea of what we're so worried about."

Jon readily agreed and called Tony's while Karen drove. Soon they were sharing one of the restaurant's signature submarine sandwiches at a shaded picnic table in the state park. He took a sip of his large sweet tea and barked a laugh. "Ha! We're eating a *sub* sandwich while we talk about a *sub* base!"

Karen shot him a withering look. "Nice try, but still *sub*-par."

"You're just jealous of my *sub*lime wit!"

"Stop, or I'll *sub*stitute your head with something else!"

They ate in companionable silence for a few moments. "This park is lovely, but what can you tell me about the fort itself? That's what we really came here to check out." Karen took a large bite of her sandwich and sat back to listen.

"I know a little. Sara Jane did a huge project on it for her history class last year." He thought a moment. "The park itself was a Civilian Conservation Corps project back in the 1930s. It's one of the oldest parks in the Florida Parks System."

"They did a good job." Karen looked around the picnic area.

"Wait until you see the fort. You'll think you're back in 1864."

They finished lunch and carefully deposited their trash in a handy receptacle before they drove the short distance to the visitors' center. Karen eyed the gift shop while Jon and the ranger at the desk talked quietly.

"Ready to get the lay of the land?" Jon asked when he had made arrangements with the ranger for a guided tour. They headed toward the entrance to the fort and stepped onto the drawbridge.

"When the CCC started sprucing up the fort, they

found the original plans for the drawbridge and this sally port." They stood in the shade of the sally port while Jon continued. "So they used those plans to make this entrance. This," he pointed to the brochure she was holding, "shows you the layout of the place. It's five-sided, and you can see the gun placements guarding the river. They built forts up and down the coast using this general plan."

Karen studied the brochure for a quick moment before she patted the thick brick wall and wondered how many people before her had touched the same spot. *Maybe some soldier—or his wife, for that matter—put a hand here to steady himself or to pause a minute.*

They walked out onto a large green expanse, which they knew was the parade ground. The five grass-covered earth bastions were topped with brick walls to form the pentagon. Along the base of the walls stood several brick buildings.

"That's the headquarters building to our right." Jon pointed and then turned to his left. "And that's the prison, I think."

He looked at the other buildings around the parade ground and shook his head. "I know that there's a barracks here, and an infirmary, but I don't know what building is which."

"That's easy," a voice said behind them.

Jon quickly turned to shake hands with his good friend, George Toone.

"Rick told me you were here and wanted a tour."

"Yeah, about twenty minutes is all. Oh, and meet Karen Newman; she works with me."

"Nice to meet you," the ranger said as he touched the wide brim of his hat. He turned back to Jon. "You're cops and it's the middle of the work day. What's up?"

"Fort Clinch came up in conversation this morning and I mentioned I'd never been here. We thought we'd check it out on our lunch break." Karen gave him her most innocent smile and Jon made a mental note to remember how well she could fake sincerity.

"Come on, then, I'll give you a quick tour." He began to lead them in a slow circuit around the inside perimeter.

"I'm sure that more than one person has told you that this place has never been finished." He waited for them to nod before he continued. "But do you know when it was started?" This time he did not wait for their answer, but continued his talk.

"You have to give credit to President George Washington for commissioning the plan that included not only this fort, but the others up and down our coast, as well." He broke off his quick summary of the country's coastal defense system to give them a quick tour of the bakery and blacksmith shop. He took up his talk again as they headed toward the Northwest Bastion and the storehouse/dispensary building that sat before it.

"By 1842, the government was ready to buy over two hundred acres on the island's northernmost tip, right at the mouth of what they called the St. Mark's River—now the St. Marys. It would guard both coastal and river traffic, as well as the very active port in Fernandina. Construction began in 1847, and the fort was named after General Duncan Lamont Clinch."

"Oh, I remember this part," Jon said. "He was a colonel in the U.S. Army during the Second Seminole War. He served under General Gaines—as in Gainesville—and—"

"Go Gators!" George interjected.

Jon shot him a grin. "I guess the colonel did well in the service. He was a brigadier general by the time he resigned his commission and came back to this area. He married a local girl, a daughter of John Houstoun McIntosh from up in Georgia, and he and Eliza had a plantation over in St Marys."

George jumped in. "And he served in Congress, unsuccessfully ran for governor, and died at the ripe old age of sixty-two in 1849."

"Is he buried around here?" Karen's genealogical studies had introduced her to several of the local cemeteries.

The ranger shook his head. "No, he's buried in Bonaventure Cemetery up in Savannah. He'd been on his way back from his summer home in Habersham County, so they just took him on into Savannah."

He led them up to the top of the North Bastion, which looked straight up Cumberland Sound, with the south tip of Georgia's Cumberland Island across the half-mile span of water. The day was so clear that they could see several large buildings at the submarine base, only a couple of miles north from where they stood.

"Any idea what those buildings are?" Karen asked.

"I know that one is a drydock at Kings Bay, but I don't know what the other one is," George said.

They turned their backs on the base and the sound to survey the parade ground. "What no one ever mentions is that this same spot of land has been used since the Timucua Indians' time to defend the river and the island," George said. They paused a moment to look at the replicas of the 19th-century cannons that stood facing the river, before he led them back down to the parade ground.

"What we usually concentrate on," he said, "is this fort's role in the Civil War, or the 'Great Unpleasantness,' as one of my more genteel ancestors referred to it in her letters to her daughter right after the war."

"Oh, my!" Karen said, "Do you still have the letters?"

George grinned. "They're passed down on the women's side of the family. Right now, they're in my mom's safety deposit box."

They shared a chuckle about George's kin and her choice of words before he continued. "It still wasn't finished when the Confederate Army took it over in 1861, but they made do with what you see."

Karen looked around and tried to imagine living in these Spartan conditions.

"The Union Army moved in the next year, right after General Lee ordered the Confederates to evacuate the fort. And then the Yankees decided they would finish the fort, which made sense because the unit based here was the 1st New York Volunteer Engineers. But they soon gave up the effort."

"Why?" Karen asked.

"Well, somebody had just invented a cannon with a rifled bore. It could throw a shot heavy enough and fast enough to blast right through the brick walls you're looking at."

Karen and Jon surveyed the high brick walls with a new perspective.

"But you know the government," the ranger said, "they just kept puttering along and the fort was almost finished when they finally deactivated it in 1867."

He led them to wooden benches in the shade and continued, "It was put into a caretaker status until they dragged it out to use—briefly—during the Spanish-American War. But it had really gone downhill by then, so they returned it to the caretaker status until they finally declared it surplus and put it up for sale in 1926."

"I've heard about that," Jon said, and the ranger gratefully turned the floor over to him. "Except I can't remember all of the names. But I do remember that Mr. Ferreira—"

"Hold on; you've skipped the first part of the story," George interrupted. "The fort went through a couple of hands before Ferreira came on the scene. First, F.W. Sadler and his wife bought it from the government, and then a man from Jacksonville, T.B. Hamby, bought it, and *he* eventually sold it to Joseph Manley Askins for ten thousand dollars."

"Yikes! How do you keep all of this straight?" Karen asked.

"Practice, ma'am, practice." George grinned before he finally finished his story. "Askins couldn't come up with the whole ten thou, so he took on a partner, W.T. Haile. And it was Haile who sold shares to John Ferreira and Glyn Waas, Sr." George beamed at them while they tried to digest all of the names.

"And then they tried to turn it into what we'd call condominiums today," Jon said.

Karen looked around and chuckled. "Well, that didn't happen!"

"Of course not," George took up the story again. "The tunnels were full of sand, there was no electricity, no water, no sewage. They finally realized that it was just too hard and too expensive."

"So then what?" Karen asked.

"You'll love it. They got the bright idea of dismantling it and selling the bricks. There were almost five million of them, so they thought they were going to make a fortune."

"That didn't happen, either," she said.

"Turned out that the mortar was stronger than the

bricks. The bricks crumbled when they tried to pry them away from the mortar. The workmen destroyed most of one wall before Ferreira and his partners stopped them."

"Yikes! Good thing," she said, shaking her head.

"Finally, they just sold the fort to the state for ten thousand dollars, plus back taxes of between eight and ten thousand dollars," George said.

"So, for less than twenty thou, Florida bought the fort and turned it into a park, just like the Loot told us." Jon concluded.

"That's true," George commented. "But the feds have taken it back a couple of times since then."

George steered them toward the visitors center while he told them about the final time the fort was pressed into service. "During World War II, the Coast Guard, along with the Army and Navy, used this place as a communications and security post. The Coast Guard even had a mounted beach patrol. You see, the Germans had subs patrolling up and down the coast, and we were pretty sure that one of their jobs was to insert spies and saboteurs into the countryside. So the Coast Guard men would ride horses along the beach to make sure no bad guys from those subs landed on our beaches."

"Do you think the fort will ever be used again by the military?" Jon asked. They were back in the visitors center, and he looked around with a new appreciation for what he saw.

"I doubt it," George replied. "We were placed on the National Register of Historic Places back in 1972, so I imagine the preservationists would squawk about any attempts to return it to active status."

Karen checked her watch and murmured something about the time. They shook hands with George and thanked him for the tour. They were quiet as Jon drove them down the tree-lined road back to the main entrance.

"The preservationists would have heart failure if they ever found out what we think the MMJ may be planning to do with their precious fort," Karen said.

Jon nodded glumly and turned on to Atlantic Avenue.

Chapter 17

Dianne inched the car up the line at the middle school. She checked Brian in the rear view mirror. He was happy with his juice box and toy.

Lisa saw her and waved as she and Sara Jane made their way to the car. "Miss Dianne!" Sara Jane exclaimed as they climbed into the back seat with Brian. "Can Lisa go with us when we look at another new house tomorrow?" The Stewarts were rapidly outgrowing their Amelia Park condominium and had been house-hunting for weeks.

Dianne smiled at her enthusiasm. "Sure. Is your mom going to pick you up after school?"

"Yes, ma'am. Can Lisa stay over?" She turned to her friend. "You want to stay, don't you?"

Dianne turned from the parking lot on to Citrona and began to shake her head "no" before Lisa had a chance to speak. "Not on a school night." She saw their shoulders slump and tried to distract them. "What house are you going to look at?"

Sara Jane's eyes lit up. "We've looked at it once before. It's called the Villalonga-Gordon House, up on North Fourth Street."

Dianne was surprised. "Isn't that a little large for you?"

"Dad says we'll grow into it. There are already three of us, and Ruby Dell will be here in a couple of months. And then Josephus needs a room for when he comes. Right now, he's sleeping on the living room couch."

"He'll be glad to have a bed again, that's for sure," Dianne said.

"And Dad's already figured out where he's gonna put stuff in his study."

Dianne silently hoped that Jon wouldn't turn into a pack rat like her husband had. "It's an old house. Do you know anything about it yet?"

"The real estate lady gave us something from the museum. It's named after two women, the one who built it and the other one who lived in it." Sara Jane said. "The lady who built it had a funny name, Miss Leonilla Villalonga. I think that's the most beautiful name I ever heard." Her clear voice sang a chorus of *Frere Jacques*; "Lee-o-nil-la Vil-la-long-a, how are *yooou*?"

Dianne laughed at Sara Jane's version of the old song. "That's great! Do you have any idea who she was?"

"Wasn't her dad some bigwig in town?" Lisa asked.

"Not her dad, but her granddad," Dianne explained. "He had a great name, too: Don Domingo Fernandez."

"I've seen that name on the tombstones behind St. Michaels," Sara Jane said.

"Look closely the next time and you'll see Leonilla's name, too," Dianne added. "But back to Don Domingo. He started the first Fernandina back in 1807 or so. He got the last Spanish land grant in America."

"You mean Old Town?"

"I do, indeed. And Old Town wasn't the first settlement on that land. The Timucuan Indians settled there, probably because it was high ground. The Spanish were actually here twice, and on their second visit, they platted the town in 1811. They changed its name from Amelia Island Post to Fernandina, to honor King Ferdinand the Seventh of Spain. They had a book that told them to center it around the fort—"

"Fort San Carlos, like the plaque says!" Sara Jane interrupted. "My mom took me there and I read it." She turned to Lisa in the back seat. "Have you seen it?"

"Yeah. The plaque, I mean. My dad says he could still see parts of Fort San Carlos when he was a kid. A section of the foundation was in the river, and you had to make sure it was low tide so you could see it."

"I'm afraid it's all gone now, girls, but when Don Domingo came along, he platted the streets right over the old Spanish ones."

The girls peppered her with questions until she said, "You know what? Mrs. Newman knows a lot more about Old Town than I do. She's the chairman of the Old Town Fernandina bicentennial celebration that's coming up in April. We'll have to talk to her.

"She and the lieutenant live in the Sharpe House," Dianne added. "I think it's even older than the one your family's looking at." She took her turn at the four-way stop at Jasmine before continuing down Citrona. "Now, do you know who Miss Gordon was?"

Sara Jane quickly explained that Edith Gordon had been Miss Villalonga's ward and that the spinster built the house for her young charge.

"Very good. And guess where they lived before Miss Villalonga built the house." The girls waited as she turned into Amelia Park and pulled to a stop in front of the Stewart condominium. "Both of them lived at the convent."

"No way!" Lisa said as Alice Stewart came out of the condo.

Dianne rolled down a window to wave at her. "They had their very own apartment in the convent, but when Edith grew up enough, she moved across the street and into the house you're going to look at tomorrow."

Alice came to Dianne's window and they chatted for a moment or two. "We were just talking about your house-hunting trip tomorrow."

Alice laughed softly. "Sara Jane is in heaven, what with all of its history. Wait until I tell her that I found out today that it's also called the Bruni House."

Sara Jane and Lisa had been talking quietly in the back seat, but now Sara Jane turned to her mother. "Why do they call it that?"

"Because a Mr. Bruni lived there when he ran the Coca-Cola bottling plant here."

"We had a Coke plant here?" Lisa was amazed.

"You betcha." Dianne now took up the tale. "You know where the hack stand is over on Ash Street, down close to the railroad tracks?"

"With that cool horse trough," Sara Jane added.

"The crumbling concrete you stand on down there is the original floor of the plant."

It had been a very long day, and Karen Millen was more grateful than ever to turn on to Lewis Street. She always felt enveloped by history whenever she entered the once black-only enclave.

She drove slowly in the deepening dusk and decided to give herself a tour. It wouldn't take long; A.L. Lewis's original two hundred and sixteen acres had been reduced to just over eighty. A large sand dune suddenly loomed tall and dark on her right. Karen loved the sight of it, and it made her think of the Beach Lady.

What a colorful character that old woman had been. She had been born Marvyne Elizabeth Betsch, but had removed the "r" as a political protest. Somewhere during her long life, "Elizabeth" had disappeared, to be replaced by "Oshun."

MaVynee, as she finally came to call herself, had been royalty of sorts, a great-granddaughter of A.L. himself, an opera singer—in Europe, no less. Her long hair was legend and trained to trace the course of the river Niger. Her living arrangements had been equally unconventional, and at one point she lived in a recreational vehicle, which she parked at various locations on American Beach.

Karen took the car out of Park and smiled as she remembered that it had been MaVynee who had named the dune NaNa—grandmother—and had declared it sacred.

She was suddenly tired and barely glanced at Evans' Rendezvous as she made the turn on to Gregg Street. She briefly thought of Dr. Gregg as she travelled down his street, and wondered where and when he'd had his dental practice.

The Hideaway looked warm and welcoming as she pulled into the garage. She could taste the tea and feel the soft cotton nightgown as she unlocked the door on the side porch.

Wilson was waiting for his family when they pulled into their own garage across the island. Dianne could tell that he was excited about something, so she sent Brian off to change clothes with Lisa as a supervisor.

"I just got off the phone with Ray. We've got a two-bedroom suite, complete with a kitchenette for breakfasts and snacks."

"Wonderful."

"There's more. I have a two o'clock meeting on Friday—I'm not sure who with, so don't ask—and while I'm doing that, Ray has arranged for a VIP tour you and Michelle are gonna take at the White House!"

"Oh, my goodness! Have you told her?"

"No, no, I just got off the phone!"

Dinner at the Wilsons' was a rollicking affair. Michelle chose and rejected one outfit after another for her White House visit, and Dianne loudly declared that she was going to buy something new for the occasion.

She was waiting for him in his study when he finished locking up. He crooked an eyebrow at her and waggled the bottle of Bailey's Irish Cream. She smiled and accepted the invitation. They were going to need it.

Dianne had taken the chaplain's advice to heart, and had spent several agonizing days waiting for the right moment to drop this on him. She hated to ruin what had been the nicest evening they'd had recently, but she was running out of time. *Now or never, girl.*

She handed him the report and spent the next few minutes watching him. His face grew darker with every line he read. She saw the white line form around his mouth and dreaded the explosion that was coming.

When he finished reading, he laid the report aside and said, "Suspicions confirmed. The man is a total waste of skin. A liar and a slanderer. I only hope I live long enough to see him go down." He never raised his voice as he spent the next few minutes refuting Khee's claims and delivering a blistering commentary on his professionalism and parentage.

Dianne sat and listened. She had expected fireworks but this was cold, deliberate rage. She was alarmed, but knew better than to confront him. Instead she relied on one of their running jokes. "You owe the Cussin' Jar a hundred bucks."

His eyes were still cold, but he broke out his sweetest smile. "How about I take you out for a fine dinner?"

She shook her head. "You're going to do that anyway, to apologize. The hundred is a separate fine for your potty mouth."

"Ain't potty mouth when you use those words on Khee; they're damn accurate."

"Another fifty cents, please."

He smiled and agreed to both the dinner and the fine, but she knew that his issues with the FBI agent were far from resolved.

The Pelican watched it all from his perch and penned the yellow note for Wilson to find on his windshield in the morning:

> *Remember what Kennedy said about*
> *Washington – it's a city of Northern*
> *charm and Southern efficiency.*
> *The Pelican*

Chapter 18

Dianne pulled into the Newmans' driveway on Estrada Street. She had packed Brian's small Power Rangers suitcase and put it in her car after Wilson had taken him to his daily battle with Sister Sue.

There was no time to admire the old house because Brian was bouncing in the back seat, demanding to see Miss Cassie. Only Brian called her that; his four-year-old tongue could not wrap itself around "Cassandra."

The lady herself stepped out on the front porch. "Do you have time for coffee?" she asked as they walked up.

Dianne wiggled her travel cup and said, "I'll work on this while you show me your latest project. Al told me that it was done."

"Well, mostly. We still have a few things to do." No one knew when the house had been built, but a shrimping captain named William Sharpe had been one of its early owners. He had been born in Fernandina in 1877, well after the town had been established.

The house had been remodeled and enlarged numerous times over the years, and now Cassandra led them to a state-of-the-art kitchen. Dianne slowly turned to take in the appliances and gadgets on display. "This is gorgeous! It's right out of a magazine!" She took another slow turn. "And the truly amazing thing about it is that all this modern stuff looks right at home in this old house."

Cassandra laughed, "Al says we're never eating out again!"

They were interrupted by a giggle from the breakfast nook. "Are these the twins?"

The girls were eating toast at a beautiful old table. "Who's that?" one of them said and pointed at Brian.

"I'm Brian," he said, and helped himself to a piece of toast. One twin glared at him and the other moved the grape jelly so he could reach it.

The friendly twin said, "I'm Bessie an' this is my sister, Sadie. We're twins."

Brian looked from one girl to another to confirm Bessie's claim. He had a smear of jelly on his face already.

"No need to worry about Brian while you're in Washington!" Cassandra laughed. "They're not really Bessie and Sadie, you know. The mouthy one's Emmaline after her maternal grandmother, and the quiet one is Cassandra, named after me. My son, Albert, Jr., swears that Cassie watches him with her big brown eyes, just like I did when he was little. He started calling them Bessie and Sadie when they began acting like the Delaney sisters."

"Bessie was the bossy one, while Sadie was quiet," Dianne said.

"Um-hum," Cassandra said as she poured a small glass of milk for Brian. "I picked up an autographed copy of *Having Our Say* at the humane society's Flea and Tick Sale last year."

"Are you or Al related to the Delaneys?"

"No, but Karen Millen is. I'm going to give it to her for a housewarming present."

Sadie spilled her milk before Dianne could ask for more details, and Cassandra jumped to mop up as she shooed Dianne on her way. "Have a great trip—and don't worry about Brian!"

Three Wilsons enjoyed an old-fashioned Southern lunch at Jasper's Porch just north of Savannah while Al Newman and his entourage sat down with Chief Evans.

Evans had moved the nine o'clock meeting to eleven, thanks to the dead battery in his wife's Buick and her hair appointment with Brenda that could not be missed.

"OK, whatcha got?" he asked after apologizing for the delay. He listened and took notes for the next forty-five minutes as Newman, Stewart, and Millen introduced him to the world of domestic terrorism. His wife's woes were long forgotten. He stacked each briefing sheet they handed to him until he had made a neat pile. "So you think these two cases, Haldad and Walid, may be related."

"Looks that way," Al Newman said. "Each case has MMJ, Navy, and Kings Bay written all over it." He shrugged. "We're still looking into it."

"I'll have to go to Khee with this. It's definitely one for the feds."

"We know, boss, and we're sorry you're going to have to deal with him again. But look at the bright side." Evans crooked an eyebrow at his lieutenant. "Khee will have to do all the dirty work. If we're lucky, his guys will get shot at, and we'll provide support, way out of the line of fire."

Evans was not impressed. "Thirty years in law enforcement and I'm reduced to being a gofer for the feds. Don't like it." He roused himself to thank them for the briefing. "Good work, all of you." His eyes swept the table. "I'll let you know what Khee has to say."

The station had quieted during the lunch hour, and Charles Evans retrieved the disgustingly healthy lunch from the refrigerator in the break room. He would eat it at his desk. It was the one time of day that his door was closed; it kept the casual visitors at bay and usually provided him with a few moments to recharge.

That wasn't going to happen today. He worked his way through the salad with its carefully measured toppings of grilled chicken strips and low-fat ranch dressing. Six dry saltines, fresh orange sections, and a cup of low-fat pudding completed his lunch. He washed it all down with a fresh cup of coffee.

Today, instead of skimming a professional magazine or day-dreaming about a pontoon boat on Crystal River, he thought about Wilson, the FBI, and the MMJ. Somewhere between the second package of crackers and the last ripe olive, he began to think seriously about that pontoon boat.

Every cop had at least one case that either made him or broke him. He'd had a couple of those, and this Wilson/Walid debacle was shaping up to be yet another. He repacked his lunch bag and hung it on the hook with his hat. Jacqueline would clean and repack it for tomorrow. *Yippee.*

He wandered about the room, straightening plaques on the wall and photos on the shelves. All the while, his mind was worrying with the various facts and facets of the case. He grunted when he realized that the thing making him tired was not Walid's death or Wilson's predicament. The very thought of dealing with Khee again made him tired. *Well, he ain't goin' anywhere, so you might as well get on with it.*

Maybe he would retire, after all.

It was almost four o'clock before he got a chance to call Jax, and he was cranky even before he punched in the numbers. It had been an unexpectedly busy afternoon; someone or some crucial piece of business had interjected itself every time he'd reached for the telephone.

"Well, well, well, if it isn't my favorite local LEO," Khee said.

"As much as it pains me to ever talk to you again, there's something developing up here that you need to know about. It may very well involve national security."

"What could possibly be 'developing' up there in that burg? Did Officer Fife lose the bullet he keeps in his shirt pocket?"

From the cackle in the background, Evans knew that Cratch was in the room. "Barney and I are getting acquainted with the Muslim Military Jihad people up here," the chief snapped. "Heard of 'em? It'll probably make us throw up, but we're willing to brief you on what we know."

"Nah, there's no need for you to leave your little island paradise. You just keep writin' them parkin' tickets and we'll take care of the mean old MMJ."

"Are you telling me that you know all about these jerks? You know that they're on the island and you didn't tell us?"

"Strictly need to know. You don't."

"Wilson was right. You are a sonofabitch!" Evans slammed the receiver down and took a few moments to find the temper he had lost before he left for the day.

He had promised his wife years ago that he would stop coming through the front door with fire coming out of his ears.

"… and so he said, 'Don't talk to the sheep; he lies!'" The bar erupted in laughter, and Shorty walked out the back door, ostensibly to smoke. His cell had vibrated while he'd been telling his favorite joke and now he checked his messages. *Call Chrissie.*

He hit speed dial. "Hey, darlin', whatcha doin' callin' me this time a' night?"

"Oh, sugarplum," Christine Mahmood cooed back, "I just had to hear your sweet voice. Can you talk? Are you busy?"

"Give me five, darlin', an' I'll be all yours."

"That was fast, *sugarplum*," she said when he called her on the safe land line at home. "Things are heating up a little. Our boy George called today, and things are developing a little faster than we like. I need for you to start keeping an eye on some place called the Addison House. Do you know it?"

"Sure. Used to be a bed-and-breakfast. What's up?"

"Several members of an MMJ cell have lived there for a couple of years. We've kept them under loose surveillance, but Khee finally got around to sending us Walid's legal pad, and—"

"Wilson's been goin' crazy, tryin' ta get a look at that thing! What's it say?"

"Walid managed to write down the plan for the cell's external operation. We'd been hearing chatter about an op, but had no details until we got our hands on his tablet."

"That's bad."

"It gets even worse. The op is a missile launch aimed at the drydock at Kings Bay."

"Damn, damn, damn."

"Yeah. And it'll be double damn if a sub's in drydock when the missile hits."

Shorty had to take a moment before he could ask where the missiles would be launched from.

"Do you have something next to water that looks like a pentagon? Walid didn't get to finish his drawing, and there's nothing to tell us what it is supposed to be."

"My Lord! It's Fort Clinch! They're gonna use the fort as the launch platform!"

"How big is the fort?"

"Big enough. And it faces the base." His voice trailed off. The more he thought about the plan the more appalled he became. "When is this supposed to go down?"

"The chatter's picking up, so it will be soon."

Shorty was planning surveillance strategy before Christine's receiver was in its cradle. *Ol' General Clinch must be rollin' in his grave, way up in Savannah!* Shorty thought as he sat alone in his living room.

Wilson clicked off the TV news and savored the quiet. He had enjoyed the two-day drive here, but it was nice to be alone for a while. This suite at the Kenwood Inn in Bethesda was pure luxury. "Don't get used to this," he'd growled after they'd given themselves a quick tour. The master bedroom overlooked the ninth green, and Michelle's room offered a wonderful view of a small, formal garden.

The clerk had handed him an envelope when they checked in. Michelle had squealed when she'd seen its contents—two passes for today's White House tour.

He had stayed out of their way this morning as they bustled about getting ready. Sticky buns and coffee in the room, and Dianne and Michelle were gone in a cloud of cologne and excitement.

He shook his head at the memory, and got up to fetch a bottle of water from the refrigerator. He set it on the desk and retrieved the briefcase lurking beside it. He selected several files to review before this afternoon's meeting and gingerly tried out the desk chair. *Good, no squeak. I can work in peace.*

When he had reread every syllable, he moved to a comfortable armchair and closed his eyes. He had several points to mull over before he discussed them with Ray and whoever else would be at the meeting.

He awoke an hour later, angry with himself for wasting precious time. He slapped cold water on his face and settled at the desk once more. He pulled the file with his list of questions to him. *Maybe that nap was a good idea, after all,* he thought as he added several questions to the list.

Chapter 19

Ray was waiting for him in the lobby of the J. Edgar Hoover building. He walked Wilson through the security procedures and rolled his eyes when the guard flipped through every file in his briefcase.

"It's really good to see you again, buddy." Ray shook his hand and clapped him on the back once they were on the same side of the security barrier.

They rode the elevator to an upper floor and Wilson realized they were chattering almost as much as Dianne and Michelle had earlier. He smiled to himself; it put a new spin on the term "increased chatter."

Wilson followed Ray out of the elevator and assumed they were headed for his office. They entered a very well appointed suite and Wilson was impressed with his friend's position.

An equally well appointed woman greeted them and ushered them into a large office. Frederick Page came from behind his desk and offered his hand while Ray introduced them. They sat around a low table which held a coffee service for four. Wilson briefly wondered who the fourth cup was for, but soon forgot about it.

Page began the meeting by thanking him first for his

service to his country as an Army Ranger and now to his community as a law enforcement officer. *Bastard's done his homework, I give him that,* he thought and scrambled to keep up with Page's rapid-fire delivery.

Alarms started their faint buzzing when Page complimented him on his perception and perseverance in this touchy matter of home-grown terrorism. *First they butter you up* ... He looked over at Ray, but he was nodding in agreement. Wilson dismissed the buzzing.

The door opened and a striking woman walked purposefully across to them. All three men stood and Page introduced him to Christine Mahmood. The organization she represented and her position in it were not mentioned. He was a veteran at sizing people up and he knew instantly that she could be a good friend—or a formidable foe.

She was small and dark with liquid brown eyes and her short hair was cut beautifully. She was impeccably groomed and dressed, but the hand he shook was rough. Ray poured her a cup of coffee as they took their seats. She sipped slowly as Page explained that her role today was to provide him with the answers he had been searching for. *And then they butter you up some more* ...

"I understand you think that the MMJ has a cell in your town," Christine said. Wilson listened to her intently for the next several minutes, but he could not place her accent.

She talked with her hands as she gave him a quick history of the jihadist organization and highlighted some of its activities. Now he saw that the little finger on her right hand had once been broken and had either been set badly or not at all. He was startled to realize that she was missing the index finger on her left hand. *This woman's been badly injured, maybe tortured.*

Wilson had started to bring his list of questions out, but she was addressing many of the points he wanted to discuss. That was fine, except she was dismissing or minimizing each one. His alarm started to buzz again.

"Actually, Captain, you would do us all a great favor if you could find your way to direct your considerable talents elsewhere."

And then they lower the boom.

"Which means, 'Go away, little boy, and let the big kids play,'" Wilson said. He heard Page's sharp intake of breath. *Who is this woman, anyway? And why is a heavy like Page so alarmed at what I said?*

"I would not put it quite that way," she began. "Are you familiar with the law of unintended consequences?"

"Intimately."

"Then do not invite it on yourself or your community."

There was a deadly pause as the two of them battled silently. Page looked at the papers on the table, but Forbes looked from one to the other.

"You wouldn't happen to be related to George Khee by any chance, would you?" Wilson narrowed his eyes.

Christine smiled and stood. She held out her hand and said, "It's been a pleasure meeting with you. Enjoy your stay." She nodded to Page and left as quickly as she had come.

There was a slight lull after her departure, and Wilson pulled SAC Khee's report on the Walid homicide out of his briefcase. "There is one other issue that I want to talk to you about."

Page recognized the FBI logo and said, "Where did you get that?"

Wilson had long ago learned to ignore questions designed to sidetrack the real issue. "This report contains several discrepancies and some downright distortions. It borders on libel. If you consider this report to be an accurate account and assessment of the Walid case, you are placing yourselves and the Bureau in a precarious situation."

Page once again stood and put his best party smile on. "It was nice meeting you. Fernandina sounds like a lovely place to live."

He stuck out his hand and when Wilson took it, he gripped it tightly and looked him right in the eye. "My advice to you is to enjoy the rest of your life and career in your very own Paradise."

Ray Forbes cleared his throat nervously in the silence left behind his boss's retreating back. "Let's go to my office so we can talk a little more." There was no friendly banter in the elevator this time.

"Well, that was a bunch of hooey," Wilson said when they were once again behind a closed door. "If you wanted to shut me down, you could have saved the taxpayers a lot of money by just telling me so on the telephone."

"Would you have listened?" Ray looked at his unhappy friend. "I had forgotten how blunt you can be. We don't see too much of that in this town."

"If that's meant to be criticism, you can stow it. I have the feeling that dear Ms. Mahmood can take it. Who is she, anyway? You and your boss treated her like she was the Queen."

"One, you don't need to know who she is. You don't *want* to know. And second, she is a queen, of sorts, anyway. The story is that her husband—long dead, killed by the Taliban—was a tribal chief in Afghanistan."

"That's it!" Wilson snapped his fingers. "I knew I'd heard that accent before; I just couldn't place it."

"They were part of the Mujahedeen, back in the hills."

"That where her hands got messed up."

"That's what I've heard. But don't make the mistake of thinking she's some simple, idealistic villager. She's as effective in the boardroom as she is on the battlefield."

"Have you seen her in action?"

"In the field? No, but I've talked to people who have." Ray leaned forward so that they were almost nose to nose. "Do not cross her. Drop this. Have a nice life. By doing that, according to Christine, you will allow others to live out their own nice lives."

Wilson had spent most of dinner listening to Dianne and Michelle rave about their White House tour. No detail was too small to have escaped their notice and comment. Michelle had been almost beside herself when she showed him the photo of her standing at the lectern in the recently-renovated press room. He knew that she had sent it to everyone she knew.

He watched her slowly wilt across the booth from him. It had been a very long day for her, and she had spent every moment of it in high gear. The waiter brought the check and asked them if the meal had been satisfactory. They bombarded him with compliments and Wilson made a mental note to thank Jon for recommending the Rock Bottom Restaurant. The department had sent Jon up to the area several years ago for a school and he had discovered Bethesda's restaurant district along Cordelle and St. Elmo streets.

Michelle mumbled a quick good-night and headed straight to her room in the suite. Dianne laughed. "I hope she undresses before she falls face down on the bed!"

"I hope she turns it down so we don't have to listen to her complain all day tomorrow about the bedspread imprint on her cheek!"

When they were in nightclothes and had nightcaps nearby, Wilson began to tell her about his meeting at FBI headquarters. She sat back and let him give his report without interruption, but began to pepper him with questions when he was done. She saved the toughest question for last.

"Did you have a chance to bring up Khee's report?"

"Oh, yeah. It was a big hit." He repeated ADDIR Page's comments almost verbatim.

"That's a nice way of saying 'Go away, kid; don't bother me.'"

"Uh-huh." Wilson leveled a look at her. "Or else."

"Caught that. What did Ray have to say?"

"I figure he's paid to listen to people Page doesn't have the time or the inclination to listen to. So I gave it my best shot. I went through the report point by point."

"And?"

"*And* I got the impression that the gods in Olympus have some doubts and reservations about their dear Agent Khee and his modus operandi. *And*," he added, "Ray basically said that he trusted Page and so should I. I don't think that anyone I talked to today is taken in with all of his bull—oops!" He broke off and grinned. "I only owe the jar twelve and a half cents, 'cause I only said half a word!"

"You doof! Let's go to bed."

"Best offer I've had today," he said and followed his wife into their own bedroom.

Michelle entertained them with her observations about the nation's capital, Arlington National Cemetery, and the Newseum during their drive back down south. When she finally ran down, her father teased her about her whirlwind tour of the city.

Dianne came to her defense. "Well, first of all, you should be glad that your daughter is so patriotic and interested in our country's history." She stopped herself when she realized she sounded a little shrill. She took a deep breath and smiled. "And all of those visits will make wonderful reports when she gets back—maybe even newspaper articles—complete with the really great photos she took." Dianne swiveled in her seat so she could see Michelle. "Don't forget to give the museum a copy of whatever you write, especially about Flossie Borden."

Chapter 20

"Do I want to know how you got your hands on this?"

Wilson had called Charles Evans first thing this morning to ask for a meeting. He was anxious to tell him everything he'd learned during the Washington trip about the MMJ and its presence in Fernandina. Now they sat in the chief's office with large mugs of coffee and Wilson's notes.

"I have my sources." Wilson pulled out the boyish grin that worked so well on Dianne, but his boss wasn't buying it.

"I should have known better than to ask." He flipped George Khee's report on his desk. "Does this guy really hate you that much? Or has he lost it?"

Wilson had given these same two questions a great deal of thought over the last few weeks. "A little bit of both, I think. The Leopard op back in 2004 was an ugly thing, a bad plan that got even worse in the field. Khee was right in the middle of it, the fair-haired child of the SAC in Jax. He could do no wrong.

"I don't know what he put in his after-action report, but I bet it was as self-serving as this one is. He got a commendation out of it, and he parlayed that into his early promotion to SAC."

"Yeah, I got all that, but that doesn't explain the Walid mess."

"Oh, well, that's easy. I'm the only one left who was on the operation, and I am the only one who knows what really happened that day on the train trestle out by the Shave Bridge."

"You were always a little cagey about the details; how about giving me a refresher?"

"You remember that the tip the FBI got from one of its informants led them up here to bust one of the East Coast's major drug dealers," Wilson said.

"The guy that called himself the Leopard ... Yeah, I remember the call from the Jacksonville FBI," the chief said. "The SAC was cobbling together a team from four or five different agencies, including Fernandina PD."

"A couple of other guys from the department and I joined up," Wilson continued, "and we all went after the Leopard and his shipment and crew."

"Then, as I recall, when the dust settled, the Leopard was in custody and one of his men was dead. So was Bill Tisher, the rep from Homeland Security." Evans looked at Wilson to see if his memory was correct.

"But what you may not know," Wilson interrupted, "is that the bad guy was killed on the Leopard's orders. He'd been the Leopard's chief of security for this op; since we busted them, it showed the Leopard that his security man hadn't done too good."

"High price to pay for failure," the chief observed.

"Puts a whole new meaning on 'early retirement,' don't it?" Wilson paused for a moment to make sure he wanted to do this. He sighed and then continued. "But what I never told you, never told anyone for a long, long time, is that Bill Tisher's death is on Khee."

"The hell you say."

"I was pretty busy that afternoon, but it looked to me like Khee froze during the gun battle on the boats. Then, when he got himself unfroze, he ducked for cover. If he'd been in position, Bill would be alive today."

"You never said anything."

Wilson shrugged. "Nothing to say. I only thought I saw what I thought I saw. I had no proof. Khee was young and green, give him a break, I thought. And he was on a fast track; the SAC was his rabbi. He was the SAC's problem, not mine."

"Now he's your problem."

"Yeah, but this time I have proof."

The chief leaned forward, looking grim. "Go ahead."

"I've watched George Khee operate for years now. I can give you chapter and verse on his screw-ups and poor performance. And I even have names of several other people he screwed over, just like he's trying to do me."

"That sounds a little scary."

"Which? Khee's shoddy performance or my documentation?"

"A little bit of both, I guess."

"You're right, of course. But I should have gotten the commendation out of the Leopard operation. And Khee should have nailed that guy before he could kill Bill Tisher."

Wilson stood and headed for the door, but stopped with his hand on the door knob. "Don't worry, Charles, I'm not going to take out George Khee. But I sure as hell am going to tell the world what a back-stabbing sonofabitch he is." He closed the door gently behind him.

Al Newman had glanced at the chief's closed door repeatedly. Those two had been behind it for a long time. Now that he thought of it, it seemed like Wilson and Evans were friends again. The chief hadn't exactly welcomed Wilson with open arms, but he hadn't yelled at him for being in the building, either.

Oh, well, Al thought to himself, *I have too much on my own plate to worry about what's on somebody else's.* The thought of full plates made him wonder how Karen Millen was doing with her own plate full of Quattlebaums. Both J. Phillip and Harlan could be difficult in the best of times.

Al had heard that their plumbing supply house had lost its bid to install the kitchen and bathroom fixtures in the new Timber Creek Plantation subdivision between Yulee and Callahan. That meant they had already been unhappy when the vandals struck their office. And hadn't he heard rumors about J. Phillip and a scheme to develop the waterfront downtown? He would have to ask Millen if she—

"Thanks, Nora, that's great news!" Jon Stewart's voice interrupted his ruminations about the Quattlebaums, and Newman asked the younger man what was such great news.

"Our real estate agent just called to tell me that the bid we submitted for the Villalonga-Gordon House has been accepted. I can't wait to call Alice."

"Guess they'll have to call it the Villalonga-Gordon-Stewart House now."

"I plan on calling it the Stewart *home*! Nora says we'll be moved in and the pictures hung before Ruby Dell gets here." He swiveled back to the phone to call his wife.

Al shook his head. He was happy for them, of course, but this would be the first place either one of them had owned. *Wait until they discover what a money pit it's going to be. Patch, patch, patch.*

And heaven help Jon if Alice got bit by the history bug. She'd drive everyone crazy with tidbits about the house, just like Cassandra did with her fixation on the history of the Sharpe House. *Ain't never gonna be called the Newman House, I can tell ya that.* She usually dug up something interesting, but sometimes he just wanted to watch mindless television instead of hearing about some long-dead denizen of Old Town.

He groaned later that day when he tried to pull into his driveway. He had forgotten that the bicentennial planners were meeting at his house this afternoon.

"And the original street names designated by Enrique White, the Spanish Governor of Florida, are still used today," he heard his wife say.

Good. She's in this century, so maybe I'll get dinner on time tonight.

He stuck his head in the dining room to say hello to everyone gathered around its long rosewood table and then headed down the hall to change clothes.

"We know that White Street was named after the governor, and that Someruelos was named for the Marquis de Someruelos, Captain-General of the Spanish Provinces of Cuba, Florida and Louisiana."

"Now that's a mouthful!" one of the committee members said, and everyone chuckled.

Cassandra blushed and apologized for telling them more than they wanted to know, and then continued with, "We've lost one street to erosion; Marine Street now lies in the Amelia River."

She paused to riffle through the papers before her and held up her prize. "If you'll look at your copy of this 1821 map, you'll see that it adds New and Towngate streets that are east of—"

Or maybe dinner will be a little late. Oh well, at least she's spending her afternoons at the museum instead of the mall. Al smiled to himself and headed for the den and the Fox News Channel.

Wilson came out the station feeling better than he had in weeks. Everyone he'd shown the Khee report to had been outraged at its libelous claims. It made him feel good to realize that people knew he wasn't the person portrayed in the report.

He smiled to himself when he noticed yet another yellow note under his wipers. *How does he get in here?* It was only when he had the engine running and the seatbelt fastened that he finally unfolded it.

> *Ponder and deliberate*
> *before you make a move.*
> *—Sun Tzu (544 BC – 496 BC)*
> *The Pelican*

He made a mental note to add this slip of paper to his growing collection as he started down Lime Street on his way home. He made a right onto Citrona and realized that his current situation resembled war. Man and warfare had changed very little in the twenty-five hundred years since the Chinese soldier had penned his famous book, *The Art of War.* He'd have to pull out his copy tonight for a quick refresher.

Alice was waiting for Jon when he pulled into the alley. He grinned and pointed to her feet. A cat sat at attention on either side of her.

"*Rrrooow*," Mary Margaret greeted him, while Amelia danced on her hind legs.

"I see you've managed to infect the cats with your excitement!"

"Yes, yes, yes! The Villalonga house is gorgeous and I can't wait for all of us to fill up every crack and cranny!"

Sara Jane came running in to see them doing a jig in the middle of the kitchen, even the cats. "What's going on? What am I missing?" She began to hop around, too.

Jon quickly told her that they would be in their new home before the baby came.

Neither Jon nor Alice would be able to recall what the dinner fare was that night. All of them laughed and chattered through the meal and paid little attention to what was on their plates.

They eventually exhausted themselves, and the nightly routine reasserted itself. Sara Jane said good-night early and retired to her bedroom.

She was deep asleep when Jon brought his wife her nightly cup of tea. He put his own cup on a side table and cradled her. They watched the silent television and sipped tea for several peaceful moments.

"I hate to break this quiet spell, but I think it's time you told me about your sister." She could feel him grow very still. "Her namesake will be here soon, and I want to know more about the original Ruby Dell."

Jon carefully lowered his mug to its coaster. "I know you're right, it's just that I have kept her a secret for so long that it's hard to share her with anyone, even you."

"Let's start with baby steps, then." Jon poked her for her unintended pun and she giggled. "Where did you and Ruby Dell live?"

"In Baltimore, in the Dundalk section, back in the eighties." He sighed and gathered his thoughts. "My mom—"

"Who you've talked about even less than you have about Ruby Dell!"

"My mom was named Della Clevenger Stewart. She had me, and then two years later, she had Ruby Dell. I know the 'Dell' part came from 'Della,' and I think her mother had been named 'Ruby.'"

"See, that wasn't so bad," she teased.

He was lost in the past and did not answer.

"When did your mom die?" she continued her gentle interrogation.

"I think I was four, or thereabouts. That would have made Ruby Dell around two." He shifted uncomfortably. "It was a hit and run, my dad said. They never found the guy who ran her down."

"Where was she?"

"Coming off her shift. She was a waitress at Bertha's Mussels, and she was crossing the street to the bus stop when he mowed her down."

"And your dad told you all of these gory details when you were how old?"

Jon shrugged. "It doesn't matter. He'd get drunk and blubber because she wasn't there to fix dinner or do his shirts or look after two bratty kids."

"What a charmer. Did he fix dinner? Take care of you?"

Another shrug. "I'll tell you about Ruby Dell now. Don't interrupt or I'll never get through it." He felt her nod against his chest. "I want you to know that I've never, ever, told another soul about this."

Tears came to her eyes at his trust in her. She knew that it hadn't been given lightly. She held his hand and waited for him to begin. Once he did, she wished he would stop.

"I remember it was a really cold winter. I couldn't get warm, not even in school. Ruby Dell and I slept together, mostly so I could keep her warm.

"And then she got sick. The neighbor lady who kept her until I got home from school, the first grade, well, she got mad 'cause her kids caught whatever Ruby Dell had. Said she wouldn't take her back until she got over it. So Dad said I had to stay home to take care of her.

"And I did, for almost a week, but she just got worse. It got so all she would do was cough and cry until she wore herself out. Then she'd sleep, but when she woke up, she'd start in again.

"Dad, he got mad. He got madder as she got sicker, said he couldn't sleep, what with all her coughin' and cryin'. Said his work was fallin' off an' his boss was gonna dock him."

Alice was mesmerized by the tale. She had never heard Jon talk like that. He sounded as if he were six years old and back in Dundalk. She finally had a full appreciation of how hard he had worked to become the man he now was.

"And then one day, the last day I ever saw her," Jon continued, "Dad came home late and really drunk. He'd brought us hamburgers and fries from the pub, but they were cold and greasy.

"I choked mine down, but Ruby Dell had trouble. The little I got down her came right back up. Messed herself and the table we was sitting at."

Alice stifled a sob.

"An' Dad, he blew. He started yellin' and flailin' about. We got under the table an' I held Ruby Dell tight, like I always did when he went crazy. 'Course, she got puke all over me, too, but I was too scared to notice.

"An' then Dad, he reached under the table an' pulled her out. She was screamin' awful."

Jon was holding Alice as tightly as he had his little sister all those years ago. She could hardly breathe, but she held him back with all of her strength. They would get through this.

"I came out from under the table an' saw he was pullin' back to really smack her a good one. 'Lousy brat!' he was screamin, 'Jus' like yer mother! Always yellin' at me for somethin'!'

"I latched onto his arm so he couldn't hit her, but he jus' flang me, an' I landed against a wall. I musta' hit my head er somethin' 'cause the next thing I knew, Dad was sittin' at the table an' Ruby Dell was nowhere to be seen.

"I asked and asked about her, but he'd just wale on my body ever' time I mentioned her name." Jon stopped and let out a long, tired sigh. "And God help me, I finally stopped asking."

"What on earth do you think happened to her?"

"I don't know. And I'll probably never find out. I think about it a lot, especially if I'm awake in the middle of the night."

They sat in silence for a few moments to let the fear and sadness retreat. He checked his mug, but it was dry. He didn't remember drinking his tea. "Lord only knows how, but I made it all the way through high school.

"Left the graduation ceremony with my diploma in my hand and hitched a ride straight to the Marine Corps recruiting station. Never looked back, never went back."

Jon roused himself and looked around his warm, comfortable home. He gently squeezed his beautiful, pregnant wife and a feeling of pure joy filled him.

"I'm desperate for another cup of tea; how about you?"

Sometimes, like tonight and its childhood memories, he felt again how novel it had been during his first days of freedom to be able to eat or drink as much as he wanted. He had almost overdosed on milk until someone had started calling him Bossie the Cow.

"So you joined the Marine Corps, came to Jax to hook up with a buddy, and stayed on. Are you two still in touch?"

"No, he walked in on a burglary at our apartment. He was DOA at the hospital."

"Oh." *So much death in his life.*

"But that's how I got to be a big, bad po-leece-man, so he didn't die for nothing. And then I met you and Sara Jane and now I'm going to meet our new daughter!"

She was delighted to have her husband back instead of the frightened six-year old who had been holding on to her for dear life. She dreamed of Ruby Dell that night and woke up with a racing heart and a nightgown drenched in sweat.

Chapter 21

Dianne had thought that this shift would never end. She had tried to immerse herself in one of the many special projects the chief had assigned her, but it was no use. Her eyes had strayed to the clock repeatedly.

She tried not to speed as she went down Fourteenth Street on her way to Publix. *That would be great—a traffic cop getting a ticket.* She could see the headlines now.

She pulled a shopping cart from the queue and started down the dairy aisle. She had spent the long afternoon planning dinner; she could taste it already. She gathered the ingredients as she made her way quickly up and down the aisles. She had just put a large bag of fresh green beans in her cart when someone called her name.

"Cassandra Newman! I haven't seen you forever! How on earth are you doing?"

"I'm fine, but I have to tell you that Al's about to have a melt-down over this speech that your husband palmed off on him."

Dianne laughed. "Well, if it makes you feel any better, Wilson wasn't handling it much better when the chief palmed it off on him!"

They both had a chuckle, and then Cassandra explained that they had decided to take Wilson's advice and make the trip to Fort Lauderdale into a mini-vacation. They were planning to drive down a day early, spend a couple of hours making nice at the university, and then stay in town for a couple of days after that. "Al has decided that Wilson did us a favor, after all. We'd never have taken a break if this speech hadn't come up."

"That's what we were going to do until the current unpleasantness fell on our heads."

There was a slight pause before Cassandra put a warm hand over Dianne's. Dianne instinctively placed her other hand on top of Cassandra's and the two women spent a silent moment in the middle of the produce department.

"Al and I had a bright idea about this trip."

Dianne had tears in her eyes by the time Cassandra had finished explaining about the weekend getaway on Cumberland Island. The Newmans had snagged a three-day, two-night stay at the fabled Greyfield Inn in a silent auction. "Since we're using Fort Lauderdale as our escape, why don't you two take the Cumberland trip?"

"OMG, as the girls would say! Are you sure? It's not really an even swap, you know."

"Oh, the men can work all of that out. We just have to figure out what to pack," Cassandra said as she aimed her cart toward the oranges. "Talk it over with Wilson, and then let him work it out with Al." She winked and left a speechless Dianne standing beside the strawberries.

She finished her shopping in a daze, and barely remembered the drive home. She changed quickly and began slicing and chopping the ingredients for the meal she had daydreamed about. She put a bottle of cheap red wine in the refrigerator to cool down just a little.

She waited until everyone had shared the events of the day before she brought up Cumberland Island and the stay at the Greyfield Inn. Wilson had just sat down with his second helping of beef stroganoff when she began to talk.

His meal grew cold while he and Dianne discussed the Newmans' proposal. The girls looked like they were at a tennis match while their parents talked back and forth. "I dunno, hon. We just spent a ton of money in DC," he said, and Dianne reminded him that the island boasted no restaurant row or museum gift shops. "Let me think about it," he'd said and turned to his stroganoff.

Michelle and Lisa exchanged glances. "What about us?" Michelle said and Lisa chimed in, "Can we go, too?"

"I'm not sure that your mother and I are even going." Wilson regretted his sharp tone, but Dianne rescued him. She had been doing that a lot lately.

"I know—we'll stay home and you two can go!"

The Pelican missed the happy family discussion. He had another house to watch, this one over on Ash Street.

Mousavi sighed tiredly as the meeting lurched its way to a conclusion. Everyone seemed cranky tonight, each man annoying the one sitting next to him. Eid and Slidell had fired zingers at each other until he had growled at them. The day after Thanksgiving couldn't come fast enough.

"Enough, ladies!" he said over the low grumbling. The room grew still at his uncharacteristically sharp tone. "We are all tired and impatient. Take the information you have received tonight with you. We are adjourned."

There was a moment of silence before the room

filled with the sound of scraping chairs and books slamming shut. Mousavi stood at the door to speak to each man on his way out.

Eid and Slidell were the last to leave. Mousavi inspected each man. Eid's face carried a smug look, proud of the jabs that had hit his opponent's soft spots. Slidell, on the other hand, looked as if he were mortally wounded. His sullen expression promised even more trouble in the future. Mousavi walked slowly behind them to eavesdrop.

"You've really messed up now, baby. You've gotten both of us in trouble. And when our fearless leader gets through with us, we're gonna have our own little session."

"Don't call me 'baby.'"

"Oooh, whatcha gonna do, have yer chubby little girlfriend beat me up?"

"That will do, Mr. Eid."

Eid had been so intent on bedeviling Slidell that he had not heard Mousavi come up behind him. He jumped at the sound of the other man's voice and grew even angrier when he caught Slidell's smirk out of the corner of his eye.

"You two come with me," Mousavi said and led them back to the training room. His abrupt gesture sent them skittering into seats at the table they had just vacated.

"Here's the thing," Mousavi said as he paced back and forth. "Your childish bullying and bickering is interfering with our mission."

Eid opened his mouth to protest, but Mousavi quelled him with a look. "You have three options. You will choose one of them within the next twenty-four hours."

The smirk on Eid's face disappeared as Mousavi talked, and both Eid's and Slidell's faces soon turned pasty white.

"Option one." Mousavi stopped pacing and held up a finger. "You will find it in your hearts to come to an accommodation so that we may carry out our mission."

He took a few steps and then whirled around with a second digit in the air. "Option two: one of you will kill the other by this time tomorrow."

Now he stood still with his hands on his hips. "Option three is that if you have not exercised one of the first two options by this time tomorrow, I will kill at least one of you myself."

Mousavi's brown eyes had turned black with anger and he pinned them with a fierce glare. "Do you doubt me?"

Both men shook their heads. He glared at them for a few seconds more before turning on his heel and exiting the room. He slammed the door behind him.

Eid and Slidell sat in silence for a long time after their leader's departure.

"Well, my brother, I vote for option one." Eid looked over at his companion to see a large tear make its way down Slidell's cheek.

"I thought you would probably kill me."

"Yer safe until ya lose yer cherry."

Slidell laughed and hiccupped. "Well, hell, the way things are goin' with the fat chick, I'll live to be a ripe old age!"

Mousavi grinned in the shadows, unaware that the Pelican was reporting the night's events to Washington.

The next day turned out to be so cold and rainy that Wilson was tempted to cancel his errands. He finished cleaning up his lunch dishes and checked the weather channel. There was a break in the rain, so he decided to venture out.

Two of his stops were along Centre Street. Now that the tourist season was over, he had no trouble finding a parking spot. He chose one in front of a pocket park. He barely glanced at the painted "Shrimp Expression" statue that stood proudly next to Amelia Island Coffee, and was unaware that his dear wife planned to bid on it at the auction later that month. There were a total of nine of these statues scattered around town that had been decorated by local artists. Money generated by the auction would go to Micah's Place, the county's only domestic violence center.

"Well, if it isn't my favorite bobby, out 'n' about this fine English afternoon!"

"Shorty, that is the worst English accent I've ever heard!" It would be months before Wilson discovered why the little guy had thought this criticism was so funny.

"Never you mind all that; how 'bout you buy me a nice cuppa tea, mate?"

"The Aussie accent's even worse. Tell you what; I'll buy you a cup of anything if you just speak American."

Soon they were sitting with steamy mugs in the coffee shop. Shorty had added a large chocolate chip cookie to his order, but only after Wilson had assured him that he was buying.

"So how was the trip to the nation's capital? Didja git 'em all straightened out up there?"

Wilson gave him a slightly edited version of his trip, which seemed to satisfy him.

"Word on the street," Shorty added, "is that young

Mr. Cratch will be gone by the first of the year."

"That's a really early transfer, don't you think?"

"Yeah, but it's good news, no matter how early it is."

"Where's he going? We should warn them."

"Uh-huh," Shorty muttered, unwilling and unable to provide any insight into the sudden transfer. He laughed and blew on his too-hot tea. "Don't do that, man. We'll never get rid of him!"

"What's the word on Khee?" Wilson tried to sound nonchalant.

Shorty was not fooled and shot him a sideways glance. "Nothin'. He's still floatin'." He looked up as a new wave of rain washed downtown. "Ya got any good news?"

Wilson told him about the proposed trip to Cumberland.

"Man, I'd take that in a heartbeat! Have you ever been there? Have you seen that inn?"

Wilson shook his head no and said, "Dianne's told me about the Carnegies—I forget their names—who built the mansion way back when, and how they used to come over to Fernandina on their yacht. Aren't some of the Carnegie descendents handling the operations of the inn these days?"

"Yep. It was Thomas and Lucy Carnegie who had the house built in 1900 for their daughter and her family. Ever'body lived happily ever after. Then, in 1962 I think it was, a granddaughter converted the old family home into the inn, and boy, is it something."

"How do you know so much about it?" Wilson could not afford to pay full price for a night there, and he knew that Shorty had even less mad money than he did. Plus, he was positive that the little guy wasn't interested in learning about history, even if it was about the area he lived in.

"Had a thing for one of them ranger lassies over there. She'd give me the grand tour whenever she could."

"Just how grand were these tours?"

Shorty smiled that predatory smile that Wilson had learned to appreciate. "Let's just say you should think of me when you get a glimpse of the Library Suite. I can testify—in court, mind ya—that it has the finest bed I've ever blessed."

Wilson wasn't about to ask what this "blessing" had entailed.

It took Wilson a long time to work things out with the special promotions coordinator at Greyfield Inn. In the end, he was successful in explaining that he was taking Mr. Newman's place for the Thanksgiving Getaway, and that he wanted to add his two daughters to the package. Yes, he understood that more money would be required for a suite in one of the small cottages dotted about the grounds. He hung the telephone up with a smile of satisfaction on his face. The four of them would arrive on the afternoon ferry the day before Thanksgiving and would depart on Sunday of the holiday weekend.

He had already talked to Al, and there had been a sufficient amount of money exchanged. Wilson had a good laugh at Newman's attempt to have him include six weeks of lawn care in the deal.

He was still chuckling when he called Dianne to tell her that they would be spending Thanksgiving on Cumberland. He'd wait until tonight to share the news that the Thanksgiving feast would be by candlelight.

Dinner in Seacrest was lively, with everyone except Brian chattering at once about the upcoming holiday. The youngest Wilson finally caught their attention with the announcement that Sister Sue wanted him to dress up like a Pilgrim for the Thanksgiving pageant, while he was determined to be an Indian.

Dianne and Wilson exchanged glances over their son's head. "My money's on the kid," Wilson whispered.

Later he made his rounds, making sure each door and window was locked. Dianne had left her car in the driveway tonight, so he retrieved her keys and opened the front door to lock the car using the remote.

He saw yet another yellow note, but this time it was under one of her windshield wipers. His shoulders slumped and he closed and locked the front door. He trudged back to his study to put on his shoes and to retrieve his personal Sig-Sauer.

He turned off the lights so he would not be a silhouette and waited a few seconds before he stepped out. He closed the door behind him and stood perfectly still, listening. Nothing. The fatal attack on Miss Blossom had made him hyper-vigilant. His gut gave him the all-clear and he walked briskly to the car with his head on a swivel. He retrieved the note and retraced his steps. He locked the door behind him and turned on the porch light once again.

He stowed his weapon and poured himself a fresh cup of tea before reading the note:

> *Man is someone that can only find*
> *relaxation from one kind of labor*
> *by taking up another.*
> *—Anatole France (1844-1924)*
>
> *Forget both kinds and enjoy Cumberland*
> *The Pelican*

The Newmans left for Fort Lauderdale as planned, but with a slight twist. About a week before their departure, Karen had mentioned to Al that she and her contractor were ready to refinish the downstairs floors. She would empty the entire floor; most of the furniture would go in storage, but several pieces were to be refinished.

"You're going to have to remove yourself, too, aren't you?" he had asked.

Karen had shrugged. "Guess I'll find me a cheap hotel."

"I got a better idea, if we can get the timing right. Why don't you house-sit for us while we're in Lauderdale? Can you and Graham get the floor people there the same week we're down south?"

Karen had spent the last three days getting her house ready for the workmen. The moving crew had removed furniture and area rugs a couple of days ago. Right behind them, the van had arrived to take several pieces to the refinisher. When the van left, she had taken the draperies to the dry cleaners, picked up her take-out dinner, and fallen into bed much earlier than usual. It had felt odd to eat in front of the television in her bedroom. Later that night she walked through the first floor to make one last security check. The empty rooms had echoed the smallest sound, making it an eerie trip. She couldn't wait to lock the bedroom door behind her.

She was up at dawn after a restless night and was impatient for Graham Lee to arrive. He pulled up in his big gray truck about seven and they shared one last cup of coffee before she unplugged the pot. She left him waiting for the refinishers and she knew that he would make sure they did a fine job. He had all of her phone numbers and promised to call if something came up. She spent the trip from Martha's Hideaway to the Sharpe House in Old Town trying to think of anything she had forgotten to tell Graham.

Al and Cassandra gave her last-minute instructions before they pulled out of the driveway. The much-dreaded speech wasn't until Friday, so they had a day or two to play before it, as well as a couple of days after.

Jon was in early that Wednesday morning. He would be the acting head of the Investigations Division while the Newmans were away. He had jumped at this chance to excel when Al had announced his temporary elevation. He looked at the other members of the division through a supervisor's eyes as they came in. He noticed that Karen Millen looked a little harried. *What's up with that?* he wondered. It took him a few moments to remember the arrangement between her and the Newmans.

He continued to watch as she settled at her desk and began to work the phone. She had just hung up from one call when the phone rang again. She scribbled a page full of notes before she stood and reached for her jacket.

He saw her eyes cut to the lieutenant's desk before they swung over to him. "I've got a break in the Quattlebaum case. Somebody wants to talk." He nodded, but she was already on her way out the door. He would be very happy if they could present the boss with at least one closed case when he got back.

Mousavi was also working the telephone this gray morning, but his conversations were not as rewarding.

"*Salaam* to you, too, Jamal." He chaffed at Said's demand for a daily report, now that the operation was almost upon them. He tried to make their conversations as short as possible.

"Yes, yes, everyone is excited. And no, there are not any glitches. Everything is on track, and the men are trained and ready. Slidell and Eid will go camping this Saturday, as planned."

Mousavi finally tired of Said's micro-management when the man questioned why they went to the state park so many days before the operation. "Jamal, there's still plenty of time for you to fly down and run this op for yourself. I can go somewhere else, where I'm needed."

He listened to Said backtrack for several minutes before he said, "Well, the invitation's open any time you want to come. Otherwise, just let me do the job you trained me for."

Chapter 22

The Saturday before Thanksgiving was a busy one in several households on the island. The Wilsons were in the last stages of getting ready for their Thanksgiving retreat. Dianne and the girls were deciding what to pack and doing last-minute laundry. Wilson was reviewing his files on the Walid case and deciding whether to leave them behind or take them along. Unlike the Washington trip, this one was supposed to be a relaxed reconnection with the family.

The Stewart household was bustling with preparations for the yard sale they would hold before moving to their new home. In a last conversation with Nora, the real estate agent had conjectured that they would celebrate New Year's in the Villalonga-Gordon House.

First Alice and then Sara Jane began to discard the remnants of their former lives. By the end of the day, there would be only a few photographs of Jocko McCaffrey, Alice's long-dead husband and Sara Jane's father.

Almost everything that related to Cletus Shanks and the rest of the clan was thrown out. Alice still felt prickles of alarm every time she looked at a picture of her murderous brother. She always said a prayer for

Laurel, the wife whom Cletus had bludgeoned to death. And she always thanked the Lord that she and Sara Jane had lived through his attack on them.

She sighed and laid the photo face down on the bureau before she put a small yellow sticker on its scarred top. She would find a place to store her brother's picture later, when she wasn't so rushed. If Jon concurred with her suggestion to dispose of this battered piece, he would put his mark on the sticker and one more decision about the move would have been made.

Karen Millen was spending this cool, gray morning in her own home. It had taken her more than a week since the Newmans' return from Fort Lauderdale to get her house in order, but now she was finally able to do her usual Saturday morning chores. The washing machine was chugging away with the sheets from her bed, and her pretty pink bathroom was spotless, as was the master bedroom.

She stood in the foyer and surveyed the downstairs. She took yet another moment to admire the refinished floor. She turned to the living room on her left and admired the window draperies she'd had cleaned while the floors were being refinished. Their dark green color complemented her reupholstered sofa and loveseat. The refinisher had done a fine job restoring the round lacquered table that sat between them.

She only took a moment to admire the sideboard as she passed through the dining room. She glanced at her grandfather's clock; ten o'clock and she was already behind schedule. She shook her head in frustration and began to give the kitchen its weekly scrubbing.

Activity at the Addison House had begun with *Fajr*, the pre-dawn prayers. Slidell had set out a cold buffet breakfast and the men helped themselves. It was Gamil's turn to clean up after everyone had eaten.

Slidell and Eid ate quickly and then began getting ready for their last camping trip. Slidell was nervous and excited, and that made him chatter mindlessly.

Eid shut him up with a growl. "I swear you're part teen-age girl." The two men had finally come to a working arrangement, inspired by Mousavi's threat to kill one of them—with an equal chance of either being the victim. Despite all of that, Eid still became impatient with the other man's immaturity.

It had been Ahmahl Walid's idea for them to plant a handy cover story at their commands: Petty Officers Cummings (Eid) and Slidell had been buddies since boot camp. That story would make their camping trips seem natural and would raise no questions.

Using that story, each man had applied for leave over Thanksgiving week, long before their coworkers had thought about time off around the holiday. Each gave out the story that they would camp at the fort, but go to a mutual friend's house for the standard feast on Thursday.

There was no friend and there would be no feast. None of the men felt particularly thankful to be an American and none saw a reason to make the day special.

Eid and Slidell quickly packed the small RV that the cell had rented for the occasion. They loaded it with enough gear and supplies for a week. They would spend Thanksgiving afternoon packing the last deadly load and attending the final strategy session.

Unlike many cells, the men in Fernandina had more than enough room. Instead of bedrooms stuffed with bunk beds, each man had his own bed and bath in the roomy Addison House. Slidell and Eid retreated to their rooms and began to make final preparations. They would never sleep here again, so they began to sanitize their spaces. Not unlike the Stewarts, they went through everything they owned and discarded all but the most essential or precious items. Those they would take with them when they left the house on Thanksgiving.

Slidell finished in time to fix lunch. Not everyone was there, but Mousavi dominated the conversation around the table anyway. He once again told them how important each man was to the MMJ and how this week's external operation would further the cause.

"The next time we are together, we will be in the final stages of gearing up for the op. I suggest that you conduct any last-minute business you have with each other now or during the next couple of days."

"Or you can do it on Friday afternoon," Slidell added. He knew that several of his cell mates were prepared to die this Sabbath, but he did not join them in their wish for martyrdom. "Those virgins will just have to wait," he always told anyone who talked about dying for Islam.

Slidell drove carefully to the park entrance and chatted up the ranger on duty.

"New RV, I see," the ranger said.

"Naw, it belongs ta muh buddy, here." Slidell jabbed a thumb at Eid, sitting slack jawed in the passenger seat. The ranger glanced over at Eid and dismissed him as yet another good ol' boy. Eid sneered inwardly. No one would ever guess that his father was a tenured professor back in Tucson, or that his mother was a successful sculptor.

Cherie was on duty at check-in, and she flushed when her favorite camper walked in. Slidell seemed to lap up her simpering, but to Eid she was nothing more than another shrill, overweight American woman who wanted everything she could con a man into giving her.

Slidell eventually extricated himself from Cherie's ministrations and drove straight to the Amelia River Campground. He had been using this campsite for months because it was closer to the fort than the one near the fishing pier. He pulled in to his usual site and they began to set up camp.

Eid was no stranger to camping, and soon he had a fire going in the fire ring, with a big blue teapot suspended over it. They would use the water from the tap at the campsite, but take advantage of the park's showers and bathrooms. Neither man had given much thought to what would happen after Friday's attack. If anyone had asked, they would have shrugged, "*Inshallah*—God will take care of it."

Chapter 23

They were late. *Figures*, George Khee snorted to himself, and drummed his fingers with impatience. His Friday had been ruined with orders from Washington to read the Fernandina Beach Police Department in on the planned take-down of the MMJ cell up there. He had waited until late that afternoon to tell Charles Evans to be at his office at eight o'clock Monday morning.

He had spent the weekend gloating over how irritated Evans had sounded. He grinned at how early the chief and his minions would have had to get up to be here by eight this morning. He looked at his watch again and smiled. *Obviously not early enough.*

Lee Marie Toohey announced their arrival twenty minutes after the hour. Khee was delighted to see that his visitors were rushed and out of sorts. "Overslept, did we?"

Evans shot him a glare that should have singed his eyebrows. "Too bad you didn't have the courtesy to tell your security goons downstairs that we were coming."

"Sorry." Khee's grin made a mockery out of the apology.

Evans suddenly agreed with Stewart's theory that Khee's lack of professional courtesy was intentional.

The meeting was off with this rocky start, and only proceeded to go further downhill. Khee made it clear that Fernandina was being invited to participate in this take-down only because he had interceded with Washington so his island friends wouldn't feel left out. He also made sure they knew that this intercession had been successful because of his "juice" with the heavies.

Chief Evans and his two detectives had done a little team-building on the drive down, and now they carefully avoided exchanging glances at Khee's outrageous claims.

"We're busy coordinating things with NCIS at the base, so there's no need for you to pester Paul Patterson any more," Khee said.

Stewart wondered if Patterson had figured out Khee yet, but said nothing.

"And Captain Wilson is to cease and desist sticking his nose into other people's business. If his meddling blows this, a whole heap of it is going to get dumped on everyone in Fernandina."

Evans had just about had enough. "Never mind about Wilson, I'll take care of him." He looked at his watch. "We got started late—thanks to your poor planning—and you've spent the last fifteen minutes telling us how great you are. So how about getting to the point so I can go back to Fernandina to complain to your boss about you from the comfort of my own office?"

Khee stared at three sets of unfriendly eyes. He was once again puzzled and frustrated that the recipients of his brand of leadership had failed to react as expected.

His cure for this situation was to deliver his demands and then dismiss them as soon as possible so they could go back to flyover country. "OK, here's the deal. We will supply all of the manpower for the take-down, and most of the equipment. FBPD will provide us with a command post—headquarters space, comm system and gear, chow, bunks, showers and heads, you know, the whole schmear—and don't even think of sticking us in some dump. You will also provide us with any equipment that is too cumbersome to bring up there."

Charles Evans hid his rage by staring down at his belt buckle.

"Oh, and we'll probably need a tactical vehicle or two. I'll have to get back to you on that one."

Khee continued to make his demands and they wrote down each and every one.

"Is that it? Are we done here?" Evans was either going to leave right now or kill the little bastard on the spot.

"Uh, I guess so. I'll let you know if there's anything else."

Evans stood and the others followed him to the door. Khee did not offer his hand to shake, and Evans would have pretended not to see it if he had. "Follow this meeting up with an official request for assistance, and I'll have my people look at it." A nod to the others and they were gone.

"I'm surprised he didn't ask for a bowl of blue M&Ms," Stewart groused as he began to drive them home.

"Don't they make you horny?" Millen asked.

"No, that's the green ones."

"Give him whatever color will make him drool," Evans said and the tension that had built up over the last few hours dissipated.

Stewart merged the car onto I-95 North as Karen Millen said, "That went well, don't you think?"

"Wilson's right," Stewart said, "the man is a sonofabitch."

Evans grunted and then said, "Be patient. What

goes around comes around. God is watching and He will get around to George Khee one of these days."

They spent the rest of the drive deciding who would work on which of Khee's demands.

"Well, one thing's for certain," Evans said as they pulled into the lot at the station. "The rest of this day is going to be a piece of cake."

Stewart delivered the punch line of the old joke; "Yeah; we've already swallowed our live toad."

Unlike his visitors, SAC Khee was rather pleased with how the meeting had gone. He had asserted his authority while irritating the three bumpkins from flyover country. A good start to the week.

He was smiling as he dialed Ray Forbes. He tried to brag about how he had bested a formidable adversary like Chief Evans, but Forbes cut him off. Forbes was beginning to think that Wilson's assessment of the man was accurate. He neglected to pass along this thought when he made his own telephone call, this one to Frederick Page. He had a feeling that his boss had figured Khee out long ago.

Page thanked Forbes and called Christine. "Fernandina's on board. We're good to go whenever you say so."

Christine called her Tactical Force Commander and told him to put a TacTeam on alert. "How about Carlin's team? We've worked on these things before, so the prelims will be quick."

Commander Thornburgh checked his roster. "Yeah, I can make that happen."

"Good. I'll be in touch."

The Wilson party presented itself at the Florida Embarkment on Wednesday fifteen minutes before the advertised departure time for the Greyfield Inn Ferry.

When Wilson had made arrangements to stay in one of the inn's small cottages, he had discovered that it contained six bedrooms. A quick discussion over dinner that night had added Sara Jane and Brian to their party.

Lisa had talked and texted Sara Jane through that evening until Wilson had threatened to lock her phone in his gun cabinet. Dianne had used the house land line to call Cassandra Newman to relieve her of her child care assignment over Thanksgiving.

The late morning departure had presented no problems. Wilson had played possum until seven, but the rest of his family had started moving well before that. A chattering Sara Jane arrived before he had finished his first cup of coffee.

"Hey, Captain, did you know that Cumberland's Indian name is *Missoe*?"

"Yeah, and they called our island *Napoyca*," Lisa added.

He shot them a look and Sara Jane beamed as she held up her Timucuan dictionary. Lisa caught his glare and saved her from an ugly death by dragging her to her bedroom.

He was very grateful for their departure and looked over at his wife. "Maybe this wasn't such a good idea after all." Dianne just laughed and headed for the shower.

The ride to Cumberland was quick and chilly, but thanks to the warning from the reservations agent, they were bundled up against cold air and sea spray.

The girls' incessant chattering stopped when they stepped into the lobby of the Greyfield Inn. Even Brian noticed the rich décor. "Is this a palace, Daddy?"

Other guests chuckled and Sara Jane jumped at the chance to explain about the Carnegie home that had grown into an exclusive island retreat.

Check-in was swift and pleasant, and soon they were claiming their bedrooms in the cottage. They gathered in the living room to pore over the information packet they had been given at the front desk. Lisa and Sara Jane wanted to use the bicycles the inn provided, while Michelle opted for the Natural History Jeep Tour.

Wilson scanned the list of sports equipment he could check out. He wondered if he still knew what to do with a fishing rod. He looked up and smiled. All of the people he loved were together in this room, including Sara Jane.

"Hey, everybody! Slow down!" he said and smiled at their startled expressions. "We're all so used to cramming the day with everything that will fit. We don't need to do that here; that's not what this place is about."

He saw Lisa and Sara Jane exchange glances and relented a little. "OK, we have a couple of hours before cocktail hour starts at the main house. So do what you want to do—"

The girls jumped up, but stopped when Wilson warned, "But remember that we want to be at the main house by five-thirty for your Shirley Temples." He held up his hand when they started to move again. "And we have to dress for dinner, remember? So get back here in time to clean up and change into your Sunday best." He watched as they reconsidered their rush to ride bikes.

Wilson announced his plan to unpack at a leisurely pace and then take a nap. One look at Dianne told him he would not be napping alone.

Chapter 24

The mood at the Addison House was not nearly so relaxed. Mousavi had called for a three o'clock meeting when he discovered that no one had to work Wednesday afternoon. Eid and Slidell had been camping at the fort since Saturday, and they would come to the house just before three.

Mousavi smiled to himself when he remembered Slidell boring them one night by telling them about Frank Simmons, the original owner of the house who had it built in something like 1876 or so. And he'd gone on and on about D.H. Grounds, who'd been a superintendent at Seaboard Railroad when he'd lived here. He glanced at the high ceilings and original woodwork. *Big deal. Those guys will be whirling in their graves later today when we finalize our plans for their infidel brothers.*

Malik Gamil was the first to appear. The *USS Indiana* had arrived on schedule earlier in the week, and he had confirmed that only the Fire and Security watch remained behind. He also reported that most of the base was now on holiday routine. Only a small number of people would be at work over the next couple of days, and most of them would be too busy grousing about their bad luck to be an effective security force. *Just like we planned it*, Mousavi thought.

Eid and Slidell finally arrived, and Mousavi started their last formal meeting before the external operation went down. He ended it with a prayer, as always, but this time he added a fervent request for success in the mission.

Shorty watched the Citation line up its final approach to the runway. A series of telephone calls from Washington to Jacksonville, and eventually to Fernandina Beach, had alerted him to this flight.

Chief Evans had briefed the Fixed Base Operator, but only about the aviation support these guests would need. If Andrew Dugan had been a little surprised to see Shorty sitting in on that meeting, he hid it well. The chief had explained his presence with a few words about Shorty and his logistics duties before proceeding to the business at hand.

Shorty had been impressed with the deft way the chief had handled that sticky item, and had said so after Dugan had left. "Purty slick, Slick." Evans had grinned and waved him out of his office.

Shorty let the other line rats direct the plane to a parking place and deploy the VIP kit. He opened a side gate so Durwood Cratch could drive a Ford Explorer up to the end of the square of red carpet that had been placed at the foot of the aircraft stairs. Shorty sneered to himself when Cratch failed to signal a thank-you for the service. *Mini-Khee*, he thought and made a note to share his witty observation with the others.

Four men in black slacks and polo shirts deplaned, each carrying a black canvas bag. *Looks like the Mafia's arrived.* Shorty rolled his eyes when the copilot, also dressed in black, followed them down the steps and unlocked the luggage compartment. They transferred its contents to the Explorer. *Mr. Personality*, Shorty thought as Cratch made no move to greet or help his guests.

"Welcome ta Paradise, fellahs!" Shorty crowed as he pitched a bag into the back of the SUV.

"Geez, it's cold down here!" one of the men complained as he put on a fleece jacket.

"And I brought my thong and suntan lotion!" another chimed in.

"Yeah, you would. At least it's not snowing like it is in DC."

"I thought the term was 'white Christmas,' not 'white Thanksgiving.'"

"Hey! I'm starving!" the copilot announced. "When do we eat?"

"You're always starving," the pilot said as he joined them.

The four-member TacTeam crawled into the Explorer, followed by the pilot and copilot. The doors were barely closed when Cratch made a particularly vicious turn that knocked them off balance.

Khee had put him in charge of logistical support for this team of buffed up cowboys. Cratch had been enraged to discover that he would have to keep them supplied with everything from toilet paper to ammo and all of the food and drink they might require.

He lurched to a stop behind a nondescript beach house. His passengers could not decide whether his bad driving was intentional or if he was merely inept.

"Help unload the gear," Liam Carlin growled as he opened the door. Cratch started to protest, but thought better of it at the team leader's glare.

He grabbed the lightest bag and said, "Who are you guys, anyway?"

"Nobody you'll ever be," someone growled from the middle of the pack.

Cratch dropped the bag in outrage but retrieved it hastily when someone prodded his shoulder. "Go!"

He could hear the boisterous greeting the Jacksonville team gave the DC contingent long before he came in through the back door. The living room was filled with fierce men with sidearms. *Even their smiles look dangerous*, he thought as he dropped the bag he'd carried in.

Khee was there, of course, dressed in black like everyone else. Cratch reminded himself to watch and learn how to handle groups like this. He listened to Khee, but he watched the men as the SAC explained that this was his plan and his op. Things would be done his way and they would follow his orders, or else. Cratch admired the way Khee bossed these guys around. He saw two of the DC types exchange glares and misread them as looks of admiration.

When Khee announced there would be a general briefing after dinner, one of Carlin's team interrupted with, "Yeah, when is dinner, anyway? I'm starving."

"Who made this coffee? It tastes like owl pee," another chimed in.

Cratch went to the kitchen to further terrorize the catering staff. Soon the dining room table was filled with warming dishes of meat, potatoes, and vegetables. A large silver tray was piled high with freshly-baked dinner rolls and the sideboard held dessert.

Cratch moved to the arch separating the living from the dining room. His announcement that dinner was ready made him sound like a butler in an old black-and-white movie. Several men snickered and Cratch's mood grew even darker.

Shorty was enjoying his own dinner in the small break area at the FBO. He munched on leftover pizza and salad from Arte Pizza, unaware that a black Chrysler 300 had pulled up to the Citation. The young FBI agent driving it got out and opened the doors and trunk. She was a small, neat woman with blonde hair that glowed in the low light. She waited at the foot of the carpet.

William "Bull" Cowper came down the steps quickly. His glances took in the details of car, driver, and the few people milling about the FBO.

He was closely followed by Christine Mahmood, who was also on high alert. She and Bull Cowper had been a team since their Mujahedeen days in Afghanistan. The *fatwah* issued against her husband had included her, and his death had not canceled orders to kill her on sight. She and Bull had survived three assassination attempts, and they had learned that the most innocent-looking situations could be the most deadly.

Christine and her bodyguard were quickly tucked into the armored sedan. Their driver introduced herself as she drove them to the Miramar Townhomes. "I am Special Agent Jo Tupper. I'll be your aide for the duration of your stay."

Her passengers thanked her for the service she was about to render while they tried to figure out how many weeks had passed since her graduation from Quantico.

"Wet ink," Christine murmured. Bull grunted in agreement, but he was not amused. Khee should have assigned a more seasoned agent to the high-value target sitting next to him. If anything went down, he was afraid that he and Christine would end up protecting the baby agent. It made him tired to think about it.

Agent Tupper parked behind the townhouse and unlocked the back door, but not before using the tactical radio to warn those inside that they were coming in.

A small group of agents was waiting inside. One man took the car keys from Tupper and went to unload the trunk. Another agent collected their coats and gloves.

Tupper pulled out her radio and reported their safe arrival to Khee. "Everyone's in and the security team is on station." She heard Cratch's snide remark about undeserved face time with the heavies, but decided to ignore it.

Tupper began their tour of the Egmont Suite at its fully stocked bar. While they fixed themselves drinks, she quickly introduced them to the other members of the team who would be assigned to them during their stay on the island.

Introductions complete, Tupper led them through every room, briefing them on the setup. By the time she came to the end of her spiel, they were once again in the living room, Christine's luggage was in the master bedroom, and Cowper's was in the room across from it.

She turned to see that a small buffet had been set up on the breakfast bar and two places had been set at the dining table. "Dinner is ready whenever you are, and if you would like wine to go with it, we have a small selection for you to choose from."

Christine moved toward the food while Bull asked to see the wine.

Several hours later, after everyone was bedded down and the security detail was in place, she finally thought of hosting a going-away party for Cratch. She turned out her bedside light and smiled in the dark. *After he's left town, of course.*

Dusk came early that day, and the cell used its cover to load the last of the weapons in the back of the RV. When the final missile and its accoutrements had been loaded, they took a few moments to wish each other success.

They gathered in the training room. Mousavi looked around and saw that the portent of what they were about to do had finally registered; all of them were nervous and one or two were just plain scared. *No matter. It is set; it is the will of Allah.*

"My brothers, let us pray. Each of us must confide what is in our hearts so that Allah may give us strength during His holy test." The room was silent as they bowed their heads. Mousavi waited patiently before he singled out the two men who would be entrusted with the weapons. "We thank our brothers Azziz Eid and Bobby Slidell for the great work they are about to do. May Allah kiss you on both cheeks."

Eid muttered a clumsy acknowledgement of Mousavi's kind words. Slidell had turned his usual bright red, but spoke up anyway. "I have something to say," he began hesitantly, but as he talked the others finally caught a glimpse of the man he was going to be.

"Y'all have been very patient with me over these last few months, even you, my brother." He laid a hand on Eid's shoulder, and the big man twitched at the touch.

"I have prayed all of these long months about the true name I am to choose for myself. I have tried and rejected many, but tonight I am here to announce that I finally know who I am."

He had everyone's attention, and several men were leaning forward in anticipation. "I am Abdul Hamid. I chose Abdul, 'the son of,' and Hamid, of course, because

I'm proud to call myself by a variation of Mohammad.

"And I can assure you, my brothers, that I am, always have been, always will be a true son of Mohammad. I am, always have been, always will be united with you in this holy war. *Allah Akbar*! Allah be praised!"

They caught his fervor and took up the chant. Mousavi and Khalidi had to quiet them, lest the neighbors hear.

"Time to go, you two, before you start a street demonstration by the faithful!" Mousavi said.

The Pelican had been on station all afternoon. He had spent most of his time eavesdropping and repeating those conversations into his cell phone. "They've finished loading and are heading out. I'll follow them and—"

"No. Return to your base and await orders."

He signed off and drove to the station on Lime Street. The town was quiet, anticipating tomorrow's festivities.

Hamid drove the RV back to the state park in silence. He had been very moved by the prayers and good wishes of the others. He sorely missed the closeness of his family back in Tennessee, but these men had filled many of the gaps. He turned to share his thoughts with Eid, but stopped when he saw the other man's lips moving in prayer.

Once back at the fort, he took them over the route they would use on Friday from the campsite to the launch site. Each man recited his role as they slowly drove the course.

They had not been inside the fort itself during this stay at the park, and for a reason: repeated trips might bring unwanted attention. They would correct their absence tomorrow morning. While most of the town was in church, they would be walking the parapets, making sure they agreed upon the exact spot to position the launchers.

They moved about quietly, even though most of the campsites were vacant. They had filled the RV with the long launcher containers, so tonight and tomorrow night they would sleep under the stars. Hamid was still too excited to lie quietly in his sleeping bag and fidgeted until Eid growled at him. His gruffness mimicked the normalcy of the past months and Hamid finally drifted off to sleep.

There was no dawn on Thanksgiving, only a lightening of the gray pallor that hung over the island. A slow, cold drizzle started just as church services began, but the communicants didn't seem to mind. They were much too busy giving thanks for another year in Paradise.

There was no such thanksgiving at Campsite 35. Hamid grumbled about the weather until Eid explained that it would keep people indoors, clustered around their dining room tables and television sets. The two of them could go about their business without notice.

Durwood Cratch offered no thanks that morning, either. He lived in a nice but sterile Jacksonville apartment he had purposely neglected to personalize. The apartment was in a large anonymous complex that allowed him the freedom to come and go without attracting comment.

He had devoted his second bedroom to a lifelong obsession with the American Civil War. Bookshelves lined the perimeter of the room, and they were filled with books and memorabilia, arranged as meticulously as a battle plan to give him quick access to what he wanted. Before SAC Khee had ruined this long weekend, Cratch had planned to immerse himself in the Battle of Olustee, fought in 1864 over near Lake City.

He was a New Yorker by birth, and Jacksonville was his first foray south of the famous Mason-Dixon Line. He had jumped at this assignment, but not because of the work or the warmer climate. He had planned to research the Southern campaigns of the war and take side trips to selected battle sites.

But on this drizzly morning, he was standing in line at the Publix Deli in Fernandina Beach instead of immersing himself in the maneuvers of Confederate Generals Finegan and Seymour.

He probably wouldn't be able to go see where Finegan's Fernandina mansion had stood, either. He had not yet discovered the mansion's fate, other than that the general had returned to find it operating as an orphanage and school for former slave children; it took Finegan years of court battles to regain control of his property.

The customer standing first in line finally left with a feast filling her shopping cart. Cratch heaved a big sigh, and the lady in front of him turned to smile in sympathy.

Finegan, he remembered, eventually sold his mansion to the Episcopal bishop, who promptly turned it into an exclusive school. The only additional fact Cratch knew was that the Nassau County School Board offices now stood where the Atlantic Avenue mansion had once been, but even that tidbit of information did him no good as he stood in line scowling. Picking up and delivering a feast for fifteen on Thanksgiving was a poor substitute for his original plan of historical exploring.

He knocked on the back door of the Egmont Suite and growled at the young agent who opened it. His irritation increased at the man's sleepy look and the mug of hot coffee he held. "Put that down and off-load this mess."

The agent's eyebrows rose and he left Cratch standing in the rain while he fetched rain gear and someone to help him. Cratch did not help. He wandered into the kitchen while the others made several trips back and forth.

His only thank-you was a grunt when they announced that everything had been transferred. He held on to the mug of coffee he had cadged as he brushed past them back out into the weather.

The agents exchanged smirks. "Mr. Personality," one said.

"Uh-huh, he'll go far."

Cratch grumbled all the way to the beach house. He was to pick up the DC team members there and bring them back to the Egmont Suite. Khee passed him, driving the Jacksonville team to the townhouse. He waved and Khee answered it with the flick of a finger. Cratch was pleased with the rare acknowledgement.

"You ready? Come on," he greeted the DC team. The agents were ready and waiting, but did not move at his abrupt order.

Liam Carlin turned from the newscast they were watching. "Wait one," he said and turned back to the screen.

"Hooray for the home team," someone said when the story ended. An FBI field office out west had taken several domestic terrorists into custody before they could commit their mayhem.

"Another day in Paradise!" another team member

said as they hurried through the rain to the Explorer.

Cratch put it in gear and growled, "After all this rain, Amarillo is going to be my Paradise."

Carlin was from the Texas Panhandle himself, and wondered if he should warn the field office about Cratch's imminent arrival. Instead, he said, "Ah, Rotor City, USA. That's where they make the V-22 Osprey. Largest city in the Panhandle. Good eats, good music, and the women ain't bad, either."

"Yeah, but you neglected to mention the blue northers they get up there," another Texan on the team chimed in.

Cratch took the bait. "What are they?"

"You're in for a real treat. Blue northers happen when the temp drops twenty degrees in an hour and the wind blows you off your horse."

"You never been on a horse in your life," Carlin laughed.

"Was, too."

"Yeah, his momma rented a pony for his birthday party last year!" a wit added.

Cratch felt himself ignored once more, alone in a crowd. January and his Texas transfer couldn't come soon enough.

Hamid and Eid left the campsite around noon and reminded the ranger at the gate that they would not be back until late that night.

"Y'all have a fine Turkey Day with your friends. I'll guard the fort while you're gone." He laughed at his own wit and waved them through.

"Huh. He's the turkey."

"Won't be so slappy happy tomorrow morning!"

The town was quiet as they drove to Ash Street. Most people were home in the middle of a day filled with food and football. Hamid felt a slight pang for a piece of his momma's famous cornbread dressing. She always cut him the biggest square. *Never mind, I'm doin' somethin' more important than eatin' dressin'.* He gave himself a little shake to focus on his holy mission.

"You sure are fidgety today. Getting' cold feet?"

"Nah. Just missed my mom's cornbread dressing for a minute, that's all."

The Thanksgivings that Eid had suffered through in Arizona, as Jared Cummings, had had a decidedly Southwestern flair, so he was not sure what dressing made out of cornbread would taste like. "Huh. Well, you got a lot more important things to think about besides some cornmeal mush your momma used to throw onna plate."

Hamid blinked at the harsh tone. This was the old Eid, and Hamid was startled to realize that the man no longer intimidated him. In an uncharacteristic burst of insight, he realized that Eid grew mean-mouthed only when he was unsure of himself.

"Here we are," Hamid announced unnecessarily as he pulled into the Addison House's parking area. *And who wouldn't be a little snippy at the thought of what we're going to do tomorrow? Allah be praised,* he reminded himself as he followed Eid up the back steps.

They walked into a house filled with tension and anticipation. And football. Most of the men were clustered around the big screen in the training room. The underdog team scored a touchdown just as Hamid and Eid entered, so their arrival was not noticed right away. Hamid quietly served himself tea from the samovar and watched the setup for the extra point.

"How are you doing?"

Hamid had not heard Mousavi approach, so the quiet question startled him. He smiled and said, "A little jumpy, as you can tell, but nothing I can't handle."

Mousavi looked over at Eid, who was reaching across Khalidi to raid the bowl of munchies. "And how is he?"

Hamid shrugged. "Irritable. Bitchy. Himself. He's OK."

"And jumpy, like you."

Hamid said nothing, but blew on his tea.

"Good." Mousavi tapped him on the shoulder. "Everything's normal, then. No doubts about tomorrow?"

"Absolutely none. I was born to do this." Hamid gestured toward his partner. "And so is he. If he falters, I will kill him and do this thing alone."

Mousavi looked carefully at the young man before him. This was no longer the immature Bobby Slidell. This was, finally, a soldier of Allah, dedicated to tomorrow's holy mission.

"As he would you," he murmured and moved closer to the game.

It was a bittersweet afternoon. There were moments of eager anticipation when this house full of young men thought of tomorrow's work. But then they would think about the danger they were about to face, and the house would grow quiet.

Weeks ago, they had agreed to avoid the traditional American Thanksgiving fare, mostly because Hamid would not be there to cook, so they feasted on lamb and wild rice fixed by the number two man. Khalidi, it turned out, was an excellent cook; he had prepared their *halal* meal to perfection.

Mousavi stood at the end of the meal, and someone

tapped on a water glass to get everyone's attention. "My brothers." Mousavi stopped and looked at each man in turn. "I have known you for only a few months. But I have come to admire and respect you and your dedication to our holy war.

"Tomorrow we are to face what will be, for some of you at least, the first test of your faith."

"*Allah Akbar*," they chanted.

"The plan that Ahmahl Walid—"

"May Allah hold him close," someone interrupted.

"Walid's plan was and is a most excellent one. It is simple, direct, and—"

"Deadly," Khalidi offered as Mousavi searched for the right word.

"Yes, deadly," Mousavi agreed and then smiled, "for the infidels!"

He waited until the whistles and cheers died down. "Make no mistake. This small thing we do tomorrow is an important part of the large war we wage. Hundreds, no thousands, of attacks like this will be mounted until the Infidel is overcome. We may not see this victory, neither may our children. But surely our grandchildren will see the True Faith and its laws hold sway over this country."

His watch gave a small beep. It was time for *Maghrib*, evening prayers. "We are adjourned until tomorrow, the Sabbath," he said.

Sunset prayers said, Hamid and Eid took their leave. Hamid once again drove them back to Campsite 35, and once again the truck cab was silent.

It was a quiet evening, with each man preoccupied with tomorrow's assignment. They were still full of lamb and rice, so Hamid made them tea, which they sipped all evening. Finally Hamid banked the fire and they began to prepare for *Isha*, the last prayer of the day.

Eid spoke up hesitantly. "I know that I've been impatient with ya ever since I met ya. I apologize fer that. I was afraid that ya weren't up to it, ya know." He looked over at the younger man to discover him gazing into his empty tea mug.

"But these last few days—ever since ya stopped being Bobby Slidell an' started bein' Abdul Hamid, ya seem ta be a totally different person. Calm, like. Growed up, even."

"Thank you, I think. Does this mean you think I can hold my own tomorrow?"

"By the will of Allah, we will both hold our own."

"Amen to that."

Prayers complete, they slipped into their sleeping bags. The temperature had dropped and each man cocooned himself deeply amongst the down of the bags. Eid fell asleep listening to country and Western music on his iPod, while Hamid listened to the exhortations of a *mullah* from the Islamic center.

Chapter 25

The Pelican waited until the campers were tucked in for the night before he headed back to tuck himself into a bunk at the command post.

The place was humming, filled with SWAT teams, tactical teams, and more brass than he cared to be around. Even the bunk room was crowded and noisy. He looked for a quiet office elsewhere in the building. Soon he was snoring on the chief's sofa.

A soft beep on his wrist woke him an hour later. He used the chief's private head to wash his face and finger-comb his hair before wandering back to the command center.

Cratch watched the command center from a vantage point near the door. Several people caught his eye. First, there was the beautiful, dark woman with the huge man who never left her side. *Who the hell is that?* He watched first his boss and then the police chief pay their respects to her. *Huh. Whoever she is, she's somebody.*

Agent Tupper's corn-silk hair caught his eye as she brought the dark woman a cup of something hot. *And there you are, my little dumpling. Yum!*

His salacious speculation was interrupted by the arrival of the shortest man he had ever seen. He watched in disbelief as everyone greeted the little man with handshakes and back slaps. Trash talk filled the air and Cratch sneered to himself. *Must be the mascot.*

His contempt turned to outrage as he watched the dark woman envelope the "mascot" in a long, rocking hug. *Who in the hell are these people?* He watched Khee watch the reunion and took comfort at his boss's sour expression. It was obvious that both of them shared the same opinion of the runt.

"OK, listen up!" Khee took the microphone and control of the room. Once the room was quiet, he introduced Chief Evans. "FBPD's our host for this fire drill and the chief has something he just has to say."

"Thank you, George; you're as gracious as usual," Evans acknowledged the introduction before he quickly explained the department's role and the resources available to them.

Khee would not allow him to speak very long and soon returned to the lectern. He turned to the short man who had caught Cratch's eye earlier. "You all seem to know Tankerville. He will be your go-to guy for FBPD stuff. Just tell him what you want and he'll have Evans over there cough it up."

There was a murmur in the room at Khee's cavalier treatment of the department and its chief, both of whom had a good reputation with the men and women drinking his coffee and eating his sandwiches. But when they glanced over at Chief Evans, they were met with a stone face.

Tankerville broke off his conversation with Christine to survey the room. They all caught his respectful nod to Chief Evans and his glare at SAC Khee before he turned and flashed his trademark grin. "Guess ol' George, here, don't wanna be associated with a ruffian named 'Shorty.'"

Cratch was incensed that this oaf would address his boss by his first name, but the rest of the room erupted. "Thigh bite! Thigh bite!" Almost everyone there was painfully familiar with Shorty's signature fighting technique.

"Enough a' that, guys!" Shorty quieted them and began to brief them about the men and materiel that the FBPD would provide.

"What's this 'Tankerville' mess? That really your last name?" one of the visitors asked.

Shorty turned to glare at Khee yet again. "Our estimable leader will explain all a' that to ya when the time comes." He left the room and headed for Chief Evans' office. Evans, Christine, and Bull soon joined him.

"Tired of being a redneck?" Bull asked.

"You have no idea." His accent was no longer Southern redneck, but had a rich British tone to it. He watched Evans closely as he continued. "It is truly wonderful to finally stop murdering the Queen's English. American is bad enough, but redneck American is bloody awful!"

Chief Evans did not join in their laughter. "Who in the hell are you? And who in the hell have I been dealing with all these years?"

Bull Cowper quickly explained. "Since Special Agent Khee so ungenerously 'outed' him, I'd like to introduce you to Sir George Grey Livingstone, the Twelfth Earl of Tankerville."

"And?" the little man said into the stunned silence.

"And," Cowper grinned, "one of Britain's most talented intelligence agents."

Evans sank into the nearest chair and glowered at the man who had exasperated him for almost a decade. "All these years, and you never said a thing."

"Couldn't."

Evans' response was earthy and succinct. He stared off into space for a few moments before he turned angry eyes back to the man he still thought of as Shorty. "I can't wait to hear what Wilson has to say when he finds out you've been lying to him, too."

"Where is he, anyway?" Christine asked. "I'm surprised he's not right in the middle of all of this."

"Cumberland, the next island up the coast," Evans growled and turned to Shorty as an awful suspicion dawned. "Did you arrange that, too?"

Shorty looked him straight in the eye. "Yep."

"Holy Mother—and the murder charges?"

"No, that was pure Khee. Something bright he thought up on the spot when he found that Walid chap dead on the floor."

"The hell you say," the chief murmured quietly to give himself time to think. "Have you found out who murdered Walid yet?"

Christine chimed in. "Yes, we know who assassinated Walid, and yes, we know what we're going to do about it."

The chief had glared at Shorty while he waited for Christine to stop talking. He loomed over the little man and demanded, "And just how do you intend to get Khee to drop this farce of a murder charge against my captain?"

Christine stepped in to diffuse the situation. "Lord Tankerville agreed to come here years ago to monitor the progress that the Muslim Military Jihad was making in setting up a cell here. He used his childhood nickname—"

"One I hate, by the way."

"And appeared on the scene as an irresponsible hell-raiser."

"Did a damn fine job of it, too," Evans growled.

"And then, about six months ago, Tankerville picked up that the MMJ was unhappy with your Captain Wilson."

"What on earth for?"

Shorty took up the tale. "He started looking into the Haldad cold case. Haldad was the first guy, in the guise of Tariq El Ramadan, who tried to establish an MMJ cell here back in 2006."

"We got intel," Christine interjected, "that the MMJ national leadership got nervous that Wilson might stumble over the cell that Ahmahl Walid was heading up by then."

"And," Bull added, "national wanted to give the Fernandina cell the external operation against Kings Bay, so first they got rid of Walid because he was turning on them, and then they went after Wilson because his work on the cold case was threatening the cell."

"And here we are, full circle," Evans said. He was no longer angry, but he still felt a little hurt that he had not been entrusted with the information about the MMJ, as well as Shorty's true identity and assignment beforehand, and said so. "And if you tell me that keeping us in the dark was a matter of national security, I will deck you!"

Their chuckle was cut short when Christine held up a finger. She listened intently to her ear bud before she stood and said, "They're moving."

Two tactical teams raced through the empty pre-dawn streets with no lights or sirens. Agent Tupper piloted the Chrysler carrying Christine and Bull at only a slightly slower speed.

The car was equipped as a command and control vehicle, and they listened as SAC Khee screamed unnecessary commands on Channel One. He had dubbed himself team leader and his Jacksonville team as Team One. The DC contingent was Team Two. It was rapidly becoming obvious that Khee's plan was to have this team, which was better trained and had more experience, act as a back-up to Khee's Team One.

"That man—" Christine began, but was interrupted by Shorty, who had joined them at the last moment.

"Don't worry. I got it," he growled. Christine sat back, satisfied.

Chapter 26

Fort Clinch lay cold and dark as Eid's wrist alarm woke him. He knew instantly what day it was and its import. He quietly slipped out of his sleeping bag, only to discover that Hamid was already awake and stirring. Wordlessly, they walked to the communal head.

Hamid got a small fire going and they said the dawn prayers while the tea brewed. They drank the first few sips gratefully, their eyes downcast. Hamid produced energy bars and they ate them quickly. Finally, when streaks of light were beginning to show, Eid stood. "You ready?"

The Pelican had been at his post for hours, and now muttered into his radio that site 35 was stirring. Christine signaled Khee to have both teams move out.

Hamid threw the dregs of his tea on the fire and turned to face his partner. Eid saw that he had tears in his eyes, but knew that they were not a sign of weakness, but the depth of his faith and commitment to the mission.

He held out his hand and Hamid shook it. *"Allah Akbar,"* they said before Hamid climbed into the truck.

The drive from the campsite to the park entrance was short and quick. Once there, he used his key card to open the gate and lead the trucks carrying the rest of the team back to the campsite.

The men moved to their chores, but Mousavi stopped them with a murmur. They stilled to listen to his final words of guidance and encouragement before they joined in a last prayer. He did not expect all of them to survive the morning and asked Allah to welcome the new arrivals.

Mousavi quickly surveyed the men and the campsite before he signaled them to load up. Hamid led the way from Campsite 35; the few spots that were occupied this time of year were still and dark. *They're gonna have a helluva wake-up call*, Mousavi thought.

"Let's go!" Liam Carlin urged when the Pelican reported that the cell was getting ready to move. They had spent most of the night waiting for this moment, and they were more than ready.

Except Special Agent Cratch. He would complain for the rest of his life that he had spent the night working instead of sleeping. Once again he had found himself in charge of food and drink. "They eat like a bunch of hogs," he had muttered under his breath more than once as he had supervised refills and replenishments.

He had also supervised one last check of the tactical gear before it was loaded into the SUVs. He detailed a junior agent to guard the two vehicles, even though they were parked in the police department's secure lot.

Khee nailed Carlin with a glare before he nodded to Cratch to move. Cratch signaled the other driver and they went to start the engines.

Cratch sat in the idling SUV and realized that he did not want to be here. He was not pumped up like the others, eager for a little action. In a rare burst of insight, he realized that he was more of a wall-to-wall carpet kind of guy than a field operative. *My God, what am I doing here? I could get killed!* He liked battle better when it was reenacted by his lead soldiers.

Hamid led the group through the fort's drawbridge and sally port constructed by the Works Progress Administration in the 1930s. He drove across the parade ground with no thought of the thousands of men who had trod across it for nearly three centuries, as island inhabitants had been using this site for coastal defense long before the U.S. Army started building the brick fort here.

They parked at the ramp close to the North Bastion. Each man grabbed the weapons and gear assigned to him. Hamid and Eid shouldered their launchers and began to walk up the ramp. Gamil and Khalidi followed them with two back-up launchers.

Eid's calligraphy on the missile containers was finally appreciated. Even in these tension-filled moments, the men found inspiration and comfort in the inscriptions. First one and then another kissed his fingers and tapped the messages. Eid grunted in satisfaction.

Mousavi had watched it all and grinned in the dark. He had had his doubts about Eid and his temper, but the man was proving himself to be a true warrior.

Eid and Hamid bent to unpack their weapons and make them ready for launch. Constant drilling was paying off; their moves were quick and efficient.

Khalidi relieved Gamil of the extra AK-47 that he carried and said a quiet word to each of them as he turned to leave. He would take up his position on the top of wall by the drawbridge and the headquarters building just inside it.

Gamil and Mousavi slung their AK-47s over their shoulders and moved along the parapet, closer to the Northwest Bastion. They would provide cover fire for the launch site from this short distance, should it come to that. They were confident in both their cause and their plan, so they had little hope of getting to fire their weapons.

A faint pinpoint of light blinked three times from the south wall. Khalidi was in place. They were ready.

Chapter 27

Khee's lead car, closely followed by the Explorer piloted by Cratch, had opened the gate to the park, and now Shorty, riding shotgun beside Tupper in the Chrysler, got out to close it once they were inside. Tupper tucked them into a lay-by and killed the lights. She kept the engine running for warmth and for power for the communications array.

The radio crackled as Carlin quietly announced that Team Two had stopped some distance from the drawbridge.

"No! No!" Khee ordered. "Move up! You're too far away!"

Carlin switched to Channel Two. "Two to *Passtana*. You up?" Christine had long ago explained to Carlin that her Pashto code name translated as "Afghan woman," which is what she was, despite the dual legacies of her chieftain father and husband.

Bull sat beside Christine and worked the radio. "*Passtana* says move half the distance, then hold." Two clicks of the mike told them that Carlin was on his way.

Carlin switched back to Channel One and caught Khee in mid-rant. "You hear me? Move up or I'll have your badge!"

"Don't get your knickers in a knot, leader. Two's movin'." He failed to mention where or how far. Christine and Bull smiled at the ambiguity.

"My knickers are none of your concern. You follow my lead or—"

"Knock it off. Maintain radio discipline." Christine's orders ended the chatter. She sat back and sighed.

Shorty stirred and muttered, "Soon, soon. It's almost over."

Cratch had grown more uncomfortable at each clash between the two team leaders. Twice he had put the Explorer into gear to follow Khee's orders despite Carlin's direction. And twice Carlin had growled at him to hold their position.

Carlin finally gave him the go-ahead to move up to the position Khee had initially directed them to. Cratch, too, kept his engine running for warmth and the communication gear.

Team Two exited the SUV and donned night vision goggles. Even though it was almost dawn, they still could not see without assistance. They crept to the fort's drawbridge. Carlin did a radio check of their headsets and then sent a scout to check inside the fort, especially the open parade ground. When the man signaled, Carlin joined him at the inner edge of the sally port.

"I count four."

"Five," Carlin corrected and pointed to a man hiding in the shadows. They watched as Khee took his team much deeper into the fort, increasing his chance of spooking the figures now swarming up the northwest parapet.

Both teams watched as two of the figures left this vantage point and returned to the camper parked at its base. When the two men returned to the launch site with more gear, one of them carried a slim case that looked suspiciously like a laptop computer.

Carlin kept his goggles trained on the high wall. "He's gonna start programming it any minute, leader."

"Stand fast. Wait for my order."

Carlin swore in frustration. *If this little shit blows it, I'm gonna pound him into atomic dust.* His ruminations ended when one of his team grunted. He watched as the two on the parapet mounted their launchers on the tripods they had unfolded.

"Now!" Carlin barked into his headset. "Time to move!"

"On my orders, I said."

Carlin watched as one man kneeled to run a diagnostic with the laptop he had attached to a launcher.

He motioned Team Two to move up, hugging the northwest perimeter wall. He kept an eye on Khee and Team One. He did not trust the man and his choice of advancing along the far wall made no tactical sense. What was he up to?

Eid booted up the laptop and initiated the short program. All systems were up and running. He signaled to Mousavi, who motioned for him to check the second missile.

Eid wiped sweaty palms on his dungarees and Hamid touched his shoulder lightly. He took a long, calming breath before checking the second weapon. He muttered a short prayer before he began to punch in the coordinates that would guide the missiles across Cumberland Sound.

Once they were programmed, Eid stepped away from the keyboard. He and Hamid turned to Mousavi, awaiting the command that would send the missiles to the drydock and the *USS Indianapolis* that rested inside.

"GO! GO! GO!" Khee screamed into his headset and charged from his hiding spot. He had waited too long to mount his attack and then had failed to warn the teams that they would be moving soon. They were taken by surprise and scrambled to follow his lead.

"*Puduu*!" Christine said from the back seat, and Bull grunted in agreement.

"Trunk," Shorty growled as he opened his door, and Tupper hit the release button. They all felt the car rock when he slammed the trunk shut. The furrows around Christine's mouth grew deeper.

"Little shit's not gonna screw up this operation like he did the Leopard," Shorty muttered to himself as he checked the weapon he had taken from the trunk.

SAC Khee was far ahead of his team as he led the charge toward the ramp. No one would ever know if it had been exuberance or incompetence that led him to abandon the shadowy safety of the perimeter wall, but he began a rapid run across the parade ground. His team followed him, but at a distance. That distance only increased as Khee raced faster and faster toward the action and certain glory.

Khalidi tracked the man's precipitous charge through the site of his AK-47.

Carlin caught a faint movement on the high wall over the headquarters building. "Swink," he muttered into his headset.

"Got it," the sniper said, and brought his rifle up. A slight *pffftt* and Khalidi froze a moment before he began to teeter. Swink and the rest of Team Two continued their cautious approach to the North Bastion and did not see the spectacular dive Khalidi's dead body made from the wall.

Khee ran on, unaware that the men behind him were distracted from the mission by having to cover him. His thoughts were concentrated on stopping a terrorist cell in mid-attack. This operation would pad his resume nicely and maybe get him a plum assignment at Bureau headquarters.

His thoughts of glory faltered when he saw a man on the parapet directly in front of him fall to the ground. He turned to see that the teams behind him were firing over his shoulder, which meant that he was in the line of fire, no matter how friendly it was. Had he known the opinion of the men he ostensibly led, he would have questioned how friendly that fire actually was.

Khee ducked into a squat and froze in the middle of the parade field for a moment as he tried to figure out what to do. He jumped up and ran into the shadows created by the North Bastion parapet. Carlin noted his flight from the line of fire, but was much too busy to remark upon it.

"Swink," he muttered into his headset a second time, and the sharpshooter dispatched a man who had emerged from the shadows above the Northwest Bastion.

Eid and Hamid turned at the sound of Mousavi's head exploding. They froze in horror as they watched the rest of his body slowly sink to the brick.

Eid was the first to recover and grabbed Mousavi's AK-47. He began to spray the black shapes coming toward him. He was only vaguely aware of Hamid screaming for someone to give him the launch order. Eid spun suddenly from the impact of a round in his shoulder. He dropped the weapon and began shrieking in pain.

Hamid screamed *"Allah Akbar! Allah Akbar!"* as tears ran down his cheeks. He watched Eid writhe in pain for a second before he turned back to the missiles sitting in front of him, armed and waiting for him to send them on their way. He could not see the launch button through his tears. He roughly swiped at his eyes to clear them and reached for the button once again.

His finger never touched it. Two members of Team One wrestled him to the ground. Another team member disconnected the USB cords from the missiles, canceling their launch codes.

An eerie silence fell over the fort. The tactical teams began to lower their weapons and looked around cautiously. A single shot made them flinch back into their defensive crouches with their weapons at the ready.

"Over by the north wall, under the launch site," someone said. Carlin and Khee's second in command exchanged glances before they each dispatched a man to investigate.

"Where's Special Agent Khee?" a member of his team asked.

Uh-oh, Carlin said to himself. *The jerk's probably shot himself with his own weapon.*

Gamil had watched from his dark spot on the northwest wall. He had watched his Muslim brothers as they prepared to unleash Allah's fire upon the nest of infidels across the sound.

And he had watched as the two teams of enemy soldiers had crept into the fort. He had covered his white teeth with his hand as he grinned and watched one of them outpace his brethren, only to freeze in fear. *Coward! But aren't they all?*

His grin vanished as he watched Khalidi fall into Allah's arms, and he muttered a curse at the man who had sent him there. He flew into a rage when Mousavi's exploding head had covered him in spatter. He stepped forward, screaming and firing on full auto. He died in a fusillade of fire, cursing in both English and Arabic.

The compound grew silent when he did.

Tupper watched as Shorty walked back to the car. She hit the release button once again, and the trunk opened, then closed quietly. He reclaimed his seat and turned to smile at Christine. Daylight was still too faint for her to tell, but she knew that his smile did not reach his eyes.

The quiet was broken again when someone keyed his radio so the occupants of the Chrysler could hear Khee screaming in pain.

"Gooood *puduu*!" Her smile was feral.

Durwood Cratch watched his boss writhing on the ground. He jumped back when Khee's flailing about threatened to sweep him off his feet.

The field medic showed up with his kit and ministered to the crying man. "Can't you give him something to knock him out so he'll shut up?" Carlin muttered.

The medic only shook his head as Khee continued to whimper. Fernandina Fire/Rescue eventually carted him off to Baptist Medical Center Nassau, and the paramedic rolled his eyes at the drama queen's antics.

Cratch watched silently as his boss was loaded into the ALS unit. No one noticed that he did not speak until hours later, when it was his turn to be debriefed.

It was mid-morning when Cratch finally left the Fernandina Beach Police Station. He spent the long drive back to his apartment in Jacksonville wondering how likely he was to run into terrorists in Texas.

Christine had temporarily taken charge of Team One and told them to go home once they were debriefed. "Take the day, but report to the field office as usual tomorrow morning. By that time, DC and I will have figured out a temporary replacement for Special Agent Khee."

"How is he doing?" one of his team members asked.

"He wants his mother." Carlin's tone was carefully neutral as he continued to fill out his after-action report.

Chapter 28

Both teams returned to the command center. "You have ten minutes," Christine said over their chatter. "Then we'll get down to business."

She spent the rest of the morning on the telephone while Bull Cowper coordinated the teams' after-action reports. He interviewed them when they turned in their reports and went over them before he cut them loose. "Keep your cell phones on. I'll call you when to come to Fernandina Municipal; you'll be out of here late afternoon," he admonished the members of Team Two.

"Yes, Frederick, I understand." Christine had kept ADDIR Page in the loop on every stage of this morning's raid, from planning to execution. "And tell the director thank you for his kind words."

"You can tell him yourself. When will you be back?"

"I'm not sure. There's something terribly wrong at the Jacksonville field office, and I hesitate to leave those people on their own. I certainly hope you pick out a good replacement."

"I'm sending one of my best men down there. He will be there until I can find someone permanent."

"When will he—"

"I've told him that he'll be wheels up on a company

plane by eight on Monday morning, and to pack for a two-week stay."

"You think you can find someone that fast?"

"No, but if I'd told him he'd be there indefinitely, I'd have two agents to replace!"

"Good theory."

"Speaking of theories, do you have one yet about how Special Agent Khee got himself shot?"

"I will by the end of the afternoon. Bull's running the show while I talk to you."

"How is young Agent Khee doing, anyway?"

"The initial assessment is that his knee is probably history. They're going to stabilize him overnight and then take pictures tomorrow. He'll have surgery one day next week."

"That ends his career, for sure."

She offered no regrets over the departure of this particular agent. "Once his doctors here give us the go-ahead, we'll fly him up to Bethesda Naval Hospital for surgery and recovery after. You'll be able to start out-processing him in two or three months."

"Great. I'll have to find a job for him in between therapy sessions. Say, why don't we have all of this done down in Jax? That'd keep him out of our hair up here."

Christine had anticipated this suggestion. "I think he needs to be removed from the area, make a clean break for him and his staff. The new guy, even if he is a temp, will not need any interference from Agent Khee, and his staff certainly doesn't need to be pulled in two different directions."

"Good enough. So how's he handling all of this?"

She let her fatigue show. "You know him, Frederick, so you can imagine how difficult he's being."

"Yes, I can imagine."

"Seems he has a very low tolerance for pain. Every time he feels a twinge, he starts screaming for more meds. And his mother."

"Ah, yes, his mother. Have you met her?"

"No, why?"

"She has a lot to answer for. We came close to washing him out of Quantico because of her."

This was juicy. She wanted to know more about Momma Khee. "How was that?"

"Little Georgie called Momma every night. If he had a rough day, he'd whine into the telephone. Then she'd call the school and scream that they were mistreating the future director of the FBI."

Christine laughed so hard she had to hold the receiver away to protect Page's ears. "Oh, I needed that!" she finally gasped. "That's the best laugh I've had in weeks! Future director, huh?"

She was still chuckling when Shorty walked in a few moments later. He waited for her invitation and then sat in the chair she indicated.

"Thank you, Lord Tankerville, for your service these last few years. And for today, of course."

"I'm glad it turned out well."

"I owe you."

"No, we're even."

"I still owe you, especially for the special assignment I gave you at the last moment."

"OK, then; I want to go home."

A British accent coming from this scruffy, disheveled man was so incongruous that Christine smiled. She realized that she was smiling a lot today, and she was pleased. "And you will. Soon, after we finish cleaning up here. And don't you have a police captain you need to talk to?"

"Crikey! I'd forgotten about that for a moment there!" His shoulders slumped at the thought. "Guess I'd better go see the chief to find out when Wilson's getting back from Cumberland."

"Guess you should. And I want to make sure you realize that there's going to be more than one issue with your captain. Of course, he's going to blow about not knowing that you've been undercover."

He nodded dejectedly.

"And he's going to be seriously aggravated that he missed this morning's little fracas."

"Yeah, and wait until he finds out that I orchestrated his Cumberland Island stay to keep him out of our hair."

"I'd wait a while before I told him that."

Shorty nodded again and left her, his small frame still slumped in dejection. It made him look even shorter.

Lunch was a quiet affair around the station conference table. There were only five of them: Chief Evans, Christine, Bull, Shorty, and Carlin.

Shorty had ponied up for a "to go" order from Gourmet Gourmet and a young patrolman going off duty had agreed to make the run. Shorty threw in a free lunch for the patrolman to sweeten the deal.

"So, Bull, is it too early to ask if you've got anything to report about this morning?" Christine asked as she swallowed a mouthful of sandwich.

"They had two missiles ready to go, with two more as back-up. They had good perimeter defense and a beefed-up security detail for the men working the missiles.

"But we had superior fire-power and manpower." Bull hesitated and then said, "I guess Agent Khee was working on a pincer movement, going along the north wall like that." He shrugged and did not mention the mad dash across the parade ground that almost got the SAC shot by his own team.

Christine looked around the table. Carlin and Shorty were intent upon their lunches and offered no theories of their own.

"What's the body count?" Carlin never looked up from his plate.

"Three dead—Khalidi, Gamil, and Mousavi. One wounded, Eid. Hamid is alive and sustained no injuries."

"Our side?" she asked.

"One through-and-through, minor damage. One twisted ankle. And Agent Khee, of course."

There was an uncomfortable pause, ended by Christine. "He's in good hands; don't worry about him. Have you found out who these guys really are?"

Bull snorted in disgust and threw an ID badge on the table. It was enclosed in a clear plastic evidence bag. "All they had on them were these."

Christine picked up the bag and read the tag out loud. "Muslim Military Jihad. Abdul Hamid. Holy Warrior. *Allah Akbar.*"

"They all had cheap wallets with these IDs inside," Bull said. "No money, credit cards, nothing. Nothing in their pockets, no jewelry."

"They were ready to die," Christine observed.

"Well, they got their wish," Chief Evans grunted. "Where's the bodies?"

Bull waited for Christine's nod before he answered. "Our clean-up crews were at the fort not ten minutes after the last shot was fired."

"I want to talk about that last shot," Carlin said, but everyone ignored him.

"The first team took videos and stills of the scene before they let anybody else start. A second crew took the bodies to Oxley-Heard for initial assessment."

"I bet Jack Denham just loved that!"

"He was a little crusty, but he came around," Bull continued. "Another team did a sweep to bag and tag everything they could get their hands on. Even yesterday's candy wrappers."

"Not many of those, I bet. The park folks do a fine job of keeping the place picked up." The chief was quick to defend one of the town's major landmarks.

"All of the forensic containers are being loaded on the plane sitting at Fernandina Municipal. Everyone but Christine and I will fly out on it late this afternoon."

"And what about Khee?" Liam Carlin would not let the subject go.

Christine decided that it was time to end this before it went any further. "Special Agent Khee is resting quietly at the local hospital. Early next week, he will be flown to Bethesda for surgery and will recover in the DC area."

"That's great, but I mean, who shot—"

"That question is above your pay grade, but I will tell you that the circumstances surrounding Special Agent Khee's injury are being investigated thoroughly. The director has taken a personal interest in this case, so you can be sure that we will get to the bottom of how this agent sustained his injury."

Liam Carlin had known Christine for a long time. He was adept at deciphering her well enough to catch her real message. Today's message was "back off."

"Thank you, that's more than I need to know," he said and returned to his meal.

Once lunch drew to its logical conclusion, Agent Tupper had returned Christine and Bull to the Egmont Suite. After they changed out of their black tactical attire and into street clothes, she drove them to the Jacksonville field office. They spent an enlightening afternoon going through Agent Khee's electronic and paper files.

Christine looked up from pillaging his desk when Bull let out a long, low whistle. "What is it?" she asked.

Bull pushed the chair away from the computer and turned to her. "It's a file on everyone you can think of, from the mayor of this town to the movers and shakers of Nassau County. Headquarters staff in DC is in here, too. He's got the goods on everybody, including us."

"How bad is it?"

"He's got my report on that little fracas along the Pakistan border, as well as the transcript of your interview with the State Department when you were trying to convince them to let you settle here."

Christine's face went still. She came from behind the desk and walked up to the keyboard. She pushed a button and the file disappeared. "The hard drive goes in your briefcase. Make sure the techs make this file disappear permanently."

Bull nodded and they returned to their work. The rest of the afternoon passed uneventfully.

Bull had released Special Agent Tupper from her chauffeur duties and had requisitioned a sedan from the motor pool. It was not armored and contained no global communications equipment, but it fit their needs.

"Did you notice that only a couple of people stopped by this afternoon to ask about their boss?" Bull asked as he drove them away from the field office.

"Yes. It fits in with the picture of him that I'm getting from going through his desk. He kept copies of staff evaluations. He was a master at slicing and dicing, and no one escaped."

Bull grunted and she continued, "The sad thing is, those reports are really dog-eared. I think he took them out and read them over and over again."

They spent the rest of the drive back to Amelia Island, as well as dinner at Bonito's, discussing how best to repair the damage that Khee had inflicted on the field office.

"Best idea," Bull growled over his shrimp and pasta dish, "is to break up that staff. They're feeding on each other, and it's seriously damaging their work.

"Khee is out of the picture and Cratch is on his way to Texas. Never did figure out what his job was around here, other than to be Khee's lackey."

"Transfer enough of them to diffuse the situation, and then put in a really strong leader to try to rehabilitate whoever's left," Bull said.

"I like it. I'll pass your ideas along to Frederick."

"And tell him to hand-pick the field offices he sends these jokers to, and then brief the agents in charge what's coming their way."

"Absolutely."

Shorty appeared at Charles Evans' open door. "May I come in? There are a couple of things I want to talk about."

Chief Evans did not answer right away, but fixed him with a fierce glare. "OK," he finally relented.

Again Shorty waited for a signal before he seated himself. "First I want to thank you for being my friend for all of these years."

"I wasn't your friend, My Lord; I was Shorty Livingstone's. I don't know or trust you any more than any other stranger sitting in that visitor chair."

Lord Tankerville looked down at his hands for a few seconds before he met the chief's glare. "Fair enough, I suppose. But you are a good copper and a good man. I always knew that I could count on you." He paused to gauge the chief's reaction, but was met with a stone face. "And I know I can count on you right now to help me with my friend Wilson."

"Oh, no. You're on your own. If you think I'm pissed, you ain't seen nothin' yet."

Shorty let the chief's threat hang in the air. "When's he due back?"

"The Sunday ferry. You have a day and a half to come up with a plausible story. But you're good at that, aren't you, My Lord?"

Shorty stood up to his full height and said, "If you would be so kind as to arrange a meeting with Captain Wilson in this office on Monday, I would be ever so grateful."

Again the chief hesitated before he responded to this politely disguised order. His curt nod and dismissive flick of his wrist were slow in coming.

Chapter 29

Wilson knew something was up the moment he walked into the station. Instead of scurrying away or averting their eyes, his coworkers greeted him warmly. He grew slightly alarmed when Rose Isabel, who was not usually so demonstrative, gave him a hug before she escorted him to the conference room. *This must be big.*

She opened the door and Wilson looked around. Only the chief and Shorty were sitting at the table, so he must be early for whatever confab was about to go down.

The chief's message had been waiting on the answering machine late yesterday afternoon when the Wilsons had returned from their Cumberland retreat. He was still basking in the renewed relationships with his wife and children and had mildly resented that intrusion of reality, even if the chief had mentioned "great strides" in the case against him.

After greetings had been exchanged, he looked around the room and said, "Where's Khee? When you said 'great strides,' I assumed that he'd be here to make his usual self-serving presentation."

"We'll get to him in a minute, so why don't you get comfortable and I'll tell you everything you ever wanted to know about this whole mess." Chief Evans was definitely in charge.

Wilson poured himself coffee from the carafe that Rose had provided and sat back. He glanced at Shorty, who merely grinned and winked. *Same old Shorty.* There was something different about him today, but Wilson couldn't place it.

"Things began to fall into place just about the time you were pulling out of your driveway on the way to Cumberland," the chief began. He talked for a long time and Wilson did not interrupt. Instead, he took notes on the tablet at his place setting.

Evans spoke about Ahmahl Walid and the assassin from New London. He talked at length about the Muslim Military Jihad and the five men who had made up the local cell. He smiled at Wilson's outrage at learning that the stately Addison House had been the cell's headquarters. Neither man saw any humor in the use of Fort Clinch as a launching pad for the group's terrorist attack.

"I don't want to steal Jon Stewart's thunder, so I'll let him tell you how he was instrumental in solving the Haldad cold case. I will tell you that it had ties to the MMJ, and that Stewart uncovered those ties. Damn fine work on his part."

Wilson was not surprised at Stewart's performance and said so. "But you still haven't told me what actually went down. Or when it went down, for that matter. Or where," he added as an afterthought.

The chief and Shorty exchanged glances. Once again, Shorty remained silent while the chief talked.

Wilson quickly realized that he was only getting big chunks of the picture. He would have to ferret out the finer details later and on his own. He added more questions to the list he had been making. "Casualties?"

"Three dead MMJ, two captured."

"Where are they?"

"DC."

"Huh. Our side?" There was a pause and Wilson looked up, suddenly alarmed. *This can't be good.*

"Uh, cracked ankle, minor scrapes." Evans paused and looked at Shorty again.

Wilson caught the look. *What is it with these two this morning? What am I missing?*

"Agent Khee sustained serious, but not life-threatening, injuries," the chief finally answered.

Wilson felt a sudden surge of glee and knew he would spend extra time at confession this week. "You sound like a 'police spokesperson.' What exactly does 'serious but not life-threatening' mean?"

"Somebody blew out his knee." Shorty spoke for the first time.

"Blew it out? How?"

"Rogue shot took out his left knee-cap, just as things were winding down at the fort," Evans explained.

Wilson tried not to smile. "I'd say that single shot blew out his career, too."

"Yup," the chief said, "he's getting a plastic knee and a pension. Already on his way to Bethesda."

"Oh, darn, and I didn't get a chance to say goodbye. Who's going to replace him? Cratch?"

"Lord, no. Cratch is being transferred to Texas. They're sending down a temporary until they can find a permanent replacement for him."

"Huh." Wilson was suddenly bored with the FBI's personnel problems. He looked over at Shorty and wondered out loud why he was in the room. "There's something different about you this morning, my man, but I sure as hell can't figure out what it is."

Shorty muttered something and Charles Evans slowly pushed back his chair and stood. Wilson glanced from him to Shorty to discover that he, too, was standing.

"Captain Wilson, I have the pleasure of introducing you to Sir George Grey 'Shorty' Livingstone, the Twelfth Earl of Tankerville. His lordship is also a card-carrying member of the British intelligence community. He has been an invaluable undercover asset for both Her Majesty's government and our own."

Lord Tankerville extended his hand and Wilson slowly rose from his seat to take it. "You have a lot of explaining to do."

The meeting reconvened after a short break. This time there were only the two of them at the table and Shorty did most of the talking. Wilson noted that he had dropped the redneck jargon and now used his natural voice. The sophisticated English accent seemed at odds with his rough clothing and minimal personal hygiene.

"First, let me say that my friendship and respect for you these past ten years have been genuine. I hope that you will continue to call me 'Shorty.'"

"Damn straight I will. There's absolutely no way I'm gonna call you 'Your Earlness,' or whatever I'm supposed to. Besides, I'm so pissed at you right now, you're lucky 'Shorty' is the only name I'm calling you."

Shorty talked steadily for the next thirty minutes. He started with the origin of his hated nickname during his boarding school years. When he got to the story of his career in espionage, he revealed his code name, "The Pelican," and waited for the explosion.

Wilson did not disappoint him. "You! You are The Pelican? I'll be a son of a—it was you sending me all of those notes?"

"I had to do something. You were coming unglued and I needed you to hold it together so I could concentrate on the bad guys. 'Shorty' couldn't very well give you words of wisdom, so I had the Pelican deliver what help I could."

They sat in silence while Wilson tried to digest this latest revelation. Shorty gave him all the time he needed. Wilson finally stirred. "OK, go on. Get to the rest of it. Don't leave anything out. So you were about to leave for the fort. Then what?"

Shorty quickly described the ride to the fort and the subsequent take-down. He provided even the smallest details because he did not want Wilson to think he was holding anything back.

Again Wilson said nothing, but made check marks next to the questions he had jotted down as the man across from him answered them, one by one.

The room was silent as Shorty came to the end of his story.

"That it? You done?" Wilson asked.

Shorty saw the white line of anger around his friend's mouth and noted the muscles working in his jaw. He carefully nodded yes and Wilson stood. He headed for the door, leaving the tablet to rest where it lay. All of the questions inscribed on it had been answered, the story seared in his memory.

"There's one more thing before you leave," Shorty said to Wilson's back. Wilson stopped but did not turn to face his friend. "I need a ride to the Jacksonville airport day after tomorrow." Shorty waited for several long minutes before Wilson growled his agreement.

The door closed softly behind Wilson, and Shorty subsided into his chair. "That went rather well, don't you think?" he asked the empty room.

Wilson pulled into Shorty's driveway at the agreed-upon time. The place looked even rattier now that he knew Shorty's true identity. He had spent the last two days trying to come to terms with the man's duplicity, even if it had been in the line of duty.

Dianne had helped him put it in the proper perspective. After her initial shock had worn off, she had shrugged. "Shorty's Shorty. Still as outrageous as ever. Doesn't make any difference if he's got a title." She had paused and her mouth had twitched.

"What?"

"My Lord, a lord!"

They had both collapsed in laughter and Wilson's anger finally disappeared.

Shorty came walking toward the car and Wilson was surprised to see only one bag. He watched as Shorty put it in the back seat. He looked even less like the old Shorty than he had the other day.

The passenger door opened and Wilson caught a whiff of nice cologne. He took a hard look at his friend while he fastened his seat belt and got comfortable for the ride. Shorty was clean and freshly shaved. He still wore jeans and a tee shirt, but both were clean and sharp creases had been ironed into the pants legs and shirt sleeves.

"You clean up purty good!"

"Drive," Shorty growled and shook his head. That's when Wilson noticed that his hair was still long, but it had been trimmed by several inches and the raggedy

THE PELICAN OF FERNANDINA

ends were gone.

They chatted quietly as Wilson piloted them down A1A to the interstate. Once they had merged with the I-95 southbound traffic, Wilson brought up one last subject. "What about Verna? Was that real or was that just a cover?"

Shorty had married Verna Ja'neen Clover back in 2006. Wilson had been busy with the Tiffany Eppes James homicide, while he had been monitoring bad guys who were using Fernandina Beach Municipal Airport as their aviation hub.

Shorty grew quiet and stared out of the window for several long moments. "Oh, my feelings for her were real. I'm just not sure what those feelings were."

"What does that mean?"

"Part of it was my desire to save the world, I suppose, one person at a time. She was a smart woman trapped in an awful package—she sounded like a yob and looked like a floozy. Her family was a never-ending soap opera and they always made sure she was in the middle of it."

"Like what?" Wilson wasn't sure he wanted to know, but he couldn't help himself.

"Well, she was trying to take courses at the community college—the Betty Cook Center—God help her."

"And?" Wilson prodded him when he trailed off.

"I paid for one course when her mother found the stash she'd saved for tuition and proceeded to use it to get her clunker of a car repainted." Shorty snorted in disgust. "And then, another time, I sweet-talked her professor into letting her take a make-up test because she'd had to drive some no-good relative down to Jacksonville instead of driving herself to class."

Wilson could tell that Shorty's anger was genuine and that it wasn't going to go away any time soon.

Shorty looked out the window again as he shared his thoughts. "My idea was to rescue her from that whole family, get her enough education so she could be self-supporting. I could only do that if I were her husband.

"And as her husband, I could physically move her from her apartment into mine; everyone had a key to hers and they came and went as they pleased. They took what they wanted and ate anything they could stuff down their gullets." He stopped again to calm himself down. "I wanted her to be educated or trained enough to carve out a life for herself—preferably one that was six or seven hundred miles distant."

Wilson wisely refrained from making any editorial comments about unrealistic goals.

"Oh, hell, I don't know what I was really playing at. And now we'll never know, will we?"

"Do you still think you were the real target of the attack that killed her?"

"Damn straight, I do. Trouble was, I couldn't figure out whether they were trying to kill Shorty Livingston or the Brit intelligence type. Afraid my cover was blown, don't you know?"

They said their final goodbyes after he had checked his luggage. "I'll be back for the trials, of course, but probably much sooner than that," Shorty had assured him.

"Enjoy yourself and have a Happy English Christmas, y'all heah? Eatin' blood puddin' and playin' with crackers, an' all." Wilson made his Southern drawl as thick as he could. He hated goodbyes and tried to lighten this one with humor.

"Fer sure. An' y'all stuff yerselfs with cornbread dressin' and pee-can pie, unnerstan'?"

Sir George Grey, the Twelfth Earl of Tankerville, clapped his friend on the arm and quickly disappeared into the crowd.

Chapter 30

Ruby Dell Stewart would jokingly complain about her birthday all of her life. She would often lament that the celebration of her birth on December 25th was overshadowed by a larger, more important observance. But she was always comforted by several extra presents under the tree that were wrapped in birthday paper instead of Christmas colors.

Fernandina Beach Police Chief Charles Evans spent his Christmas surrounded by everyone he loved. Last night's New Year's celebration had been with friends who gave thanks for the old year and eagerly anticipated the new. Who knew what it would bring?

What, indeed, he snorted and carefully placed his snifter on a coaster. His wife had presented him with a bottle of Dakota Winery's finest port, and he couldn't wait to savor its taste. Now he understood why she had been so eager accompany a girlfriend on a drive over to Chiefland, Florida, last month. He took a sip and rolled it around on his tongue while he closed the door to his study.

He rolled his chair up to the desk and pulled out a legal pad. He had a letter to write. He and Jacqueline had spent the last several months talking about retirement. His joke about a pontoon boat on the Crystal River was rapidly turning into a full-fledged plan.

He had laughingly told Wilson about retirement and the boat, and Evans had warned him that he would recommend him as his replacement. They had had a good laugh before Wilson observed that he would be ready for his own retirement by the time the chief got around to putting in his papers.

I hereby resign my position as Chief of Police of the Fernandina Beach Police Department …

He and Jacqueline had also discussed the timing of his resignation.

… effective the first day of February 2011.

He had explained to her that he was not up for yet another Shrimp Festival, especially since the subject of waterfront development—and its possible effect on the festival—was heating up again. "Mark my words," Evans had said just the other day, "J. Phillip Quattlebaum is right in the middle of that project; he'll wheel and deal until that piece of real estate along the river has his name all over it." It made him tired to think of it.

He quickly typed and printed the letter on his personal stationery, signed, sealed, and stamped it. He threw on a jacket and walked the envelope to the mail box at the end of the drive. He smiled as he flipped up the little red flag.

J. Phillip was no longer mayor, so the letter was not addressed to him. He would not be privy to this juicy bit of news until the mayor shared the information with him and the rest of the city commission. He fully expected a telephone call to arrive within the week from an outraged Commissioner Quattlebaum castigating him for his failure to provide the man with the inside knowledge he craved so much.

He grinned and settled at his desk one more time. He took a sip of port and pulled out the pictures he had taken of a pontoon boat that a neighbor was trying to sell.

ABOUT THE AUTHORS

David Tuttle — Cara Curtin

DAVID THOMAS TUTTLE, Sr.
February 17, 1941 — August 22, 2008

DAVID TUTTLE used his varied talents and experiences to add flavor and authenticity to his writings. A twenty-eight-year military veteran, his U.S. Air Force career took him to Africa as a member of a NASA recovery team, and his decades in the Florida Air National Guard kept him abreast of the latest advances in avionics.

While living in Fernandina Beach, he worked for a time at Publix and managed the photo lab, which allowed him to use his expertise in photography. Samples of his photographic skill can still be found on the covers of several books bearing his name.

An experienced rock and gem hunter, David served as president of the Jacksonville Gem and Mineral Society. He was a saxophonist with the New Horizons Band, affiliated with the Amelia Arts Academy.

David put his considerable writing skills to good use in many different disciplines. The international gemological newsletter he produced for several years was a consistent award winner. His writings reflected his interest in and knowledge of a wide variety of subjects.

He was an already successful writer when he proposed the story line of *Murder in Fernandina* to the Nassau County Writers and Poets Society, and he was lead writer for the ten members who developed the book introducing Lieutenant Wilson. The success of *Murder* led him to write its sequel, *The Leopard of Fernandina*, and he went on to co-write *Fernandina's Lost Island* with Cara Curtin. His collection of short stories, *Pirates, Gamblers and Scalawags – Fernandina Tales*, was published in 2007.

The Pelican of Fernandina is David's last work, which was destined to be completed by his friend and co-writer after his death in 2008.

CARA CURTIN

CARA CURTIN got her B.A. in English and promptly found a job as a copywriter at an advertising agency in Norfolk, Virginia. It took her three years of writing billable copy to discover that she was starving to death. She joined the Navy when the recruiter promised her a living wage. When she completed Officer Training School, the Navy first sent her to Public Affairs School in Indianapolis and then to Pensacola, Florida, as a public affairs officer. She used her writing skills every day of her twenty-year career.

After retiring, Cara opened the Sailor's Wife Book Exchange in Fernandina Beach and began to write about her community. Her by-line appeared regularly in *Amelia Now* and *Amelia Islander Magazine* and she became active in the Nassau County Writers and Poets Society.

She and Foy Maloy, publisher of the *News-Leader*, coordinated the PR for the first Book Island Festival, later renamed the Amelia Island Book Festival. It was from that successful collaboration that Cara was invited to write her *City Sidebar* column for the paper. She continues to make her irreverent observations about life in Paradise. *City Sidebar: The Book* is a distillation of over ten years of her columns.

Her book writing career began when David Tuttle led the Writers and Poets Society in producing a group novel. *Murder in Fernandina* was an instant success, and soon people were asking for more adventures of Lieutenant Wilson. David wrote and Cara edited the second book, *The Leopard of Fernandina*.

The Tuttle/Curtin writing team collaborated on the third, *Fernandina's Lost Island*. As they worked, they wondered what would happen next to the intrepid lieutenant. Cara soloed in *Fernandina's Finest Easter,* showcasing Wilson's next adventure and introducing his protégé, Jon Stewart. Meanwhile, David began Wilson's foray into international intrigue with *The Pelican of Fernandina*. Cara is busy plotting Captain Wilson's next adventure, *Fernandina's Last Treasure*.

ALSO READ...

Murder in Fernandina

Lieutenant Wilson wants to escape Miami and its high homicide rate, so he takes a job heading the Investigations Division at the Fernandina Beach Police Department. His first day on the job proves to be pure murder, and soon the lieutenant is caught up with treasure maps, a beautiful redhead, and some of the island's more colorful characters. Readers also get a peek into Fernandina history and its notable inns, homes and churches.

The Leopard of Fernandina

Wilson's murderous adventures continue, again woven around the island's rich history. Wilson objects when his new chief volunteers him to be a member of a joint task force, but he finally gets to meet the Man in Green, and it is not love at first sight. The book was written by David Tuttle, lead writer of the first Wilson Mystery, and edited by Cara Curtin.

Fernandina's Lost Island

Co-authors Tuttle and Curtin plotted this third adventure while they were busy working on the lieutenant's second one. This time, Wilson discovers that the bad guys are using the Fernandina Beach Municipal Airport in their skullduggery and Dianne, now a police officer, discovers a new—and risky—interest in pre-Columbian art.

Fernandina's Finest Easter

In the fourth book of the series, authored by Cara Curtin, Sue Nell Borden finds a Labrador puppy on her porch one Easter morning. When the local veterinarian discovers the pup's amazing secret, he realizes it's going to take both him and the dog, as well as some sleuthing by "Fernandina's Finest," to save Sue Nell from a web of danger.

City Sidebar: The Book

For the first time, Cara Curtin has collected favorites from her long-running *News-Leader* column into book form. Laugh along with Cara as she finds the funny side of life in Paradise.

All books are available at
www.CaraCurtin.com

CPSIA information can be obtained at www.ICGtesting.com
Printed in the USA
LVOW131309030613

336596LV00001B/1/P